No Matter What

No Matter What

A Novel

Mary Elizabeth Gillilan

Independent Writers Studio Press
Bellingham, Washington

NO MATTER WHAT

For Those of Us Who Carry On,
No Matter What

I've been absolutely terrified every
moment of my life—and I've never let it stop
me from doing a single thing
I wanted to do.

—Georgia O'Keeffe

1

Exposed

I stared at my alarm clock. It was 3 a.m., and I woke with a start. A boot stuck under my collar bone and my yellow puffy jacket that I used for a pillow lodged in the small of my neck. Upward, I saw my two print sundresses. So, that's where they are—first thoughts. I wanted to wear the elephant print yesterday and ended up in a t-shirt and jeans.

Honeydog waited on the other side of the closet door. "You're a good girl," I scratched the back of her ears. "OK, yeah, I'll try to sleep in bed the rest of the night."

At least the panic attack was over. I couldn't remember much of the dream that landed me in the closet, but its consequences hung in the early morning air. I pulled up my comforter and tucked it under my chin. Arizona nights chilled in October, and this particular October of 1993 was breaking weather records for chilly nights. Funny how my mind turned towards the weather as I tried to recover from my racing heart, shaky knees and sweaty palms.

Ever since moving to the ranch, panic attacks had haunted my nights. I'd go to bed, go to sleep, and wake up after dreams

about my mother or my ex-husband. After a series of nightly attacks over six months, I'd timed them. (Timing an attack
helped me endure the terror. At the peak, halfway through, I'd
want to call for help, imagining myself dead in the closet and
no one here to take care of the girls. It was like being on an out-
of-control ferris wheel on amphetamines. That's why I always
took my alarm clock with me into the closet. Twenty-two minutes into the attack was always the worst moment—Give it five
more minutes, I'd whisper to myself, and then I'd watch my
body's reaction slow as the clock ticked off the minutes, and
when that pertinent five minutes passed, I'd know I could ride
it out.)

This one lasted the usual forty-five minutes, then I slept in
the closet because I was too worn out to go back to bed.

My bed felt safe enough in the moment. I lay still and
practiced breathing. Ironic that anyone practices something as
mandatory as breathing. You either do it or die. In the distance,
thunder roiled; I threw off the covers, dressed in my sweat-
pants, tossed on a sweatshirt, then padded through my small
ranch-style house, careful not to alarm my other two dogs, Yul
and Deb. I poked my head into my daughters' rooms. Both
slept. Good, I thought. I hadn't screamed in my sleep. Another
clap of thunder brought me back to the sheer anxiety I shared
with the open desert skies. I unlatched the front door and slid
outside like a thief. Lightning broke across the horizon, but the
sky did not break.

I sat on the wide porch steps and watched CollinCamp
silhouetted as the lightning strikes pummeled the heavens.
We'd been here a year. I assessed my situation again. Allen,
my ex-husband, was yelling at his second wife, not me, and
they were in Japan. My mother was in Vancouver, British
Columbia, deported years ago. Neither of them would ever
wake me up again in the middle of the night. Well, that

wasn't true; they woke me up nightly. As long as I kept my cool in the ranch office, played the role of an accountant, and tucked the past deep inside, everything would be OK.

As an art major in college, I planned on moving to the Southwest to paint, like Georgia O'Keeffe, but Allen did not want to move. He worked all over the world and claimed to hate traveling. He was full of contradictions and half-lies. I shook my head as an owl interrupted my reverie. Allen's mother owned our Seattle house overlooking Portage Bay. He made tons of money, or so he said, but he was delinquent on child support. He forbade me to take this job, pissed as hell at me from his house in Japan. I intertwined my fingers as I witnessed the storm. I thought I'd take a shower before the girls got up.

Blood smeared the ripped edge of the envelope in my hand. I tried to rationalize what I had read. The Vancouver lawyer informed me that my mother was in the hospital and not expected to live. A car struck Vivian crossing the street in front of her apartment past midnight the week before. I had no idea that she knew where I lived. Maybe the lawyer found me in Oracle, Arizona? I wiped my paper cut off with a tissue from a box on my desk.

My mind went white, and my ears buzzed. I sat stalk-still, my back straight, and my eyes focused on the interior of my thoughts.

The day moved around me; something or someone relayed that I still was Tansy Daniels, bookkeeper at Col-linCamp, Allen's ex-wife and mother of Clea and Janey. The girls' voices came in on waves propelled by the ceiling fan, moving the hot late Arizona afternoon around and around.

Blood dripped from the paper cut from my finger onto the letter I let fall to my desk. Gratefully, no guests were around, and Glen was out on the property. The memories tumbled through the white wall of hopeful forgetting.

Like fast-moving high water suddenly flooding the desert, I relived the memories from over twenty years ago when my out-of-control, drug-addicted, and trust-fund-baby mother and librarian father were divorcing. She wanted custody even though I was sixteen and opposed it—the battle continued with countless court filings. She lost each one, and with each failure, her antics escalated. Mother bounced in and out of our lives, coming home only to sober up, shower, and be on her way. My dad rarely raised his voice, which compelled her to scream louder. In late spring of that year, while the divorce proceedings continued, she and Dad fought; I woke up to something crashing against the wall, and I heard her yell my name. Her habit of coming home drunk or high and waking me up "to talk" had gone on for years, and had morphed into crying apologies and promises to be the "best mom ever." When I heard Mother come upstairs, I turned my head to the wall and covered myself with a blanket, pretending to be asleep. She turned on my light: "You are mine," she claimed. "Get up. You're going with me."

For a change, Dad was steps behind her. "I've called the police. Leave, or you will be arrested."

"This isn't over." Mother raised her hands and backed out of the room.

And the court wars went on.

Dad concluded the safest place for me was with my

boyfriend, Allen, at his mom's summer mountain house near Mt. Rainier. Mother had never met Allen or any of the Daniels family. Dad and I spent two summer weeks annually at a campsite he had purchased years before next door to them. It was where I met Allen, who later became my husband. Allen was a sophomore in college; I was on my way to my senior year in high school. I felt safe at Allen's, and we were in love.

That day, Allen and I returned from a swim at the lake. We were dripping wet and needed towels. Allen popped into the house to get them when Mother drove up. I should have run, but I froze in place. I remember a flume of gravel floating in the air as she ground the gears to stop but not turn off her Audi. She left the motor running and grabbed something before charging toward me. My wet bikini stuck to my shivering skin, and my hair dripped into my eyes.

She said, "I have something for you." That's when I saw the knife.

She pointed to the car with it. "Get in the car," she said, "we're going to go fly on clouds,"

I yelled, no, and turned to run, but she caught me by the hair. I felt the knife under my chin.

Allen saw the scene unfold from the cottage porch, took the stairs three at a time, and shoved my mother away from me. I tumbled to the ground and rolled under the car. As that memory filled the guest ranch office, I touched the scar under my chin where the knife cut me.

Mother lost custody and eventually was deported to Canada, where she has lived off her trust fund. Allen saved my life.

We married, he cheated, and we divorced. Sounded

simple, but I didn't go into marrying Allen thinking about how or why we might divorce. He saved my life. Allen promised that he'd take care of "everything." What a blissful concept! I welcomed the feeling of security and protection, Allen's words gave me. He never liked Lara; she was far too confident for him. We argued when I met with Lara for a run or lunch. When she came over unannounced, he'd nod, claim he had a headache, and ask me for a massage or aspirin, anything to maintain my attention on him. Eventually, Lara and I saw each other when Allen was out of town. Allen thought my dad was too needy, but put up with family dinners every few weeks, and again, like Lara, I saw Dad more when Allen traveled. When he claimed migraines, he was unbearable. I kept everything quiet in the house. Sometimes, he disappeared for a few days, visiting old school friends. In retrospect, I assume he was seeing other women.

When he wished, Allen could charm fleas off a dog, and he supported my art and my work with Brette. He always knew the right thing to say or do, and even though he could be arrogant and rude, I went along with what he wanted because it made life easier. Because of his travels, I wasn't privy to much about Allen's life. Slowly, living with Allen became a source of anxiety, a guessing game in dealing with his mercurial moods and his fist pounding the table when he aired his complaints.

Allen petitioned me for divorce to marry Julie, and Lara was the one to do the cleanup. After the divorce, Allen promised that he'd be there if I "needed a friend." He wanted to control my life and the kids' lives, while in the meantime, he went on searching for shiny objects worn by beautiful women.

That's Allen. My darling dad, the librarian, worried

about how I'd get along but was happy about the divorce. He hadn't lived to see how Mother's life ended, a blessing, I supposed. He died a couple of years back.

"You alright, Tansy?" Glen Newbauer in his beat-up Stetson came into the office through the back entrance from the kitchen; he pulled up his chair at his desk facing mine and let out an audible sigh.

I folded the letter and shook my head at CollinCamp's chief cowboy. "It's about my mother," I waved the letter towards him.

Glen looked at me quizzically.

"Anyway, she got hit by a car and is not expected to live." My shoulder muscles tensed. "I may have to go to Seattle for a few days to take care of things."

"The kid and I'll keep the ranch up if you and them girls have to go." He waved to Janey and Clea outside.

"Thanks, Glen." Guests entered the ranch office as I rose to leave.

I walked outside to where the girls had drawn a hopscotch on the courtyard patio. "Come here, you two," I felt like an executioner whose job was slowly to kill my babies' innocence. "I got a letter with some sad news in it."

"Is Daddy alright?" My preteen daughter wrapped her arm around her little sister.

"It isn't about your dad. Vivian is dying." I picked up the chalk and squeezed it tightly.

"Who's that?" Janey asked.

"That's Mom's mother," Clea answered. "The lady in the picture with the big hat, holding Mommy's hand at the beach when she was a little girl."

The lady in the hat with the little girl. Who were they,

and oh God, where are they now?

We walked home. Saguaro and brush lined the gravel pathway. All the buildings at CollinCamp seemed low compared to the Santa Catalina Mountains above the ranch. Unlike other dude ranches, Glen kept a few head of cattle, from which came our beef supply. We used pork he raised as well as eggs from chickens he kept. Our path meandered across a little rise, and a prickly pear jutted out like a signpost down a small gully. The first thing Glen did upon our arrival was to put cyclone fencing all along the perimeter of my yard, which permitted my dogs the freedom of cool shade under a paloverde tree.

I saw remnants of a life lived too fast as I entered the house. Newspapers and my journal were in a small chair by the floor lamp left on this morning. I neglected to block off the garbage container under the kitchen sink to protect it from the dogs. All three scrambled when they saw me, a dead giveaway for what might lay ahead. I started cleaning the kitchen floor and noticed the laundry piled on the washer and dishes in the sink.

"Looks like a hurricane went through here," I said. "Clea, will you walk the dogs up the ridge and back? And Janey, why don't you go pee pee? I bet you have to go!"

With Clea outside with the dogs and Janey in the bathroom, I had a few minutes to myself; I filled a large black refuse bag and hauled it to the garbage can, an area locked off to protect it from critters outside under the awning.

"Mommy, I'm all done," Janey called.

"Good job!" She pulled up her pants as I entered the bathroom. "You want some juice?"

She ran to the kitchen. I filled a glass of apple juice and

handed it to her. She gulped it down and gave me the cup. "Read to me, Mommy."

"I have to straighten things up, sweetie. Why don't you find a book in your room, and I'll read it later?"

I ran the washer by the back door, then returned to the sink. Hot water caused a shot of pain from the paper cut; my thoughts jumbled. I needed to call Lara. I ran my finger under cold water as Clea returned with three bounding dogs awaiting their dinners.

"That didn't take long—thanks, honey." I began fixing the dogs' bowls, a mix of kibble and canned dog food; three pairs of eyes stared at every move my hand made. "I've got to talk to Lara about Vivian's condition, will you—"

"Mom, I have homework. I have to finish reading *Tess of the d'Ubervilles*. It's so stupid."

"Give me fifteen minutes. You can put on the Winnie video for Janey."

"Mom, I am not your slave."

The dogs followed me as I carried their dishes to the small hall by the washer. "Eat, you guys!"

Janey ran from her room with a copy of her flower fairy book. "Read to me, Mommy!"

"We're going to find your Winnie video, and sister will sit with you for a while. I need to talk to Lara on the phone."

I went over to the VCR and plugged in the video. "Fifteen minutes, I'll be back. I'm going to my room." I left before either of the kids could complain. My twelve-year-old black lab mix, Honeydog, followed me and jumped on my bed while I dialed Lara Sloan. From the look on Honeydog's face, I understood she was the number one culprit in the garbage-on-the-floor incident, and she knew I was in trouble, too. She put her head in my lap. "Good girl," I said as Lara's phone rang.

Lara Sloan is my best friend and an attorney. It was a great combination when I was getting a divorce. Today, her assistant answered as Janey burst into my room. I barely heard the secretary say Lara had left for the day.

"I want gummy worms, Mommy."

Lara's assistant laughed. I told her I'd contact Lara later and turned my attention to my four-year-old. "Honey, I don't think we have any. Let's go check." I picked Janey up, hugged her, and then walked into the living room, where Clea watched the movie. "We're going to go search the kitchen for gummy worms."

"There's some in the cupboard above the fridge," Clea said. "You put them up there last Friday."

"I totally forgot," I yelled from the kitchen. "Your memory is so good."

"There's some Hershey Kisses up there, too, " Clea said, joining us in the kitchen.

"That explains your good memory!" I handed the bag of Kisses to Clea and gave Janey five gummy worms. "I think I'll walk over to the office to call Lara. A little walk might clear my head. And, Clea, only take a handful of candy and put the bag away.

"Mommy, stay!" Janey said.

"Janey, your sister is staying with you for about half the movie, and I will be back to see when Christopher Robin gets Winnie out of the window."

"Bring me a prize," Janey said.

"Yeah," chirped Clea, "a desert rat."

I rolled my eyes, threw my backpack over my shoulder,

and headed out. As soon as my feet landed on the last stair, the impulse to run struck me; the heat struck me, too. It was still in the high eighties with a little breeze, but the weight of that thin envelope, not the backpack, urged me on. So I ran, the bag thumping against my back. My mother was dying. Given our history, someone should throw me a parade with floats, clowns, and jugglers dancing along a crowded street.

Instead, I found myself in the riverbed that bisected Glen's ranch. How the hell did I get here, I mused. And I meant more than the riverbed; I meant Arizona with the kids. I chose the Southwest so that I could paint. Allen told me I was fooling myself. And a fool to leave the Seattle house where I paid no mortgage or rent, a weird divorce settlement, perhaps, and probably a generous gesture from Allen's mother, who owned the house.

The day I called CollinCamp, Glen answered the phone. We talked and I told him I was a good bookkeeper and wanted to raise my kids and get a fresh start at a place like his ranch. I didn't say I'd called a list of ranches in Arizona asking about job openings. Glen was the only hit. Glen offered me a job based on that conversation. I think he pitied me. I landed somewhat on my feet. The job was a state short of Georgia O'Keeffe's New Mexico, but the smells and wonder of the American Southwest informed me that I could paint here.

I rubbed my nose on my sleeve and looked back the way I had come. CollinCamp stretched around me. The white, aged wood of the corral stood in contrast to the henna-colored horse standing mute and staring at me. "You're lovely," I said as tears blurred the horse and the corral until I could not distinguish one from another.

How could she be dying today? What was the date? I

should know that, I thought. What did she look like? Jesus, she was only fifty-nine. I touched my head. I should be wearing a hat; certainly, I should be wearing a hat. The sun will ruin my skin. No one's touching it these days. Who cares?

I sat on a rock and watched a lizard sun itself. "It's easier for you guys," I said to it and hiccoughed back a wave of grief. While I sat there, my ex-husband, Allen, was sleeping with his second wife, Julie, in Japan. "Well, now, that's what I call a comforting thought," I said to the lizard and laughed.

2

Is It Alright to Run

Tansy Daniels, what the hell are you doing down there in that dried-up drink?"

I looked in the direction of Glen's voice. "I'm not down in it; I'm up it." I smiled.

"Where are them kids of yours?"

"At home."

"Alone?"

"Clea is almost thirteen; I think that's old enough to babysit."

"I can't hear a damn thing you're saying; it's like talking to the ass-end of a steer."

I waved to him again.

He stood with his hat in hand, staring at me with his mouth in a perfect "o" as if he were going to speak but then thought better of it.

I shrugged my shoulders, turned around, and started back the way I had come. I slipped into an empty office and called Lara. I read the letter to her; I heard her scratch out notes, including the lawyer's name and the hospital's contact information. We made tentative plans for the kids and me in Seattle. Before leaving the office, I tried to call the hospital, but no one would give me any information. I stood and stretched, then headed home.

Glen met me on the porch. He winked at the girls and tipped his hat at me, leaving without saying anything.

After putting Janey to bed that night, I sat on the floor by Clea, watching one of Glen's World War II war movies. "This was one of John Wayne's earliest movies, Mom. I think he looks sorta stupid. You know how his helmet is always kinda cocked on his head like the Army couldn't find one big enough to fit it."

"Don't let Glen hear you say that—he and the Duke are tight."

"Glen's pretty nice, though, Mom. He just looked shocked when I told him I hadn't seen the Duke in a war flick. I promised I'd watch it and give him a report tomorrow." Her voice filled with reproach. "And he did keep Janey entertained while you were gone."

I decided to play it safe and stick with John Wayne. "Well, what do you think of the Duke?"

"He's pretty good once you get past the hat. You gonna watch it?"

"No, I'm going to run a wash and maybe get back to Lara. Funny to think we'll be in Seattle tomorrow night. I'm hoping she'll figure out where we stay—you might be with Brette."

"I won't bring anything for Patricia to steal, then." Clea peered up at me as I stood. "Can I stay here?"

"We go as a block," I laughed. "Enjoy the Duke! I'm going to wash clothes."

"Does Dad know?"

"I don't think so."

"I wish Dad would come to the funeral."

"Who knows?" I shrugged.

"Is she sorta dead or really dead?"

I brushed Clea's dark hair back; she jerked away from my hand. "I called the hospital and talked to a nasty lady who said she could only confirm that 'Vivian Carson was a patient.'" I held my nose. "Then, she hung up."

"She's going to die?"

Honeydog brushed her tail against my legs. "The letter said there was little hope of recovery and that the 'family should be so informed.'"

"Why didn't you talk to the guy who sent the letter?"

"He's a lawyer, sweetie, and he wasn't at the hospital. I mean, his office isn't there, and it didn't impress anyone that I was a family member." I shrugged.

"But Vivian's your mother." Clea pressed for more information.

"It's complicated, darling."

"Are you going to see her if she is still alive?"

"I don't know. Lara can find out all we need to know as my attorney."

"Well, I don't want to see her. I never even knew her, Mom."

"I don't think I ever did, either."

"She was your mother!"

I ran out of words, and tears laced my cheeks as I peered over my daughter's shoulder. I still wanted to protect Clea from my childhood.

"Sorry," she muttered and turned away from me, her eyes steady on the flickering TV screen.

"I better get busy with the wash so we have clean clothes for Seattle," I said. "No matter what, always know that I love you." My voice sounded pinched as I wiped my face with my hand.

"Can I call Dad? I love calling international," Clea said as I retreated. "Daddy should know."

I clenched my fists and stiffened my shoulders. Allen might still be mad about me taking the kids to Arizona. He couldn't hit me over the phone. An inner voice cautioned against exaggeration. Allen never actually hit me, and he should know about my mother. "OK. You might get Dad before he goes to work."

"I'm stopping the movie right here—I get the phone first."

You really want to go to this dance? The words glazed my consciousness as I watched Clea dial a call to Japan as if she were calling someone in nearby Tucson. Usually, this ended in frustration of too many calls on too many lines, but tonight it all worked. When she said hello, I wondered what to say to Allen. He was no longer my husband; he was someone else's husband.

Clea delivered the basics in one rushed sentence: "Vivian, Mom's mom, is in a hospital in Vancouver (the Canadian Vancouver), and we're flying to Seattle tomorrow." Then her voice erupted in a sweet giggle as Allen responded with lighter news from Japan. When she said goodnight, I imagined Allen telling her, "Sweet dreams," Clea extended her arm with the phone out for me.

"Tansy," he said. "How're you doing, babe?"

He hadn't called me that in years. "Never thought it would end this way, you know? The Vancouver letter said she got hit by a car and is not expected to live."

"I'd say I'm sorry, but that's hard to do after what we went through."

"That was like a lifetime ago, you know? No matter what else," I waved my hand as if erasing a chalkboard."No matter what else," I started again, "you saved my life that day." My voice cracked. His manner sounded so familiar. In that nanosecond, I wished he were here, the old Allen, to take care of everything.

"Is Clea listening to you?"

She lay on a floor pillow with her elbows propped under her chin, staring mutely at the paused video. Of course, she was listening. What was I doing, taking her down this rabbit hole? I walked with the cordless phone into my bedroom. "Clea's in the other room now."

Honeydog opened the door with her nose and flopped herself at my feet beside my bed. "It's so weird," I heard the whine in my voice and continued. "Oh, God, Allen. She was only fifty-nine. What a wasted life."

"For your sake, I wanted as much distance as possible between Vivian and our family. At least she honored that." He paused. "Are you sure you want to handle this?" Allen sounded sincere.

"Yup." My tone was surprisingly firm. "A night flight. Tomorrow, Tuesday. We'll stay with Brette or Lara."

"Drag the kids? Whoops, sorry. Why did you move to a place where you knew exactly no one? I know we had that conversation, but you could've dealt with this easier had you stayed home in Seattle."

"The move's made, Allen. Home is CollinCamp, now." The ocean between us grew wider.

"Did Mother dearest have a will?" Allen shifted topics with practiced ease.

"We'll see. Lara's trying to find out." I scratched behind Honeydog's ear; her head was in my lap.

"Does this lawyer have a name?"

"Yeah. Charlie Trucker. Why?"

"I could make some inquiries."

"Lara's handling it. I'll be fine."

"Good ol' Lara." His tone smacked of disdain. "Not about this, but I'm coming back to the States. I miss you guys—family. Miss Seattle. I don't miss Lara. I miss the kids. And you. I miss you, Tans. Do you want an I-told-you-so moment?" His voice drifted. "I'm sleeping solo these days. It's over with Julie and me." The line went quiet. "See what I mean about you staying in Seattle?"

"Apples and oranges, right?"

"What do you mean?"

"Your breaking up with Julie has nothing to do with my move. One is an apple, and the other is an orange. Are you staying at the house, or did your mom rent it out?"

"Mom's been doing renovations in the house. She may sell it. I'll stay with friends." Allen's tone indicated that he was finished answering my questions.

"Well, sorry to bust into your day with my news." From down the hall, I listened to warfare on Glen's video. Allen always acted like he struck wife-gold with Julie. "I'm sorry things haven't worked out," I said, "let's talk in a few—"

"Wait, Tans," Allen interrupted. "I have a question for you: If what I offer you has no consequential meaning in your decision-making, why did you call me?"

"Good question. Better go," and I hung up.

Why the hell had I called?

I took the phone back to the living room. Clea peered up at me from her perch on the floor. "Mom? Was Vivian a bad person?"

"I think she was troubled."

"Are you scared of her?"

I swallowed hard. "Not anymore."

"What did she do to you?"

"There's no reason to talk about it. Ancient history. And I'm not scared." Every pile of bullshit commences from a kernel of corn. Glen said that the other day. I had to agree. I wanted to protect Clea from my night terrors, and I was without a manual for how to do that. I did my best. I slid to the floor and put her feet in my lap.

"Watch the movie with me, Mom?"

For a moment, I pretended that it was an ordinary weekday night. The dogs, clearly done with their day, stretched out and snored softly on the floor by us; Honeydog draped herself over my feet. I don't know what John Wayne said to Forrest Tucker, and Clea and I did not chat, but the quiet felt good.

The dryer turned off, a call to action. I patted Honeydog and tapped Clea's leg. "Hey, sweetie, I need to pack," I said to my sleepy daughter, intent on seeing the Duke save the world. I wished he was here.

With a basket of clean clothes to fold and pack, my bedroom door shut, and Honeydog on my bed, the phone rang. I ran to the living room to grab it.

"Tansy?" Lara began.

"Call you back in a sec," I have to get Clea to bed."

Clea was sound asleep; it took a parade of trumpets and drums to wake that girl, but I managed, and she left for her room. I turned off the VCR and TV and listened to Lara's updates.

"The nurse told me Vivian was awake when she first arrived at the hospital and wanted to talk to her lawyer. Your mother had a major stroke shortly after their conversation." The nurse described Vivian's condition as critical; she remained unconscious.

I didn't ask how Lara got someone to talk to her, however; she can make people open up to her as if she were the sun and they a day lily. I tried to mimic her demeanor in the past, and I often failed. She spoke to Mr. Trucker, and he was helpful. Vivian had a will with directions for cremation, my name, address, and who inherited what.

"I'm kinda stuck on the phrase, 'quite fond of her.'"

"Mr. Trucker sent his 'genuine regards' to you."

"Well, thank you very much," my sarcasm unmasked.

"How are you doing with all this?" Lara asked, "I know this dredges up old times."

I felt my voice tighten. Damn it. I cursed myself; stop feeling sorry for yourself. "A long night, yeah?" I thought about Clea and all she witnessed this afternoon. "A lot of dredging—I called Allen," I said, "actually, had Clea do it."

"Why?"

"Clea wanted to talk to him."

"Oh, come on." She turned down the radio, blaring, "Take it Easy" I wished I could. Back on the phone, Lara continued. "Let me be clear: It's awesome that he talks to Clea, but don't delude yourself." Her words were sharp, and I was unused to hearing this heightened irritation in her voice.

"No, I get it." I felt the same defeat the day Allen married Julie. I waited all night for his call that it had all been a mistake and that he was coming home to Clea and me and our new baby. And yet, the lies he told, his screaming voice, I couldn't hide from that. "I think he broke up with Julie."

"Are you surprised about that?"

"In a way, maybe."

"Did he mention anything about what he owes in back child support? Or the notice you got from the bank about foreclosure?"

"The house was in Allen's mother's name; she took care of it before we left. I think she might sell it." I sounded defensive.

"Probably to recoup some of Allen's debt. Remember what we discovered after you kept receiving notices from debt collectors? Besides his gambling debts, he maxed out five credit cards. He was supposed to make mortgage payments."

"I repeat. His mother took care of the payments."

"And gave you shit for not contributing more," Lara said. "If they sell, you need to get some of his back support. We'll have to file a lien. How much is he behind?"

"I don't want to get into it. I kept a record and the checks like you said to do, and like I said, I get it."

"A ballpark, how much?" Lara pressed.

"I asked him for some money when we moved. He was behind twelve grand and gave me two—then stopped altogether. Around twenty-four thousand. I know it sounds like a lot."

"Good God, why didn't you say anything?"

"He gets so mad, and I'm doing fine. I'm making do here. My house comes with the job. Not the time to talk about money stuff."

"There's going to be a court date in that boy's future," Lara sighed, returning to the Seattle trip's details. "Oh, and Tansy," Lara reminded me, "I'm meeting your flight. Brette and Patricia are coming in Brette's car. She's all set for both girls, leaving us free to go up to Vancouver on Thursday. "And," she paused, "when this is all over, find yourself a cowboy."

I burst out laughing. We both fantasized about the perfect guy in college: cowboys topped our lists. "I'll save one for you should that happen," I said. "You're the one who loves horses."

We said goodnight, and I folded the rest of the clothes, then tiptoed down the hall to check on the girls one last time. I leaned over Clea and kissed her forehead. I vowed I would never lose custody of my daughters. "I love you," I whispered to my sleeping child and left her room. Janey slept soundly with her arms wrapped around Winnie. I tucked a blanket around her, kissed her forehead, then walked softly through the living room and stood on the front porch.

The winds howled outside. A woman I might recognize was dying in some hospital. I was out of tears. I peered out into the vast, empty, screaming blackness and wondered if the moon was out or hidden under clouds of sand. It scared me to think it didn't matter.

3

Becky Who?

I awakened with a fervent urge to clean. I brought out the small buckets from the back porch and my gallon container of Simple Suds, the advertised elixir for all my cleaning woes, and began in the bathroom, then worked towards the main living areas. All the while, the three dogs followed me. I started at four-thirty, and by the time the girls got up at seven, the house smelled like mint as breezes through the opened windows aired the place out. I fed the dogs and ground French roast coffee beans for my pour-over brewer. The lovebirds chimed loudly from the back hall, fed and in clean cages. The girls and I feasted on fresh cantaloupe, kiwi and orange slices, cinnamon toast, and yogurt. Whatever lay ahead, we would come to it with full stomachs and clean clothes.

I called the ranch office and told Glen I would arrive around nine-thirty and that Alex was taking the kids and me to the airport after school was out. Janey and I walked Clea to the bus stop at the top of the winding road into CollinCamp. It was a lovely morning. We watched a spotted bird camouflage herself in the scaly arm of a saguaro.

She was nesting. Clea had watched her each morning on the walk to the bus, and she was happy to be able to share this with us.

"Mommy?"

"Yes, Janey?"

"Can we take the bird home to live with our birds?"

"No, sweetie," Clea interjected. "You see, this bird has little babies under her wing. The saguaro helps her protect them."

"But the cactus hurts me when I touch it," Janey replied.

Clea wrapped an arm around her little sister. "The mama-wren doesn't want anyone touching her babies, that's how the cactus helps her out. Besides, they're free birds. They wouldn't understand living in a cage."

"I would never hurt her babies," Janey said.

"I know that, but the mama-bird has rules, and we have to mind them."

"Can I hold your hand, Clea?"

These sisters loved one another. I had to let that guide me. My awareness shifted sharply as the school bus roared around the corner and stopped. We waved goodbye to Clea as she walked up the steps and greeted the driver.

After delivering Janey to Rena Flores' place for her preschool program, I returned home. Usually, I went straight to work. That day, I stood outside the house; the air was so still I imagined I might hear the ants rustle. Inside the house, I sat in my favorite chair by the lamp, read for ten minutes, and gave myself another five. I drank a glass of water and called Lara to see what was new with my mother. Her vital signs had slipped during the night. The nurse said she might go at any time. I felt removed from Vivian as I changed into a light cotton sundress and ambled quietly to the office for work.

"Well, where is that goddamn son of a dog's hind leg, anyway?" The high-pitched nasal wail came from inside the office door. I thought about turning around and going home. The woman yelled at Alex Warren, the next thing to a manager we had at the ranch. Glen referred to him as "the kid."

Alex took the lady's verbal assault with ease. "I told you, Becky, I don't know where he's at. We didn't know you were coming in today."

Whatever perfume Becky had on was as forthright as her mouth, which, by the way, was painted bright red. The color matched her nails, making the zircons shimmer in her cat eye glass frames. Her store-bought bouffant wig shone in the morning light. And like the old gospel song preached, she had a firm foundation.

"I want his signature on this here paperwork, an' I want it now!" She noticed I was in the room. "Who's her?"

"Tansy Daniels," Alex said, "I'd like you to meet Becky Newbauer, Glen's former wife."

She puffed out her pinkened cheeks and put her hand out to shake. Her inch-long nails cut into my hand. She apprised me from head to foot. "And what's yer business here?" she asked.

"None of yours," Glen bellowed from behind me.

Becky stepped back and opened her mouth to speak, but Glen beat her to it. "Becky, if you want to talk to me, let's do it civilized. Let's go up to the house, OK?"

"Are you referrin' to my daddy's house?" She peered around coyly. "Alright. I am sorry I was so abrupt, but I thought you was tryin' to run out on me, and I got to get back to Vegas this afternoon. I have an engagement tonight."

She walked over to Glen, who held the door open. She passed through. Glen looked back at us, shook his head, and popped a couple of antacids in his mouth.

"So, that's the famous ex-wife," I said.

"In full armor!" Alex answered. "It's so eerie in here this morning. Do we have any guests?"

"Wasn't there anyone at breakfast?"

"Marty Chicago and the honeymooners."

"Sounds like a rock band." I smiled. "Well, we'll have three units booked for business tonight. With our minimum of four-day stays, it's something."

"We're going to have to do something to pump business up a little," Alex stared at the door.

I didn't know the scenario between Becky and Glen, but it felt threatening. I had an idea. "You know that kid at the Arizona Tourist Bureau? The one Glen knows? Let's see if he has any thoughts?"

"Jimmy Andrews?" Alex liked the idea; the kid was a "graduate" of CollinCamp. Glen had hired local boys to help with ranch chores for years, usually fatherless teens on the edge of adulthood without role models to guide them. Tucson is a tightly-knit community; word-of-mouth brought these boys to Glen's ranch. Glen teased and ridiculed the hell out of each. No one was as dumb or stupid as the current kid, and the next kid would never be as smart or intelligent as the last kid. Glen filled their heads with stories of the early West, the Native people of the Southwest, stories from Glen's early life, and the war stories that shaped him. When tending the cows, he'd make the kid quit everything else to listen to a cow eat straw. These young teenage boys came to share Glen's code of ethics. Glen preached loyalty. Loyalty to the family—he said there wasn't much else without that. And then there was loyalty to yourself, to the principles that guided you must guide how you deal with others. Alex had explained this to me in my early days at the ranch.

Glen was straight with my daughters, teasing them just as he would the boys. Clea and Janey were welcome any-where on the ranch at any time, and when they called him Rancher Glen, he beamed.

Alex was as close to a son as Glen had. I knew Alex grew up here. He went away for college and then later came back. He was building a house higher on the side of the moun-tain on land purchased from Glen. Another graduate, Pablo Sagasta, recently returned to the ranch. Glen told me that Pablo was a metal artist making a piece for the courtyard. He camped by Alex's place and worked out of an old barn. I hadn't met him yet. All of Glen's boys turned into fine men. The man running the Arizona Tourist Bureau was no excep-tion and was only too happy to help if we could get Glen on board.

Alex thumbed through the guest ledger while I spoke to Jimmy Andrews on the phone, and then Alex left to tend the horses. Since so few people were at the ranch, I helped clean the units awaiting guests. Peter, our unreliable cook, arrived and gave me a food order to pick up. I didn't see Glen all day. We were in for a busy weekend. I hoped all would go well without an extra hand in the office.

By late afternoon, I had fed the dogs and made a list for Alex about their care and feeding. He promised to cover the birds at night and give them fresh water. The girls and

I were ready when Alex drove up to my house. We loaded into the ranch van. Alex struck a handsome profile with his sandy-colored hair, high forehead, and Roman nose. He wore a red t-shirt, jeans, and leather sandals. Alex smelled like Ivory soap. On the way to the airport, he told me about Glen's visit from Becky, which wasn't good news. Glen refused to sign a partnership agreement.

"What does that mean?" I asked, watching a dust devil whirl across the freeway.

"It goes something like this," Alex said, "her ol' man owned the place. She sold Glen her share for a percentage of the ranch earnings each year. 'Cept things have been slow. Now, she wants to be a partner—wants to come back and do your job."

I breathed out with an audible sigh.

"Don't worry about it. Becky always makes threats when she's after money, never carried anything out." Glen took her out to lunch and drove her back to the airport. She's gone home to Vegas." He peered at my daughters in the rearview mirror. "Now, girls, we'll get your mom on a horse when you come home." He turned off the freeway to the airport and turned his attention to me. "I am so sorry about your mother, Tansy. We'll take good care of your dogs and the birds while you're gone. Not for you to worry."

"Who's the 'we'?" I asked. "I thought you were going to stay with them."

"It'll be either Glen or me—he has the key."

"OK," I said. "Honeydog's getting to be an old lady. Be gentle with her."

"Don't give them another thought. They'll be fine." He pulled up in front of our airline and helped me organize the kids and luggage. We waved goodbye. I longed to be in that van going home to CollinCamp.

I paid for our tickets inside the terminal and got us to our gate, then stared through the large glass windows at airplanes taking off. We lined up to board the plane and waited. People milled. Some ate. I saw a teenage boy wolf down a hamburger, ball up the wrapper, and toss it in a receptacle in what seemed like one move. The smell of fried meat and french fries turned my stomach. Because the airport was air-conditioned, it felt cold to me. I held Janey's hand and shrugged at Clea. And we waited some more. Soon after, Clea tapped me on the shoulder while Janey tugged on my purse strap. "Mom," Clea said, "they're calling our flight."

Set for north, the pilot propelled us home. A nagging thought recurred: What if Glen lost and Becky came to CollinCamp? Where would we go? I knew we would not return to Seattle. But what would I do to support us if Glen lost the ranch?

Clea read, and Janey watched the night sky, fascinated by the stars and the sheer size of the heavens. None of us felt obliged to eat, and after the flight hostess took our trays away, I told Janey one of our magical stories—Puff stories— the dragon, made famous by Peter, Paul, and Mary. I usually start by singing the song to induce the mood, and I found myself on a 737 singing "Puff the Magic Dragon" as discreetly as possible. When the guy behind us said, "What is this a goddamn camp?" I sang louder. I was almost done with the song, anyhow.

When I finished, I nudged Clea and said, "Puff doesn't like critics."

She laughed, and Janey said in her full alto, "What doesn't Puff like, Mommy?"

I felt the kick of a shoe in the middle of my back. I stared over the seat and said, "Sorry."

I could feel Clea's eyes rolling around in her head without looking. "Please don't get us thrown off, Mom." She lowered the seat back, "we didn't pack parachutes," and then, she pretended to sleep.

4

Seattle Mist

Lara and Brette met us. We hugged as our children stood on one foot and then the other, waiting for us to finish our public display. Lara's eyes filled with tears. We small-talked as we waited for the luggage to get off the plane. Brette dressed windows for high-end boutiques and stores like Frederick & Nelson. She called herself "artsy." She was a lifelong friend of Lara, whom I met at college. Brette and I formed a women's art collective in the late seventies. Allen and my dad chiefly supported us. We re-purposed an old church in Ballard and set up galleries for artists. We had Lara write a grant, Brette handled the day-to-day management, and I found the artists. Brette's interest dwindled when she met a man with whom she traveled for two months, and came home pregnant. In fact, we both were pregnant. As time progressed, the artists could not afford even a nominal fee for space. We couldn't afford the rent and wanted more time with our new babies. Brette married for a second time, and I saw her less and Lara more. I sorely appreciated her coming to the airport tonight.

Brette's daughter, Patricia, picked up Janey and kept repeating, "You've gotten big."

"You girls all get to stay with Patricia and me. I've got a special bed just for you, Janey. Mom's going to stay with Lara." Brette knelt low to be eye-to-eye with my youngest.

We all stared at Janey in silence to see how this piece of information would digest. She appeared pretty serious as she weighed her options. "I want to go with sister."

We each breathed a collective sigh, and I felt liberated.

Lara and Brette had parked a few cars away from each other. Lara and I went to Brette's car with the girls, and I kissed them goodnight.

Lara remained quiet as we walked to her car. The cool, damp Seattle night contrasted with the harsh sound of her heels against the concrete floor of the garage. "I gather you have an update from the hospital?" I said, trying to ease into what I was sure would come next.

"Yes, I do." She paused, turned on the ignition, looked over her shoulder, and said, "Tansy, she's dead."

I stared off into the night. "You forgot to turn on the lights," I tried to remember the photo of Vivian Carson, my mother, and me at the beach, how our laughter might have sounded together, and how her voice sounded at all, for Christ's sake. But my mind was numb and cold. If there were memories, I wouldn't retrieve them now. It was too late. Rain began to fall. "It was a good flight," I said, "a guy was sitting behind us, and —" I closed my eyes as I visualized my mother's face, and she was screaming — "Damn," I said and cried as Lara drove us into the Seattle skyline.

We arrived at Lara's house, and I thought I should tell someone, but who? I shivered inside my fleece jacket while

Lara went to the kitchen. Before leaving for the airport, Lara had pulled out the couch bed and made it up for me.

"When did it happen?"

"Early afternoon." Lara walked into the living room with an open bottle of wine and two glasses. "I called the hospital just before six, then tried you, but I guessed you were on the way to the airport."

"Yeah, we were."

"You want to talk about any of this stuff now?" she asked.

"What happens to her?"

"The hospital had the release from her lawyer, so her body was transferred to a funeral home for cremation. You and I can go up to Canada the day after tomorrow." The fourth-floor apartment's sliding glass door opened to a deck onto the quiet Green Lake neighborhood. Two high-backed bamboo chairs sat side by side, facing the lake. Lights shimmered off the still water. Rain fell. Lara set the wine glasses and wine on a small table between the chairs. "I have mac and cheese warming in the oven."

"Sounds good: I don't know when or if I ate today." I sat down in one of the chairs.

Lara took the other chair, poured the wine, and handed me a glass. "I propose we drink a toast. Vivian was your mother, and the good news is that she gave birth to you."

I took a breath. "I'll never know how it all turned out for her."

"Let's drink to her soul," Lara said, raising her glass.

"To Vivian Carson's soul," I said, and Lara and I touched glasses and drank the wine. The rain mesmerized me. A streetlight cast shadows on cars parked along the avenue.

"What are you thinking?" Lara asked. She curled her legs under her and smiled.

"About that crazy day," I said.

"Your dad did the right thing by having you stay at Allen's mom's house," Lara said.

"I never felt safe after that day. I'm still listening to bumps in the night. I had to testify against her in court." I sipped the wine. "When I spoke to the police and the judge at the trial—hearing or whatever you call it, before they took her away, they kept asking me to identify the knife as they held it up in my face. 'Yes, yes,' I said, 'that's it.' When I left the stand, I glanced once in her direction, and she looked away. After I sat down, I heard someone I didn't know behind me say, 'They look so much alike.' Dad squeezed my hand and kept saying he was sorry." I took a breath and sat back.

"Damn hard day." Lara patted my hand. "Your dad must have felt so bad about you testifying." Lara stood.

My face felt hot with grief. Was it for me or my mother or Dad. I wasn't sure. The silence between Lara and me grew awkward.

"Let's head to the kitchen, and have some food. Bring your glass."

"Follow the melting cheese," I said. "Oh my God, it smells good." I was glad to change the subject.

We sat on chrome and red vinyl barstools nestled into her kitchen counter and ate mac and cheese with slices of wholewheat toast. "I haven't thanked you for all you've done the last few days. I want to make another toast to friendship. I am so grateful, and the food was delicious."

We finished the bottle of wine, and I insisted on washing

the dishes while Lara dried and put them away.

"I remember you used to dream about the knife," Lara said, toweling off the bowls.

"Sometimes it's a knife, sometimes Allen, and sometimes Mother. The dreams continue."

"And that actual day Allen saved your life was the one noble thing he ever did." Lara put away the serving dish and the loaf of bread while I rinsed off the silverware.

"Mother went to jail for a few months. As soon as she got out, they deported her to Canada."

"Yeah, I know. How'd your dad end up being her guardian?" Lara dried the forks and butter knives and put them away.

"Dad never went through with the divorce, and she could never handle money, so they struck a deal. He withdrew the divorce petition and managed the trust fund. Dad was the only person she trusted. No matter what Mother did, he loved her. From what Dad told me, she got sober. He set her up in an apartment and handled her finances officially through the court. When Dad died, she must have petitioned the court to break the guardianship."

"I think the lawyer I spoke to, Mr. Trucker, took over the guardianship. I know he's the executor. You were named a beneficiary; I think you and the girls." Lara hung the dish towel over the oven door handle.

"I hadn't thought about the will until Allen brought it up." I wiped off the counter. "Done!" I tossed the cloth to Lara.

Lara shook her head. "Nothing surprises me about Allen, and he still surprises me. Of course, his first question would be about your inheritance." She rinsed the rag and laid it over the sink edge to dry. "You want a cookie?" She held up a box of gingersnaps she had retrieved from her pantry shelf.

I shook my head no. "I'm good."

Lara crunched on a cookie, waving the box in her free hand. "The lawyer is the executor; he has a copy of the will for you. The money might be sizable, and then again, maybe not. Mr. Trucker only said he looked forward to meeting you." She returned the box of cookies to the pantry and patted me on the back. "Let's go look at the night sky before bed."

Settled into our wicker chairs, the curtains open to a quiet night, I sighed. "Aw, this is better." We drank Perrier now; Lara refilled my glass. "I never wanted anything from Mother. Never asked any questions. I let Dad handle the details. He discussed it with Allen, probably."

"You are the decisionmaker this time. I imagine Allen will call you as soon as you return to Seattle—do not ask his advice about what you should do with anything you inherit. Promise me."

"OK," I said, too tired to debate the point, but I remembered the chaos of that long-ago day at Allen's. Dad arrived and offered to take me home now that Mother was in custody. I agreed to go with Dad. By my dad's Renault, Allen hugged me close, "I'll always be there, babe. Always. I promise. I love you." Through adultery and loan defaults, I had clung to that moment—even when things got ugly with Allen, I didn't tell Lara about it; I was sure she would find another glaring fault in Allen's character when I needed a hero.

5

Get The Popcorn

I phoned the girls early Wednesday morning; Brette answered the phone. In the background, I heard Patricia and Janey. "I told the girls that your mother died," Brette announced.

Brette had no right to tell the girls about Mother's death. "I wish you'd left that to me."

"They're not that upset," she said, handing the phone to Clea.

"How're you doing?" I sipped my coffee seated, looking out at Seattle waking up.

"I want to go home," her voice plugged with emotion.

"We're going really soon, honey," I answered. "Lara and I have to go to Vancouver to take care of things tomorrow, but this afternoon, I figured we could go to Woodland Park Zoo."

"I missed a math test today, Mom." The tension in her voice was not about missing a math test, but that was where the conversation started.

"Honey, I told the school you would be gone, so your

teacher knows. You don't need to worry."

Janey yelled in the background. She wanted the telephone, and Clea handed it to her without a reply.

"Hi, sweetie pie," I said. "We are going to the zoo today. OK?"

"OK, Mommy."

In the background, Patricia told Janey, "I'll be a tickle monster, and I'm going get you."

"Mom, when are you coming over?" Clea regained control of the receiver.

"Why don't we have lunch at the zoo? I can get you guys around eleven, OK?"

"Brette said I had to go to school with Patricia." Clea's voice flattened.

"Let me talk to Brette."

"Hey, Brette," I said. "The girls and I are hijacking Lara and going to the zoo. I'm picking them up at eleven."

She paused before speaking. "Oh, I had planned the day differently. I thought Clea would like to see some of her old friends at school, and I could take Janey with me on errands."

"Maybe that'll work best tomorrow. Do you need me to come earlier than eleven?"

"I think my plan would be more beneficial for the girls," Brette said.

"Does eleven work?"

"If you insist. Patricia is going to be so disappointed."

"I'll be over at eleven."

The sun peeked out of ragged clouds at the zoo, and the wind stirred from time to time. It was early October and invigorating with deciduous leaves in full color all over the park. The monkeys delighted us, and a lion roared. I didn't dwell on Vivian Carson's cremation in Vancouver for the entire day.

We ate dinner at Brette's that evening. She served sourdough French bread she made and froze in advance if she needed something for a so-called spontaneous dinner. It was hot and crispy and strictly her recipe—she always managed to remind us. And that she had tweaked the recipe from The *New York Times*; the trick was in the aging of the sourdough starter.

I said once again, "I do want that recipe." Asking for the recipe was due diligence.

She smiled enigmatically, refreshed her wine glass with a cabernet sauvignon, and asked if I wanted more spaghetti.

The house lay down a winding lane tucked between Portage Bay and Lake Union. Western Hemlock bounded one side of her property, and a tall Douglas fir marked the other side of her front yard, making for a grand entrance to a stylish treasure. The cedar-sided dwelling featured porches on both floors of the home. In the distance, boat lights twinkled on Lake Union.

After dinner, Brette sent the kids downstairs to watch a video while the three of us lounged on couches in the living area off the dining room. I declined more wine.

Brette Archer's dark hair, artfully streaked, hung just above her shoulders in a pageboy. She wore a blue and silver silk kimono over black leggings. She had been married and divorced two times and claimed she was so bored with men that she considered taking up women.

The green glass clinked with ice cubes when I sipped water. Brette set wine glasses down for Lara and her. The expansive windows brought the outdoors inside as the day cast golden light at sundown. We settled in, and for a moment, save for the click of the ice, all was quiet.

"Allen tells me he's selling the house," Brette said softly. "You knew he was doing that?" She rolled her shoulders back and continued. "I caught him up before we went to the airport to get you guys."

"He told me before we left Arizona. I think he was already 'caught up.'" I glanced over at Lara, whose composed face gave nothing away. "The house is in his mom's name, so she is selling, not Allen."

"How did he know the kids were here?" Lara asked.

"Oh," she raised a sculpted eyebrow. "He called after talking to you, Tans. Apparently, he's coming back to Seattle." She seemed to know more than what she shared about Allen. I wondered why. "We talk now and then." Brette paused as if she were thinking about how much she wanted to add. "We, ah, he wants an even playing field," Brette said. "He's asked me for advice, you know, his marriage to Julie—"

"He told me about that." I studied the melting ice. Did Brette and Allen—I rejected the thought of those two together. I filled the awkward gap by thanking Brette again for caring for Clea and Janey. Lara stood and suggested it was time to say goodnight to the kids and be on our way.

"Do you know if Allen and Brette ever?" Lara started her car; the unsaid question dangled between us.

"She flirted with him." Rain drummed quietly against Lara's windshield. "But like sleeping together? Ugh." I rubbed the mist off the passenger window. "It's a bit ironic for her to advise him about relationships. That's a hoot. And selling the house? It was only mine if I lived there, and I left it. Like we've talked about."

"Brette never intimated about an affair with Allen. She is more than capable, and he is, too," Lara said.

I frowned. "He called me 'babe' on the phone and said he missed me."

"He'll be super sweet because he thinks you might inherit a bundle."

"God, I hate it when you make sense," I said, "but he used to complain about her perfume. Funny memory, huh?"

"He must've been in pretty close proximity to notice that," Lara said. "I haven't seen Brette in months. She sure pulled it together for tonight. I wonder if she was trying to impress Allen or give you fair warning?" Lara sounded amused. "Get the popcorn."

6

The Cat & The Money

Lara pulled into her condo's parking space and she shut off the BMW. "Well, I'm glad I'm not responsible for his debt load, that's for sure." I slammed the car door louder than I intended. "I said goodbye to the house on the hill when we left it. I miss the rope swing from the old cherry tree the most. Allen made it for Clea when she was two or three, and he used to tell stories to her as they swung on it, and now the house is all about money." I felt defeated. "Sometimes I wonder why we have to remember so much."

The elevator opened to Lara's floor, and we entered her condo. The next day would come early. We hugged goodnight, and I settled in my pullout bed and stared into the Seattle night, a Seattle fading slowly away.

Lara and I headed for the Canadian border before the morning traffic jammed Interstate 5. Somehow, we managed to find Charlie Trucker's office. Lara pulled into the small parking lot that fronted the building. "God, this has to be so hard, Tans, and you are equally strong. Let's go get this over with and back to Seattle."

A receptionist greeted us and led us to an office with an overlarge watercolor painting of the Capilano Suspension Bridge on one wall. An Emily Carr framed print centered another. I loved the depth of the forest colors and the movement in her work. A wall of books, a leather chair, and a reading lamp created a cozy touch to my right. The lawyer in a steel gray suit wore red-framed spectacles attached to a gold chain lanyard around his neck.

He stood as we entered. Long hair curled around his earlobes, a small diamond stud in the right one. He shook my hand. "From what your mother told me, you two were long-estranged," Charlie Trucker said in an even warm baritone voice. "She wanted me to tell you how sorry she was and that she takes full responsibility for the family break. Vivian told me the circumstances." He paused, smiled, then added, "I sometimes do not know how we survive our families when we're all alive. Let alone when a parent passes." Mr. Trucker went on, "My deepest condolences." He bowed his head and motioned us to sit in wingback chairs facing his desk.

As Charlie Trucker took his seat, he added, "Her death was so senseless. She walked to a late-night market to fetch a carton of milk for her cat, and a drunk driver hit her in the crosswalk in front of her apartment building."

"Milk for the cat?" was all I could utter.

"What do you mean?" Mr. Trucker said.

"I imagined her dying in a high-speed chase, or perhaps, in a bad drug deal, murdered or overdosed, alone on the street, but going out at night to get milk for her cat and hit by a car—seems like the death of a librarian—ironic, you know? My dad was a librarian." I tapped my foot. I wanted to be out of this office and see my kids.

Charlie Trucker raised an eyebrow. "Life comes with ironies, yes? I knew your mother quite well," he said with tears in his eyes. "She hired me after your father passed, and I handled her trust fund. But we became friends."

I stared out the window behind the lawyer's desk and into the street, where traffic took families on outings. Who knows where those cars were going or whom they carried? I wanted them to have happy moms and dads with excited children on the way to Granville Island or Stanley Park. I never had happy moments with Mother, at least ones I could conjure sitting across from her lawyer.

"You look a great deal like her, Ms. Daniels, same eyes, hair, a bit wild and untamed." He raised an eyebrow again. "Let me show you." He opened his desk drawer and withdrew a framed recent picture of Vivian with her cat.

"Oh," I said, startled by seeing a photograph of my mother. She had parted her hair in the middle and pulled it softly into a high bun with small curls springing at the edges. She teased the camera with wide green eyes, and her lips were closed with only a hint of a smile. Her Maine Coon cat, with its over-large paws, filled her lap and seemed right at home. "What's the kitty's name?" Tears popped. I felt like a child trapped inside an angry woman's body. The child wanted to know the cat's name.

"Mama Cass Elliot," he said. "She named her for the singer."

"I named my dogs Yul Brenner and Deborah Carr—I guess we both had a penchant for entertainers, or at least we saw our pets like that." I stared at the photo and cried— I felt empty. Mr. Trucker cried, too. He handed me a box of tissues, even Lara appeared weepy.

"Mama Cass Elliot lives with me now. She's grieving; the cat is. Hopefully, her heart will mend. She's a charming, long-haired, huge girl. And I'm taking my allergy pills."

I nodded and stared at my hands. "I'm glad she had a happy life then, I mean Mother, and the cat. I'm glad Vivian had a friend like you."

"Before we get to business, I have a favor," Charlie Trucker said. "May we keep in touch?"

"You can write me, but I don't know if I'll write back. I can't promise."

Charlie Trucker cleared his throat, wiped his eyes, and blew his nose. "I have a copy of Vivian's will. I'll tell you the highlights: The trust expired upon your mother's death. She gave me the cat and a thousand dollars for her care. There was fifty thousand dollars left in the trust. She had no out-standing debts. She had some quirks, your mother had," Mr. Trucker licked his lips and paused. "She left five thousand to Safe-cat, a no-kill cat shelter, and forty thousand to a non-profit's building fund. It's called Reinvest; they are revitalizing the east side of Vancouver, one dilapidated structure at a time. The money is earmarked for the community center they plan to open in the new year. It's a great organization. Your mother was on its board." Charlie wrinkled his forehead as he peered at us over his reading glasses. "She left you four thousand dollars, Tansy. I have a check for you."

I listened to what appeared to be a sea of words. Raw nerves made my fingers tingle. I could have used fifty grand, well, who couldn't? However, though I couldn't express why, I felt fine about the money. It was never mine in the first place. I replied, "Thank you."

"I want to read a note your mother left for me to read

to you; she put it in her will. Charlie Trucker adjusted his reading glasses and read from the document: "'Dear Tansy, I had too much money, and it never made me happy, but getting kids off the street and giving shelter and food to hungry cats makes me happy. I hope you agree that I've made a good investment. With the money I leave you, I hope you do something special. I never stopped loving you. You are in my heart eternally.'"

"The will sounds recently composed." Lara cocked her head toward Mr. Trucker.

"A coincidence, perhaps." The lawyer peered at Lara and then at me. "Vivian gave me the details about revising how she wanted the funds distributed upon her death ten days before the accident. She was sitting right where you are, Ms. Daniels, the day before she died. Signed her will and gave me the letter. And then the accident. I saw her the day after she was hospitalized. Then the stroke." He shook his head as one does in contemplation. "I'm sorry you are not inheriting more."

"I kind of feel relieved," I said. "I didn't come here expecting a windfall, and no amount of money could fix the past."

"She lived with deep regret. She became a devout Christian. I think that helped her." Mother's lawyer and friend opened another drawer on his desk and held a mahogany box. "She wanted you to have her ashes, to do with what you wish."

I stood and took hold of the box carrying my mother's cremains. "Mr. Trucker—"

"Please call me Charlie," he said.

"Thank you, Charlie," I whispered. "We'll have a ceremony. I'll do it properly."

Charlie handed Lara the copy of Vivian's will and the check. We shook hands and said goodbye.

"I had no idea what was in the trust fund," I said to Lara as she pointed her BMW southward, and we said goodbye to Vancouver.

"Play money," she said.

"More like paying off my credit card money." I shrugged. "The photo of Mother and the cat's name, then what she did with the money. And he wants to be my friend?" I stared outside. Lara played the Whitney Houston album *The Body Guard.* As "I Will Always Love You" played, I wept. Mother had to leave. Always. I knew it, but it hurt to the core of my being. I touched the scar under my chin. Lara said nothing and quietly drove. We stopped at McDonald's near Marysville, got milkshakes and french fries, and then returned to Seattle. Lara paid.

Brette arranged for us to go out on a boat owned by our Seattle friends, Jonny and Emma Buffet. Early the following day, they took us out onto the Sound. Ferry boats chugged on their route from Bainbridge to the City. The water ruffled under the rudder; seagulls squawked in the light fog. Jonny stopped at a place as the sun pierced a cloud above us, shattering light through the misty air. "A good place," he called.

We stood together. Emma sang "Amazing Grace," and we said The Lord's Prayer. I threw a wreath into the water and poured the cremains into the sea. "May you rest in the peace you finally found. Goodbye, my mother." My voice felt like it came out of someone else's body as the boat bobbed up and down in the silent wake of death.

Brette, Lara, Brette's daughter, Patricia, and my kids stood in a semi-circle around Lara's and Brette's cars in the marina parking lot, the exact positioning we were in on the Buffets' boat a short while ago. Clea stared at the sidewalk, and Janey cried when Patricia tried to pick her up. Brette patted Janey on the back, and Janey cried louder. "She probably needs to cry it out," Brette said. "Let's get you guys home."

I held Janey as Clea got into the middle seat of Brette's new minivan. I buckled my unhappy Janey into her car seat. "I should get hazard pay," Brette quipped as she started the vehicle.

7

Bumped Knuckles

I bit my lip as they pulled out of their parking space. "I don't think the kids can take another night at Brette's," I said as Lara put her BMW in gear and we headed out. "I'm going to change our reservations. Get on a night flight. We'll arrive too late for Alex to pick us up, but he'll do it tomorrow afternoon. We can stay over at a place the ranch does business with, Spring Vista Inn. It has a pool. It'll cost more, but it'd be nice." I peered at Lara, drained of color and appearing tired herself. "You want to come for the weekend? No cost for the stay at the ranch, and I'll cover the inn. I'm a rich lady! Looks to me like you could use a little sunshine fix yourself."

"Mm-hmm, it sounds tempting. A pool and horses, I wish," she chuckled. "I might be able to pull it off. I'll check my Monday calendar and call my assistant when we get home."

While Lara handled her scheduling for the next few days, I made tea and steeped it in a large Brown Betty teapot. I set cups out with gingersnaps, then packed my bag. Lara returned from her bedroom smiling, "I'm coming with you! Sheryl said she'd put me on the plane— herself— to get me out of town for a few days. Being the most marvelous assistant ever, she said she'd clear my calendar until Tuesday morning."

After Lara left and I made the calls for the airline and the inn, I opened the terrace slider, looked out onto the lake, and thought about Charlie Trucker. I was glad that Mother had someone to mourn her, mourn the woman she became, the lady with the cat in her lap. The cool air refreshed me as I snuggled under a maroon cable knit afghan Lara had made, and dozed. The doorbell ringing woke me up. Brette arrived with the girls and left with a quick goodbye.

Lara returned soon after. While she packed, we watched an episode of "Mister Rogers' Neighborhood" on TV. Janey sat on my lap, and Clea thumbed through *Time Magazine* and *Better Homes and Gardens*. Lara came out of her bedroom, "I'm packing jeans and a swimsuit. Will I need a dress for anything? Shorts?"

"We're the same size, so if you need anything, you can borrow from me," I said.

"You have sun lotion?" Lara asked.

"Yes, I do."

We gathered our bags and my girls and then loaded into a taxi heading to SeaTac. I bought a box of apples for the ranch at the airport, and we boarded the plane.

The Spring Vista Inn's courtesy van appeared ten minutes after we retrieved our luggage. As the bus pulled into the night of twinkling lights and airplanes, I sat back and sighed. Lara reached over to me, and we tapped knuckles, a sign between us expressing that all was well. We made it safely back. Lara was in vacation mode. I felt relief about my move to Arizona. I loved the wide-open sky and swaying palms lit by the street lights. Janey fell back to sleep, and Clea's head nodded. The children jolted awake when the bus stopped at the inn's entrance. The driver helped us with the bags, and we trundled into the narrow lobby with its bright red carpet festooned with abstract yellow flowers. We rang the bell on the long counter, and as we waited for someone to show up, I shook my head at the display of CollinCamp's brochures on top of the desk. "That thing must have printed twenty years ago," I said.

"What?" Clea asked.

"The brochure has to be pretty old. Look at the picture of the dining room. It's not even the same color. We need a facelift." I turned to Lara, who had opened the brochure. "CollinCamp doesn't exactly look like the photos."

"Mom, Glen tries real hard," Clea said, "he's really nice to us." She turned to Lara. "We have horses, and I like my school. It's cool."

"Point taken," I shifted Janey onto my other hip. I was happy to hear how Clea felt about CollinCamp.

A young man appeared from swinging doors behind the counter and checked us in. With the key in hand, we exited the lobby and found our room up one level. Two queen beds met us, or we met them, weary travelers coming home.

We woke early, ready for the complimentary breakfast

hour. Clea brought swimsuits for herself and Janey; Clea was always hopeful that a hotel swimming pool would be part of the occasion when we traveled. While the kids changed, I called the ranch and spoke to Alex. He had a pickup at the inn at 12:30 and was glad, he said, that we were home. He perked up when I said I brought a beautiful blonde with me.

As the girls played in the swimming pool, I dangled my feet in the water, and Lara swam laps. Clea also wanted to swim laps, so I jumped into the pool in my cutoffs and green tank top. I piled my hair into a high ponytail, but curls sprung loose from my heavy mop as I bounced Janey up and down. Afterward, we hustled to our room; Clea jumped at the opportunity to shower first. She emerged with her hair dried and gelled in a curve across her high forehead. Lara was next. She parted her flaxen bob on the side. She looked model-perfected with red lipstick that accentuated her mouth against her Nordic pale skin. I showered with Janey, and we were ready for the day.

Clea and Janey walked around Spring Vista's lobby while waiting for the ranch van. Lara and I sat on green vinyl lobby chairs across from a couple from Oklahoma who I recalled booking at the ranch a few weeks prior. The woman wore pink stretch pants and a lacy sleeveless tunic; her husband sported corduroy slacks and a short-sleeved cotton print shirt. He wore a watch embellished with gold nuggets and dozed in a hat propped onto his head.

"Who's the mama to those girls?" The woman asked.

"I am," I said.

"You waiting for the CollinCamp van?"

"We are," I answered. We had piled all our gear together while Clea kept Janey entertained. The woman wanted to have a conversation that I tried to avoid.

The kids rounded the corner toward me. "Mom, Janey wants to use the bathroom."

I smiled at the couple, picked up Janey, and headed to the restroom. On our return, Clea and the lady were talking. Lara was missing. Clea turned to me, "When is Alex getting here?"

"Should be anytime," I said. "Where's Lara?"

"She wanted to get a hat or something from that little gift store." Clea motioned to the tiny galley-style Arizona Treasures store on the other side of the lobby doors.

"Can we wait outside?" Clea asked.

"Yeah, in that green area with the swing, right over there." I pointed outside to a small playground visible from where I sat.

"How hot do you think it will get today?" the woman asked. "My name's Loretta, and your daughter says you work at the ranch?"

"I think we may have spoken," I said, "I'm Tansy Daniels, and yes, I think maybe mid-eighties—I haven't seen the forecast for today." I kept an eye on the girls and watched Clea push Janey in the swing.

"I'm so sorry for your loss," Loretta said.

What was she talking about? My mind spun, and then I realized Clea must have told her why we were in Seattle. I didn't want to extend this conversation; Loretta's husband, Ron, roused from his nap while Lara crossed the lobby to join us.

"Yeah," I said quietly. "You're never ready, I guess."

"Ready for what?" her husband Ron asked.

"Oh, for God's sake, her mother died, Ron." Loretta turned to me. I noticed a smear of hot pink lipstick on her front tooth.

"Isn't that our ride?" Ron checked his watch. "Damn near ten minutes late."

We all stood. "We do our best," I said. "Alex will take care of your bags."

We watched as the couple heaved themselves into the van, and then Alex greeted us. "Hi, you guys!" When he caught sight of Lara, I smiled. Here's your cowboy, Lara, I thought and introduced them. The girls hugged Alex and helped load the van. We buckled Janey in her booster seat, with Clea and me in the row behind the Oklahoma couple. Lara rode shotgun with Alex. I stared out at the desert as the air conditioning chilled the van's interior. Mirages created waves of undulating sand in the distance. The hot world opened — infinite spaces — ambling on. I thought about my mother — how quickly her life was over, as quickly as the shape of a dune that morphs and disappears. How do you paint that feeling? I wondered as the minutes clocked on. How do you hold a mother whose arms you feared? I listened to Alex chat with the guests and Lara about air conditioning, the telescope, and side trips to the Grand Canyon, but my mind floated with the changing tides of the sand.

As we neared the Oracle Junction, we heard tunes playing in the outdoor arena at Ringo Nogales Dance-A-Rama & Grill, famous to locals. "What's that?" Lara pointed to what was probably Tucson's hottest nightspot, fifteen minutes from the ranch and fifteen from town. Lit only by an electric lantern above a small sign and surrounded by a tall fence, you might overlook Ringo's if you didn't hear the music.

"You really have to go to Ringo's," Alex chimed. "Great live music all weekend and good food. Sunday afternoons are awesome there."

"Did you like it?" Loretta peered back at me.

"I have only heard stories about Ringo's. Someday, maybe, I'll go," I said.

Alex left the couple at the office, Glen at the door, and then buzzed us over to my house in a hurry with a group horse ride booked for later. Before leaving, he said to Lara and me, "We should go over to Ringo's. I'm surprised you haven't been yet, Tans. And Lara, you don't want to miss out."

"I hope we can work that out," Lara said.

Oh, God, she's falling for him, I thought. And he's definitely falling for her. The four of us stood on the porch and waved to Alex as he turned the van around and left. I was so caught up watching Alex and Lara meet that I hadn't realized how quiet my house was. The dogs should be barking greetings. And nothing. I held my breath before going inside. Were the dogs OK, and what about the birds?

"Hello?" I ventured inside, but no dogs were in sight. The air conditioning was on, and the house was cleaner than I had left it. Someone vacuumed the couch, stacked my books neatly on an end table, and left a small bouquet of daisies in a mason jar on the table.

"Wow, Mom," Clea said, "it feels good to be home."

I nodded, and I heard the back door open. My dogs thundered in, and a teenage boy I did not know followed them. Honeydog jumped up on me while Yul and Deborah circled us.

"Hi, Ms. Daniels," the teenager said, "my aunt, Maria, she just left."

"So Maria took care of my house—flowers and all?" I asked. "Bless her heart."

"Yes," the boy seemed more at ease. "I work for Glen sometimes on the weekend and sometimes after school, and he comes over to check the dogs and lets me in and out to walk them. The two young ones are goofballs."

"I know!" We all laughed. "And you are?"

"I'm Diego Doran."

"Thank you, Diego—you did a great job!" The dogs pranced gleefully about. "Would you do me a giant favor and take this box of apples over to the kitchen?"

"Yes, sure," he said, "Glen has your key."

"Who's Maria?" Lara asked after Diego left.

"She's one of our housekeepers," I said. "What a sweetheart."

We unpacked, and the girls and I took Lara for a stroll around CollinCamp. Glen met up with us and explained some of CollinCamp's history to Lara. He waxed poetically about the sacred trust he felt toward the land, emphasizing the indigenous history of the land's earliest settlers. The Hohokam were the earliest inhabitants. Glen called them highly advanced. They were seasonal farmers, hunters, and gatherers of acorns and grasses, which they wove into some of the same designs you see in Apache artisan baskets today. Glen pointed to some of the grasses along the route we took around the ranch. He cut a piece of devil's claw and held it up to Janey. "That there's a basket," he said. "What they made them pretty baskets from."

He went on with the history as we passed the small dairy barn. The Hohokam people's descendants, the Apache and the Sobaiparis tribes, fought over the land about the same time Father Kino, a missionary, arrived in 1698, "Almost three hundred years ago," Glen emphasized. "You take note of that, Clea." He told us about the Apache who lived around Oracle and how a vigilante group massacred two hundred elderly tribespeople, women, and children. The government relocated the Apache to the San Carlos Reservation.

"I bet they were glad to leave," Clea said.

"This was their home, their land, so no, I expect they wanted to stay. And a few families did, claimin' their land. And they won it." Glen stooped to the ground and picked up a handful of dirt. "We're travelin' on other people's property, and we keep it up. It means something. Knowin' the history. So don't you forget it, Clea."

"I'll remember, too, Rancher Glen," Janey said.

"I bet you will, little one," Glen tousled her hair.

Glen left us at the corral; we toured the low building, stopping to pet one of three horses in their stalls when we heard the riders return. We watched Alex help some of the least experienced off their horses. The guests returned to their bungalows, and Alex led the horses to a large trough where they drank heartily. Clea wanted to introduce Lara to the horses; she knew all of them by name, and Janey and I tagged along happily.

"What have you been up to?" Alex directed the question to me with a nod toward Lara.

"We took a walking tour of the ranch and happened to run into Glen. He told us all about the Apache and the early times of Oracle."

"He'll talk your ear off," Alex said.

"He knows his history," Lara said. "He loves this place." She patted a dapple gray who nudged her hand. "You are a beauty," she said to the horse, "so gentle."

"That's Demon Savior, Mom, the horse you said you would never ride." She laughed. "Do you know Mom's afraid of riding horses, Lara?"

"I've heard rumors about that," Lara replied. "I'd call you

Sugar." She spoke directly to the horse.

Alex had hauled off the saddle from a second horse; he pivoted to Lara. "You like to ride?"

"Yes, and I'm no city slicker amateur." She pointed her index finger at me.

"Are you an early riser?" Alex asked Lara.

"I am," Lara responded.

"We could go out at seven tomorrow if you're interested?"

"I will meet you here," Lara and Alex smiled at one another.

"Can we go, too?" Janey wondered.

"No," I answered.

On the way back to my place, Lara and I bumped knuckles.

"We are lucky to be here—I feel like a guest. It's great to have you here, Lara."

The phone was ringing when we got home. It was a short vacation.

8

One For the Team

Clea grabbed the phone, said hello, peered over her shoulder at me, and said, "Dad." She listened to Allen, put her hand over the receiver, and said, "He just got to Seattle!" When she asked when he could visit, she paused and handed the phone to me. "He said he has to talk to you about that."

Allen wanted a party at CollinCamp. "Friends and family!" he said. "Mom wants to be there, naturally. I've invited Brette and Patricia, too."

I repeated what he asked aloud so that Lara understood the gist of the conversation. "I have to check our bungalow situation; probably the week after next will most likely be open. I can give you dates tomorrow. That OK?"

"Yes, I'll call you tomorrow around noon," Allen said, "we can nail the dates," then paused. "Before you go, did you talk to the lawyer handling your mother's estate?"

"I have a copy of the will."

"And?" Allen asked.

"Nothing much was left in the trust fund, if that's what

you're asking. But Charlie was nice."

"And Charlie is?" asked Allen.

"Charlie Trucker. Mother's lawyer." Lara motioned me to end the conversation. "Let's talk tomorrow, Allen. Bye-bye," And I hung up.

The camp cook, Peter, was sober enough to make chili and cornmeal muffins. It wasn't the greatest, but I appreciated Glen inviting us for dinner with the other ranch guests. In the library adjacent to the dining room were board games and tables set up for people to play. We played Monopoly. Janey and I played together.

At home, Clea called her best friend, Franny, to see what she had missed at school, and the day ended on a sweet note. Lara and I shared my bed with Honeydog. Lara was up before sunrise, getting ready for the horse ride with Alex, and gone before the girls roused.

"We're going to Ringo's tonight," Lara purred when she entered the office, where I"d been catching up on paperwork for the last few days.

"You are?" I smiled, "I figured a while back that you and Alex—"

"You, me, Alex, and Pablo," Lara interrupted. "I met him at Alex's after the ride. Pablo's a metal artist, Tans, and he is like drop-dead gorgeous. An artist-cowboy?" She added, "You can't make this stuff up— he's perfect for you."

I held up my hand. "I just got off the phone with Allen. I don't think I'd be very good company."

Lara shrugged. "C'mon. This is one night."

"I'd rather have a root canal."

"What did Allen say to you? You know, or we highly suspect, he's hooked up with Brette, and his divorce from what's her name isn't final. What whiny story did he give you?"

"He gets this tone of voice that throws me back to when we were kids, confiding in each other. He told me the divorce from Julie took all the wind from his sails, and driving by our old house depressed him."

"Where's the poor soul staying in Seattle?" Laura smirked.

"He didn't say."

"Did he mention your mom's will again?" Lara was in full lawyer mode.

"He told me that I should've verified all the funds—he thinks Charlie might have skimmed from the top. He wondered about the charities."

"Tansy, for God's sake, you read the will. Your mom was clear. And what were you doing telling him any of the specifics?"

"Allen sounded genuinely interested in the kids and my well-being on the phone. I think he was trying to look after me like he used to."

"Like when you were pregnant and he divorced you? Or when he let the house go into foreclosure? That man is about control. Allen's interest is in how much money you might inherit because he wants it. So, yeah, he's going to be all chummy until he's not. You know that, and I do, too."

"Yup. A moment of weakness. I want to believe—"

"I'm making you go to Ringo's. If the date's a dud, so what? Ringo's has live music, and it will be fun, a story, anyhow."

I wanted to hide in my closet, but I thought maybe I should go out, and then I balked at the idea, so I changed the subject to Allen's visit. "I booked the bungalows for Allen."

"Long-suffering Allen may be finding some relief from his good friend, Brette, the relationship counselor." Lara widened her eyes. "You think?"

"Could be, but since Allen's inviting friends, I decided I could, too, so I booked a bungalow for you—no pressure." I toyed with a strand of hair that fell loose from my braid. "I told Glen I reserved three bungalows, full price, and he was one happy rancher." I stared at Lara's passive face. "You will come, won't you? You'll stay for free. The heater might not work, but I don't think that'll bother you. Come for the weekend—your own place so you'll have more privacy." I coyly blinked at my friend, "You would like to ride horses some more?"

"Well, I always like to help a friend," Lara said sagely, and we burst out laughing. "But this means, Tansy Daniels, that you are coming with us to Ringo's."

"I have kids, and this is a school night, and after talking to Allen, I think I'm over men forever."

"You said you wanted to go and …"

Maria poked her head in the door from the kitchen. "I will stay with the children. I overheard," she grinned. "I babysit on the side, and I love your family. And Pablo is cha cha cha." She winked with a broad smile.

"OK, you two, I'll go to Ringo's."

We decided to meet Alex and Pablo at Ringo's. The boys had pickups, and I drove a small sedan, nothing that comfortably fit four adults. I thought they were going together but was unsure of the plan. I heard Maria chat with Lara as I finished getting ready. I wore a beige tank top and my skinny jeans. I brushed my hair back from my face and put on small copper-hooped earrings. "Time to go," I said to a nervous reflection. "This is just a casual date." I didn't look like I believed myself. I sucked in my gut. I hadn't been on a date since my divorce four years ago. Nothing felt casual about it, and I never imagined going on a blind date.

I kissed the girls goodnight. Maria picked Janey up, and she hung onto the short, loving woman with deep brown eyes and strong hands. Everyone appeared contented as Lara and I drove out of the ranch. Lara seemed on air while I glanced at my watch. Home in less than three hours, I thought. A blind date? What do you even say on those things? *God, I'm sorry you smell wrong.* I prayed to get through the evening—after all, I was there for Lara.

9

Dancing With Pablo

I pulled into one of the five spaces in front of the heavy wooden door at Ringo's and took a deep breath. How was this going to go? A couple holding hands left through the door and passed by my car. They appeared comfortable with each other, laughing, maybe at a shared joke. I couldn't remember going on a date with anyone but Allen twenty years ago. I'd rather be walking my dogs, I thought, or going to the dentist. I shook my head and laughed.

"What's the joke?" Lara asked.

"For one, my tank top looks better on you than me. Violet is your color. And second, I haven't been out like this except with Allen twenty years ago. It feels awkward."

Alex knocked on my window before Lara could answer. I opened the door as Pablo appeared.

I was dumbstruck because I had seen him before, a guest, I thought at the time out for an early ride. I didn't know his name then; I witnessed the horse, its rider, and a small dog running in sync with the horse. The horse tail's white brilliance caught in an Arizonan sunrise; the rider's straight back as he rode. They all belonged together, that's what I thought. Who was he? I didn't see the rider's face. Was he young, old, or somewhere caught in the middle like me? I heard the palomino's hooves only on the cobblestone walkway, then horse and rider chose the worn desert path, and a spray of dust lit in the morning light as they disappeared in the full body of sunlight. And now I said, "Nice to meet you," after being introduced to Pablo Sagasta. Lara had not exaggerated. Lean and tall, young with laugh lines established around deep charcoal eyes, his shaggy head of black curly hair framed a caramel-tanned face. "I think I saw you ride one morning. Do you ride a palomino?"

"His name's Jeremy," Pablo said.

"You have a dog?" I asked.

"That's Diamond. She's Jeremy's buddy."

Alex offered his arm to Lara, "Let's do this!"

Pablo followed Alex's lead, and I curled my arm through his. The heavy door opened onto a man dressed in black sitting on a barstool behind a small counter. Western swing doors on our left led to what I believed was the bar itself. "Hola, Alex, and who is the lovely lady tonight?" He walked around the desk to shake Alex's hand. Alex introduced us to Chucho Gomez, a greeter at Ringo's.

"Ray is practicing a new set tonight. Enjoy." Chucho led us into a bowl-shaped room with a peaked ceiling lined with ponderosa pine log paneling. Large barn doors framed the outer side of the seating area; the doors opened onto a dance floor and arena on the weekends. Chucho said they planned to open it up in another hour. The honey-toned wood and cobalt iron hinges caught in low light, enhanced by table

candles, made the room we entered feel intimate. A ceiling fan moved slowly. We followed Chucho up four or five
steps, where he seated us by the cedar pole railing on this
elevated floor. Below us was a small stage where I guessed it
was Ray, whom I saw fingering a guitar.

"Navajo tacos tonight? She's got the fryer going," Chucho
offered.

"You have to try the tacos! Rosa is a master," Pablo said.

"I think I better," I said.

"And beer?" Chucho asked.

"Perfect," Lara said.

"I'll bring a pitcher and four glasses, yes?" We all nodded
yes, and Chucho was off to run the order.

"So, what is this we're going to eat?" I asked.

Pablo smiled. "Instead of tortillas, Rosa makes fry bread.
We'll get a platter of tomatoes, avocados, lettuce, and sea-
soned meat to load them. Rosa usually makes Navajo-style
for celebration events, so we are in for a treat."

Alex gave a thumbs up.

"Do you like to ride?" Pablo asked me. Alex and Lara
laughed.

"They aren't being fair. Stop laughing. I do like horses,
but I—"

"That's a start," Pablo said. "I hear you're an artist."

"I try to be, " I answered.

From below us, Ray began singing "Forever Young." I sat
back, smiled, and relaxed. I loved Pete Seeger's songs, and
here we were listening to one.

When we applauded after the song, I was surprised by
how many people were at Ringo's. I wasn't aware of anyone
coming in, but there were other tables with folks in secluded

corners. "You weren't kidding about Ringo's," I said to Alex. "And a Pete Seeger song, too. But just one song?"

"There'll be more," Alex said. "Ray's warming up."

Over beer, we chatted about what brought us to the Southwest.

Pablo and I began to talk about landscapes and art. "I love to ride because I sometimes feel what I create—I'm always looking at structure, whether it's a cactus or a cow."

"Lara said you're a metal artist; I guess you would be looking at structure."

"Yeah, I do welded sculptures from found objects—that's how someone at a gallery described a display of my work." He shrugged. "What kind of art do you do?"

"If we're speaking gallery-talk, I guess you'd call it mixed media. I love watercolor, pastels, and some oils. Whatever the canvas wants. I love the idea of what you do, by the way, how fire changes something. I'm drawn to that." I continued, "Or the depth of what is out there to create. I find myself on my porch absorbed in the desert sounds every night, well, most nights—like a magnet pulls me there. Distant lightning, sand storms, or the purest sky imaginable. Owls and coyotes."

"And the colors," Pablo began when our food arrived.

The yeasty bread beautifully browned from the fryer nearly filled my plate, and the heavenly smell filled the room. "The food looks as good as the music sounds." I laughed. "I don't think I ate today."

"I'm glad it meets with approval," Pablo lifted his schooner of beer and said, "Thank you, Alex, for bending my arm to come here tonight."

"I had to bribe Tansy," Lara said.

"I'll drink to that." Pablo and I touched schooners. "God, we're brave."

Fry bread tacos puff out, and after I filled mine with the delectables from the platter we shared, I paused. "If I figure out how to eat this taco, I think I might love it—I don't know how I'm going to get it in my mouth," I said. "I might need a fork."

"Just go for it!" Pablo said. "That's why we have these generous napkins."

"Well, I have a four-year-old, so I do know how to go for it." I grabbed the taco, folded it the best I could, and plunged it into my mouth for a generous bite with dubious success. Trails of sauce spilled, but it was so delicious I didn't mind. I wiped my mouth and continued eating.

When I peered over my plate at Pablo, he said, "You missed a spot." He took his napkin and gently wiped the tip of my nose. "So Glen tells me you drove fifteen hundred miles to get here with dogs, birds, and kids? What kind of woman does that?"

"Maybe a crazy one?" I shook my head. "I rented a small camper trailer in Seattle, and a really nice man at the rental place hitched it to my car, and I drove to a nearly empty house where I put the birds in pet carriers, loaded them, and Yul and Deb, my younger dogs, in the camper, put the kids and Honeydog, my old girl, in the car and we set off with a road map of campgrounds between Seattle and Tucson. " I smiled at the memory. "In one place, I forget where, maybe Wyoming, we stopped at a motel. Anyway, Clea wanted to pet the birds. I had seven birds in two carriers. She opened the crate with Cecilia and Starlight, parents of the other five birds, and out they flew. I brought a bird net for such an occasion. I figured they'd roost together when we went to bed, and they did on top of the curtain rod in front of the main window. We slept with the curtains open. I had the bird net by my hand. I waited until things were dead calm, captured them, and put them back in their crate. Cecilia bit me. She's a nasty girl but loves Starlight, so all was well."

"Where did the dogs sleep?" Alex asked.

"In the car. No pets were allowed, but I talked the lady into letting us stay. I'm glad I didn't have to explain the bird poop on those shiny pink curtains."

"You and Tansy have known each other a long time?" Alex asked Lara.

"Twenty years," Lara said.

"We go way back, too," Alex pointed at Pablo. "Back when we got into a whole lot of trouble."

Pablo shook his head. "Let's not go there." And they began to laugh. A story ensued about the night they took Pablo's mother's car to the desert to drink beer. They were thirteen, rolled the car on the way home, were arrested, and spent the night in jail. "Remember when your mom bailed us out? We said goodbye to two old guys sobering up. One guy looked up—no teeth, he yelled at our backs as we left. "You'll be back." They laughed at the memory. "Amazingly, we're not dead," Pablo said, laughing more.

I finished my glass of beer. "Alex tells me you were traveling. Where was that?"

"Short story: I met a woman who lived in Toronto. Lived there with her and a beagle named Diamond for six years. You guessed it. I got the dog in the breakup and began traveling west in my 1952 Chevy pickup. Eventually, we got home."

"That's a pretty old truck."

"It's a great truck when it wants to be. I rebuilt it in Canada—it got us here."

"I don't know why you don't get something newer," Alex said.

"I'm sentimental," Pablo deadpanned.

Alex shook his head.

"Does Glen keep your horse here?"

"Yes, he does."

A male voice over the intercom interrupted our chat. "As some of you know, this is Rosa's sixty-fifth birthday. She wants a dance party. We're opening up the outdoor dance floor, and Ray and the Three O'Clocks are going to play a few sets."

Chucho appeared. "You guys go on down while Ray gets things going. I'll clear your table." Chucho was directing, not asking; he spoke with authority. I heard the barn doors open to the outdoor patio, and people were already going there. Lara and I insisted on paying for half the ticket, and Alex and Pablo reluctantly agreed.

"I haven't danced in a long time," I said, changing the subject from the bill.

"Let's give it a go," Pablo said. "You did alright with the tacos."

Lanterns lit the fence around the small arena. Toward the left was a raised platform where Ray and his band set up. While they were at work, Chucho joined them with Rosa, a small woman with voluminous hair piled into a bun. "Let's everyone sing happy birthday to you, Rosa."

We stood in a semi-circle and sang Rosa the birthday song. Then Ray began playing an Elvis Presley love song, and without a word, Pablo put his hands on my shoulders and turned me around. I put my hands on his shoulders. We faced each other as we moved in circles. He moved his arm around my waist, and I nestled into his shoulder. Ray sang, "… and I can't help falling in love with you." And I remembered the feeling. Ray was not through with the love songs. For another, and another followed. Pablo and I did not speak. I don't remember anyone else on the floor.

When Ray stopped playing, it was as if I woke up from a dream. We stood in a dancer's embrace. God, this man can dance, I thought. He dropped his arm, and I took a step back. He put his hand under my chin, lifted my head, and kissed me. Had I waited my whole life for that kiss? And it happened here at Ringo's in Oracle, Arizona? Life comes with ironies. Ringo Nogales Dance-A-Rama & Grill was palace enough for this latter day Cinderella. I nearly laughed aloud at the thought.

I guess Ray noticed because he began playing "Love Me Tender." We danced again. We were the only ones left on the floor. At the end of the song, Ray blew us a kiss. I giggled and did a little curtsy. I caught sight of Alex kissing Lara not far from us. Whatever else happens, I thought, I will remember this night always.

We held hands leaving Ringo's and didn't speak until we stood on the other side of the door. The date was over. How could that be? "That was magical in there," I said as we stood by my car.

"You're beautiful," Pablo said. "The light, the night. How happy I am." And he kissed me again. He hugged me closely. "I better get out of here." He let go and glanced at his watch. "You know it's almost midnight?"

"Holy cow, I've got to get home," I said.

Alex and Lara said goodbye at his truck, then walked over to us arm in arm.

"Will I see you again?" Pablo asked.

"I'd like that," I answered.

"Me too," Pablo said. "Take it easy driving home." He kissed me on the forehead and both cheeks. "Bye for now." He waved to Lara, and we watched Alex and Pablo walk away.

"I know it's late," Lara said, "but drive home slowly. What a night."

10

The Cat

Maria met us on my porch. I paid her. Maria appeared worried. "Is everything OK?" I asked. She tucked her shawl around her shoulders and assured me that all was fine with the girls, but her husband called with news that her mother had fallen. She worried about missing work. "My cousin Consuela could work for me," Maria added. "Glen needs more help, anyway."

"Send her over in the morning, and I'll work it out with Glen," I said, "give your mom my best."

Maria turned as she left for her car. "Allen, he called twice," Maria said. "He asked where you were, and I told him you and Lara went to dinner." She smiled broadly. "I think you had a good time?"

The following day, the phone rang before I was up. Lara was riding with Alex again. I answered on the fourth ring. "What time did you get home? And why is Lara at the ranch?"

"Well, good morning to you," I said to Allen. "We're getting up here. Everything is fine. Have to run, so let's talk later." And I hung up.

Both real and imagined, my mind spun a hundred scenarios as I hustled the girls through breakfast and to their schools. The one set in sepia tones with gold glimmers when I danced with Pablo at Ringo Nogales' Dance-A-Rama & Grill lingered.

For me, it was a work day. By mid-morning, the coffee was hot in my mouth as I paused from paying bills in the safety of the dude ranch office. Lara peeked in earlier to tell me she was back from the early ride with Alex and packed to go home. She was coming over for lunch with me before her return flight to Seattle.

Meanwhile, the sun played solo in a steady blue sky. While Glen was at his lawyer's office, Peter, the cook, came in sober, I was happy to see. The ranch hosted our Oklahoma guests, two couples and their families, as well as Marty Chicago, our resident writer.

I wondered if Maria's cousin was coming in for work. Alex took an apple from a basket I had on my desk and left to continue his ranch chores. He was floating on the same cloud as Lara. I wondered what Pablo was doing. The phone rang, and I thought it was Allen, but it was a potential guest checking out our services. I recognized the dread I felt about speaking to Allen, quizzing me like a child. He hadn't called yet. I turned my thoughts back to work and bit into an apple. Juice dripped on my chin as I pondered my line of attack on the remainder of the bills.

With not enough cash flow to cover everything we needed to pay, I had to figure out what vendors needed prompt payment from those who could wait until the current (and hopefully) new guests had paid for their stays. Sometimes, I wondered how CollinCamp remained in business, winter or summer. I sighed and looked up from my work. Some guy in cutoff jeans, with a sunburned back and overhanging belly, threw a cigarette butt down by the old saguaro that centered the courtyard. Was that Ron, the Oklahoma guy? He stomped the butt out and began walking away. With its arms upturned toward heaven, the cactus appealed to some authority beyond us for help. Well, today, it was me. I went outside with a tissue and picked up the butt.

Faint lines of the children's hopscotch bleached in the sun remained on the patio. I stepped over the squares in a fruitless effort to halt time and returned to my desk. I sketched the saguaro in the margin of an unpaid invoice. Becky Newbauer's father built the courtyard around the cactus. I doubted the man had completed the fifth grade, yet he understood the saguaro's importance. The saguaro lived fully-saguaro, and its vitality inspired art.

I noticed a new woman fitted out in an apron pushing a cleaning cart in an animated conversation with Glen. I stared at them with my eye on the giant cactus to their side. What stories it could tell. I wondered if that was Consuela, Maria's cousin with hands on her hips glaring straight up at Glen.

"That damn cactus telling you anything you didn't know?" Glen said as he came through the door.

"What's up?" I asked.

"The new person. Says she's Maria's relative."

"Her name's Consuela, she's filling in for Maria. Her mom fell. Hurt herself."

"How do you know?"

I told Glen about my conversation with Maria the evening before.

"Dora or Consuela wanted me to pay her before she

started working, practically threatened to go on strike before she'd been here ten minutes."

I stared back. "Glen," I said, "you fired her?"

"I wouldn't dream of doing that," he said in mock sincerity, "but I did think you might be able to talk to her, god damn it." He wiped his brow with a handkerchief from his back pocket.

"Watch the phone." I saw her walk right past Bungalow Five. It had a tricky air conditioner that only Maria's husband, Jesse, could fix. Right then, the unit contained a family who prepaid their vacation. I hadn't seen them yet and was grateful that the weather remained good because the cooler was down, and as soon as Jesse got the parts, he planned to fix it. We couldn't afford to offend Maria's family.

"Hello," I said to the maid. "You're filling in for Maria?"

"Yes, I'm Consuela Doran. Maria's cousin. She sent me. But this man, he doesn't have me fill out papers—no W-4, nothing. He hands me a mop and tells me where the cleaning supplies are. If he doesn't hire me legally, I get paid first."

"Mrs. Doran, I'm Tansy Daniels. And I'm so sorry. I handle the paperwork. Come with me." We walked into the office; Glen nodded and left the room. "I met your son, Diego, I believe? He walked my dogs, charming boy." I brought Glen's desk chair around by mine. "Please sit. I'm sure Glen was waiting for me to do the application and the government forms. Have an apple from Washington and a cup of coffee, and I'll get the application and the W-4. How's Maria doing?"

Consuela was an intriguing woman. She had four kids. The oldest was a teacher, and Diego was "in and out" of high school. She volunteered at WomanSpeak, a shelter for abused women and their children. Consuela liked the apple, filled out the forms, and went happily and legally back to work. I walked her over to Bungalow Five and then returned to the office. I thought about her kids supporting each other through college. Her husband was dead. They were a refugee family from El Salvador that started life in Tucson in the back of St. Agostina's Holy Trinity Church.

I saw that she had left her sweater in the office and raced back to the bungalow before she was through. She nodded and smiled thanks as I left her and crossed the courtyard again. Consuela and I were single mothers, sisters more like, I mused. A stray gust of wind blew a lump of sand in my eye. Christ, what was I thinking? Consuela learned what was necessary by having everything taken away. I had nothing taken from me except a philandering husband and a mother who left me four thousand dollars. As dramas played in my mind, mine was minor. I squinted as a tear ran from my eye.

"Are you OK, Tansy?"

"Got a little sand in my eye," I said to Alex. "That's all."

"Let's wash it out in the kitchen." He put his arm around my shoulder, and we walked through the office to the kitchen. Pools of water felt cool as they surrounded the sand and washed it away.

"Is she alright?" Glen said as he passed through.

"I think she'll make it," Alex answered.

"I feel like one of your horses the way you guys go on." I heard Glen answer the phone while Peter, the cook, offered me a glass of what he called cooking wine. I declined the offer and listened to him tell Alex and me about his new job. I didn't know he quit.

Alex asked Peter for a towel and handed it to me. "Speaking of horses, I brought a special horse up from my place that's perfect for you. Pablo thought you'd like her."

"Well, we'll see." I dried my face and placed the towel in the dirty linen container.

Glen buzzed the intercom to say that the phone call was for me. I picked up the extension, and Allen said, "You are the hardest person to get hold of."

"I am at work. Call me when the kids are home."

"I want to talk to you now."

"Can't. Call at six." I hung up the phone and felt queasy.

Glen walked into the kitchen. "Who was that on the phone?"

"My ex-husband, Allen. Sorry about him calling—he's been out of the country."

"I don't like him," Glen said.

"He was the one who rented the bungalows for a week, maybe two," I said.

"I like him some better," Glen said. "God, what a craphole of a day. Speaking of which, I left you a note to start lookin' through the books when Becky ran 'em. For my goddamn lawyer." With that, he banged his way out of the kitchen

"Do you know where they are?" I asked Alex back in the office.

"Yeah, in the safe. Do you have the combination?"

"I'm glad I asked before I spent all afternoon searching for them, and yes, I have the combination."

"I don't think he got the best news from his lawyer today." Alex polished an apple on his jeans and took a bite. "Third one today."

"Lawyer or apple?"

Alex shook his head. "Very funny. Becky conveyed through Glen's lawyer that she'd drop her bid for partnership if he came up with a million five."

"She must know that Glen can't do that. What's her game?"

"She wasn't serious, but Glen doesn't know that. It was her way of saying her case is ironclad."

"Poor guy," I said.

"Glen hates working with a lawyer."

"Well, he seems to like Lara—maybe he should hire her."

Alex blushed. "She's something else!"

"Could we talk about the cook for a minute? I know Glen's a good man—you've told me how he helps troubled and forgotten kids from Tucson out on the ranch, and I love his humor and his heart—my God, he puts up with me. But why on earth does he antagonize good people like Consuela and patronize you know who?" I pointed toward the kitchen.

"Another soul to save. Peter's a buddy from Korea; they were in the Army together. They go way back."

"I think he quit again," I whispered. "You can't have a drunk in the kitchen. I'd like to hire someone new. I might just put an ad in the paper and tell Glen about it later."

Alex laughed and shrugged. "It might work." He stood up, "I have a trail ride booked in a few, then I'm taking Lara to the airport. We're still on for you and the girls on Sunday, right?"

"Clea would kill me if I canceled the horse ride."

Lara and I shared lunch at my house before Alex took her to the airport. Over toasted cheese sandwiches and apple slices, our conversation turned away from Alex and Pablo and back to Allen. "You said you kept a record about ali-mony and child support from Allen?" Lara said. "Let me go through it. He owes it to you, and especially the kids."

"Yeah, I have it in my closet. Follow me. Allen's going to call again tonight. He's asking questions about what I am doing, why you were here, how late we were out, and where we went." I pulled a jacket off a box at the rear of my closet. "Here it is!" I held the red folder before handing it over to Lara. "Can we keep this out of court? Maybe negotiate with Allen's lawyer, take a little less or something?"

Lara took custody of the of the papers. "I will talk to Max. I know you hate court filings, but you can't let Allen get away with this BS. Try not to talk about money with Allen until I figure out how willing Max and his infamous client, Allen, will negotiate with you. Be friendly." Lara ex-tended her fist for a knuckle bump. I returned the gesture.

The phone rang. "Hey, Tans," Alex said. "Grabbed a call from Reno Air. They wanted you to know the cat arrived safely. I'll pick it up when I take Lara to the airport. Speaking of Lara—"

"What cat?" I asked. "No one told me about a cat. Lara is here, and we're coming over to the office now. See you in a few." We said goodbye.

Lara came out in jeans with her backpack over one shoul-der. "Was that Alex?"

"Yeah," I said, "Guess what? I think Charlie Trucker sent me Mother's cat." I tousled Honeydog's furry head and gazed at Yul and Deb."Well, this is going to be interesting."

11

Mama Cass Elliot's Got Lungs

The afternoon didn't go as I expected. Lara and I returned to the office, and Alex said, "We better hustle," to Lara, and then directed his attention to me. "You hung up too fast—Peter is sober enough to make dinner, but I grabbed Pablo's keys to his studio out at my place. Can you run 'em over there?"

"Who's covering the office?"

"Glen's talking to Peter, and he's got the front end covered. We better scoot." He tapped Lara on the shoulder.

I hugged Lara goodbye, and she and Alex headed for the van.

It was a ten-minute walk to Alex's place, and the small red pole building was hard to miss in the valley below. Set out to the side where Alex's double-wide trailer stood, a barn behind it, and pasture where three of his horses and several of Glen's pet cows grazed. I noticed a goat in there, too. I passed one of Glen's wells; he had two, with water supplemented by a state program. I loved the shush-shush sound of the water generated from its metal tower as it pumped into the cistern next to it.

Pablo sat on the porch steps. A small beagle with a waggling tail sat next to him.

"I hear you needed these," and I tossed Pablo the keys. "And you must be Diamond!" The dog jumped up on me, pranced around us both, and then took off in a dead heat for the field.

"Well, hello," Pablo said, "I wondered where these were." He yelled for the dog, and Diamond returned reluctantly.

"She's a beagle—amazing she came back on command." I watched the pup; her ears hung low—busted. "Alex had your keys."

"He helped me load a few pieces I took into town for my show. I think he locked up after I left and took off with them." Pablo paused. "Why don't you come in the barn and see what I have going on?" He directed his attention to Diamond, who I petted while he spoke. "You, little lady, are going inside. No barn for you." Diamond followed him to the front door and, with mournful eyes, went inside. "I keep her away from welding for her safety." I loved how gently he handled Diamond.

A large brass barn bell held by a filigreed bracket was attached to the side of the entrance; I rang it as Pablo unlocked and slid the door open. "Well, that's cool." I peered at shelves lined with metal objects, tools, paints, and resins. The only bright light came through the doorway and overhead where Pablo worked. "What are you working on?"

"Watusi Sally."

"It looks like the head of a cow," I said. "Watusi Sally's a cow?"

"One of Glen's favorites. She's out in the pasture. Glen wanted me to create a metal version of her for the patio."

"By the saguaro? Oh my God, I love it," I said. "Can I peek at some of your sculptures?"

"Just delivered most of the finished stuff. It's a pain in the neck to truck the large pieces."

"Like what?"

"I have a saguaro and a Corvette, smaller than full-sized but large. They're in town."

"Does the car come with a story?"

"My dream car before I met Glen," Pablo shrugged. "He gave me the truck after he taught me how to drive it so I could go to college at Arizona State."

"Glen. He's a puzzle—he's as gruff as he is generous. I wonder what made him that way."

"He had one of those life-changing moments. In Korea, the war, he served with Peter—"

"Alex told me something happened in Korea but didn't explain. Something to do with a sniper incident."

"That's right. Glen and Peter were out on patrol—returned fire from a sniper and killed him. Turns out the sniper was a kid. Changed them both—Glen helps any kid he can, and Peter can't find the bottom of a bottle of booze—his solution to brutal times. Glen keeps trying to save Peter, and Peter abuses the hell out of Glen."

"That explains a lot," I said. "Peter's the perpetual lost soul, I guess."

"I feel for the guy—for both of them."

"You can't save everyone." I wondered if Charlie Trucker saved my mother like Glen helped so many kids over time. What does being saved mean? Vivian had no one. We all shunned her after that fateful incident. What had her life been like? The past crept up on me as I stood there with Pablo, and I wasn't ready for it. I turned my attention to Pablo's workbench. "When's the show?" I asked. "Is it hard getting space large enough for it?"

"Ten days," Pablo said. "Yes, finding space for it is always a problem. I'm using a courtyard, basically, for the gig in Tucson."

"How many pieces are we talking about?"

"Seven big ones, six Glen kept in storage while I was away, and others that are fragile like the crows and the clock." Two metal crows forged onto a metal tree branch stand, one bird higher and larger than the other, were on a table in the back of where I stood. Next to it was a coyote clock about half a yard wide formed with the coyote's muzzle centering it. Blue shone through copper and silver tubing. "Decorative but functional," Pablo said. "Made for the outdoors.."

"The crows have a whimsical view of things—and the coyote telling time, great!"

Pablo shrugged in response. "Thanks. Why don't we visit Watusi Sally and her friends out back."

Pablo filled a shoulder bag with some carrots from a bin under the eaves of Alex's porch, and I walked with him to where a metal gate led to the pasture. The weathered wood fence enclosed what Pablo said was over an acre of irrigated farmland.

I edged around some cow pies. Pablo whistled for Sally's attention, and she strutted over to us. "She comes to you. That's so cool."

"Hand her a carrot, and she'll be your friend forever," Pablo said.

I offered a carrot to Miss Watusi Sally. She took it, and I swear she looked at me appraisingly, perhaps to see if I was suitable for the job. "Glen has NEVER uttered a word about you, Miss Sally," I said. "Excuse the udder reference." I patted her. "How old is this girl?"

"She's about thirteen," I think," Pablo ruffled the top of her head as she munched on a carrot. "Glen delivered her; her mother died. I raised her, and she's a smart cow. You see how she looks at you? You can tell she's thinking. We have a big ball she loves to play with." The other cows and horses ambled our way, and we gave them carrots as we chatted.

The animals followed us to the gate. Pablo's horse, Jeremy, nudged him at the entrance. "OK, you get one more carrot."

"Thank you for the tour, and I'm looking forward to the show," I said. "Hey, can I see your famous truck before I go?"

On the far side of the small barn was a carport where Pablo's '52 metal gray buffed-up pickup with a gleaming grill was parked.

"That's a pretty truck."

"Let's go for a ride sometime," Pablo said.

"OK," I checked my watch. "I gotta get back. Alex is bringing me a cat if you can believe it. I have to explain things to my dogs."

"A cat?"

"It was my mother's. You know she died." The words caught in my throat. I put my hand over my chest; I had no idea I was close to tears. I sucked in a breath and apologized for the emotional display. "We were estranged, the word I guess you'd use. Hadn't seen her in twenty years—and all weekend with Lara here and Ringo's? That cast a spell, but Mother's dead and left a cat. I thought her lawyer adopted her. Alex is picking the cat up at the airport."

"I've been to Ringo's many times, and it's special, but you are the one who cast the spell." Pablo touched my nose. "And it's still working." We kissed. From the house, we heard Diamond howl. Pablo hugged me and shook his head. "Diamond—"

"—wants out! I'll see you soon." I smiled as I jogged back to work, smitten by Pablo's touch. I wanted more of that.

Alex chuckled when he came in with the cat carrier. "I think Miss Kitty is OK, but she's not very happy."

The cat yowled and appeared scared as she huddled inside.

Alex handed me her paperwork, which included a letter from Charlie and an additional box of supplies. As the cat yowled louder, I read the letter aloud to Glen and Alex. "Every time I look at her," he wrote, "I cry—she needs to be with you, with family—she misses your mother. She's lost weight. Please accept the thousand dollar check for her care—all supplies included—inc. a new cat box and scoop. Regards, Charlie T."

"Get that cat out of that damn carrier," Glen boomed. The cat's yowls escalated into a howl. Glen lowered his voice. "She's scared half to death."

"Guests have been in and out of the office all day," I

said. "If I let her out and someone comes in, I'll never see her again."

"Put the closed sign up and let that poor thing out," Glen said. "A man's gotta get some peace around here. I'll go get a bowl of water for her." He went to the kitchen.

Alex put the closed sign up and shut the blinds. The rear gate of the cat's container stuck when I tried to unlatch it. Through the latticed door, I eyed Mama Cass, an oversized kitty with piercing blue eyes and golden red fur trimmed with pure white paws backing further into the cage. She pressed her body against the back of the crate.

"That carrier opens from the top," Glen said. "Reach in and pick her up and hold her." Glen had an open can of tuna fish and a bowl of water.

"She might claw the hell out of me."

"That might happen," Glen said.

The three of us stood around the crate as if we were about to perform surgery. "OK," I said, "I'm going in." I opened the latches on the top of the carrier and spread them apart, and with one sweep, I brought out the cat. "You're beautiful!" I said.

Mama Cass jumped from my arms and raced in circles. The three of us stood with arms up, surprised, as surprised I imagined as she was. She meowed and yowled, then went toward the slider, hiding under the shade.

"You guys leave through the kitchen," I said. "I'm going to sit here with her 'til she calms down. Alex, could you open that box of supplies, put some kitty litter in her box, and stick it in here?"

Alex nodded, and they left.

I shut off the bright overhead light and sat on the floor

with the tuna not far from Mama Cass. "Honey, I know you're scared," I said quietly. "Please stop crying, OK? I'm Tansy, and you, Mama Cass, are going to live with me now. You'll be safe." Tears fell as I spoke, so I stopped talking and cried. What kind of crazy karma is this? I heard Alex tiptoe in with the box and leave. Mama Cass stopped crying. "I know you've been through a lot, and you'll have to meet the dogs. Don't worry about them. A big girl like you can handle them. When you get ready, I have tuna for you, OK?" Poor cat, I thought. "Poor little girl," I said. "I'll take care of you." I closed my weepy eyes and then felt a nudge on my hand. Mama Cass was saying hello.

She looked quizzically at me, tilting her head right, then left, and sat by me. I patted her. We sat side by side for a good five minutes without a word from me. I moved the tuna over to her, and she ate it. After she ate, I began to stand, and she pawed at my hand, wanting me to stay on her level. She drank some water. All the while, my tears formed and flowed. She approached me, gave me that questioning look I had begun to recognize, and plunked herself onto my lap. I kissed the top of her head. "Mama Cass Elliot, I miss her, too."

12

Allen the Giant Hairball

Alex took Mama Cass's belongings to my house, and I carried a nervous cat. As a favor, he picked up Janey at daycare. Maria's son, Diego, walked Yul and Deb, leaving Honeydog with me and the cat. Honeydog was the alpha, and she liked all kinds of critters.

Honeydog jumped onto the couch and stared at Cass, who sized her up, then went to her cat box, where we set it up in the alcove by the back door. I was as relieved as the cat was. Diego brought in Yul and Deb, and things intensified. Yul lowered himself, rump up, challenging, ready to chase Cass, who lounged on the sofa back. She licked her paws, but her eyes stayed on the dogs. Diego motioned with his hand, "*Deja de tonterías,*" he said. Yul quit his antics, and Diego gave him a treat. Deb appeared oblivious to the goings-on but got a treat, too.

"Whatever you said worked," I said. "What does it mean?"

"Cut the crap," Diego laughed.

"I'll have to remember that."

All went well after the first evening, anyway. We did have another incident. The girls adored Mama Cass, and Cass moved easily between them. I asked Cass if she was hungry as I filled her dish and placed it on the dryer on an old blue flannel bath towel. She meowed in response, but it was conversational, "Yes, I could use a bite." We all went to bed, and Cass wanted to be with me and Honeydog. Shortly after the lights were out, I jolted as a screech woke everyone. I ran out of my room, the girls from theirs and Honeydog and Deb alongside us. Yul was in full pursuit of Cass. They whipped around us out to the back door, then inside Janey's room. We heard a bloodcurdling shriek, and then Mama Cass strolled out, rubbed against my legs, and went into my room.

"You guys stay here," I said. "I'm going to check on Yul." Dogs and kids watched as I entered Janey's room. Yul sat on Janey's pillow, his head down and paws crossed in front. I leaned over my defeated dog and pulled out a claw directly between Yul's ears. "Oh, sweetie," I said. "I think you lost." Yul followed me out, and Cass walked out of my room. Yul stopped, allowing the cat to pass in front.

The next day, I checked in with my four-legged crew off and on. They appeared content with one another. Yul acted as if there was no cat at all on the sofa. Mama Cass wanted to leave with me and meowed each time I got close to the door.

Midmorning at the office, as I started to schedule our ranch duties, the guests from Bungalow Five entered the office. "May I help you?" I said to the neatly mustached man holding their young son.

The wan-faced wife spoke in a cold, articulate voice. "We prepaid for four days, and we wish to leave."

"You do not sound happy," I said.

The husband glanced at the floor and then in his wife's direction. She went on. "We feel compelled to leave. The service has been terrible, and I believe you told us that this was the busy time of year, but the only companions I've seen for our son have been the roadrunners. The air conditioner still does not work in the room. None of us have slept well. The food has been simply terrible. You show a swimming pool in the brochure, but yours is empty. I could go on, but do you get the point?"

"Would you like to move to Bungalow Three with a ten percent discount?"

"No!" The woman said.

"And you want to leave this morning?"

"If it's not too much trouble," the husband said.

"I have a problem," I said. "Glen Newbauer is our owner, and I feel uncomfortable issuing a check without his approval."

"But you can issue a check—you have the authority?" said the wife.

"Yes," I answered, "but—"

The wife interrupted. "I don't want to be difficult, but we are packed." She appeared desperate, and the husband's forehead broke out in a sweat.

I added and subtracted and said, "Gosh, I'm sorry things did not work out for you on your trip here. I'm making out a check for your last two nights, and you can be on your way. Jesse tried to fix the cooler when you were at dinner last evening, but he was working without the parts he had ordered." I handed the woman the check. "You can cash it at the branch in Tucson. I wish you a happy holiday," and I did my best to smile.

Glen came in two hours later and noticed Consuela cleaning out the infamous bungalow. "Hey, what goes?"

"It's what went," I said. "The guests departed."

"They better had died and not taken any of their deposit with them."

"C'mon, Glen," I said, "they weren't any fun, anyway. The wife looked wilted, and the man was polite, but it looked like he had his hands full. Who wants a pain in the ass around, anyway?"

"Is there anyone else coming in?" Glen's face resembled a tomato.

"Yes, sir!" I said. "Four women are coming in for a college reunion, and I'll pick them up in a couple of hours. We won't put anyone in Five until Jesse fixes the air conditioner." I peered at his worried face and wished I had had better news. "Glen, you need to emphasize what you do so well here. You are the quintessential cowboy, giving guests a real look at a working ranch. You provide guests with home-grown foods in a setting where writers to senators have stayed." I pointed to a picture of Zane Grey on the opposite wall. "This ranch has a seventy-year history. I called that guy you know at the tourist bureau, Jimmy Andrews? He's coming out to see you next week. Says it's been too long. When you talk to him, remind him how special CollinCamp is."

"I can't afford to lose business. You know, I should fire you." He pushed his hat back and wiped his brow with his handkerchief. His lighter tone betrayed the threat in his words. "How's the kitty?"

"She's working out, and it'll all work out," I said. "Most things do." I hoped I sounded more convincing than I felt.

That night, Mama Cass burrowed under the covers,

leaning into me, stretched her long body until she got the right fit, purred briefly, and fell asleep. I realized Allen hadn't called, and my thoughts drifted back to Ringo's and Pablo and dancing; if it could always be so—but life shifts, breaks open, creates chaos and passages to the unknown. The ruptures arrive unannounced—sometimes announced, I thought. Allen. I sat up, raced to the bathroom to vomit, washed my face, and returned to bed. I hadn't noticed, but Mama Cass followed me. She cocked her head as if trying to figure out what sort of hairball I puked up, then jumped back onto the bed and crawled under the covers next to me. I patted her furry side. "Yeah, Mama Cass, Allen's a giant hairball." I fell asleep imagining the drawings I could make in a book titled *Allen, The Giant Hairball*.

13

Scorpions

There's a story about a saguaro, its arms turned downward. The owner called the nursery where she bought the cactus, and they told her to evacuate. She started to, but the saguaro exploded before she left the door, scattering thousands of nesting scorpions all over her living room. After falling asleep, I had dreamed about scorpions. Scorpions and hairballs? I shook my head.

I'm at work now, I told myself. *Put away the sketchpad.* I stared at my ink impression of a tangle of fur and wire with scorpions climbing in its mass. One to burn, I thought. Allen and his mother were on the way to CollinCamp. Oh, God, his mother, too. Fur and wire, indeed.

Agnes Baker Daniels, my former mother-in-law, came from a family whose lineage she bore with the tilt of her upturned nose. Her great-grandfather, an entrepreneur during the Gold Rush, later had one of the first vineyards in Santa Rosa, built hotels in San Francisco, and entertained the likes of Mark Twain and Brett Harte. The Bakers traced their ancestry to The Mayflower. Agnes married Peter Daniels, Junior of an equally distinguished Seattle family. Peter Daniels, Senior, was one of Seattle's early mayors and ran unsuccessfully for governor. A beautiful downtown Seattle theater was named for him because he laid the groundwork for it. Allen Daniels never knew his father. Peter Junior died in a boating accident with his only passenger, a beautiful young actress from a traveling company performing at the acclaimed Daniels Theater a week after Allen was born.

Agnes held forth in her mountain home near Mt. Rainier during the summers. I met Allen there. My dad owned a piece of land where we camped in a tent for two months near the Daniels' estate at Wood Lake when schools were out. Allen went to prep school in California, and his mother doted on him on his summer visits. Agnes never remarried and lived in San Francisco.

When I was married to Allen, she visited and wrote frequently. She wanted me to believe the sun could not rise or set without consulting Allen first—always quick to point out how grateful I must feel to be married to "our Allen." She blamed my lack of gratitude for our divorce. Even if I had told her the litany of angry Allen stories, the words that, as a woman, you cannot unhear after your mate berates and belittles you, Agnes would figure a way to make it my fault for his bad behavior. I don't know what Allen told Agnes about his marriage to Julie or how he explained leaving me when I was pregnant, but I imagine Allen impressed his mother with how long he endured our marriage. After the divorce, she lavished the girls with gifts and openly questioned my ability to raise the children by myself. She commented frequently about me pulling "my poor boy" into court. When I told her we were moving to Arizona, her response was to ask

for temporary custody of the kids while "I got my head together." I declined the offer, full stop. "You're crazy to leave
Seattle. You live rent-free. But I do think you need to get a
job. Pull your weight. You have to think of the children."
We stood in the kitchen of the Seattle house, coffee mugs in
hand, the kids just out of earshot. She believed my art was
frivolous now that Allen and I were divorced; it certainly
didn't count for work. She never mentioned Julie, but she
attended the wedding in Japan.

I was quiet around her, nodding frequently, letting her
advice float like clouds that I pictured evaporating in the
desert heat. My heart focused on Oracle, Arizona, and CollinCamp in the Santa Catalina foothills. "Breaks my heart
you're leaving all this," Agnes's arms widened expansively
around the kitchen counter.

"You want more coffee?" I asked.

I saw Allen's devotion to his mother as an inherited
weakness—both waxed each other's egos while singing to
the superficial. I rationalized that witnessing their interaction
was a primer to learning small talk for cocktail parties. She
doted on him and would do, I am sure, whatever he asked.

I pulled my shoulders towards my ears, circled them
backward, and thought no wonder I'm dreaming of scorpions. I picked up my sketch pad and put it down under my
desk.

I took a breath and placed an ad for a new cook. I had let-
ters to write to people confirming holiday stays at the ranch
and Becky's books to peruse. The sun blanketed the office,
but it felt thin; a chill ran through me that I could not shake.

I kicked my sketchpad back further as Alex strolled in. "Good morning," he said, "guess what, Tansy? Peter is in the kitchen. The boss threw out all the booze last night—he raided every cupboard in there, and Peter swears on the memory of his mother and the Virgin Mary that he will go to AA."

"You're kidding. I'll be cooking tonight, for sure. I just phoned in an ad to replace Peter an hour ago. I get Glen's loyalty, but Peter probably keeps supplied." I tossed my hands in the air. "Peter won't stay sober because Glen tossed the booze. He needs help. More help than Glen can give him."

"Glen says this is it—he either stays sober or gets out."

"Great. Another cowboy solution."

Glen banged the door as he came into the office. "With all this chitchat, I don't see how anything gets done around here."

"Good morning to you, too," I said.

"Alex," Glen turned his attention away from me, "got to talk to you. Let's take a look-see at the horses this morning."

"Any rides scheduled?" Alex asked as they both focused on my messy desk.

"Yeah, the reunion women signed up this morning."

"Any more than that stayin' here?" Glen asked.

"Quiet today," I answered. "The honeymooners and the Wisconsin couple left this morning. They both had their own vehicles." Glen shook his head dolefully. "But tomorrow, we have two families coming in. One of them already requested the observatory tour." I tapped my pencil. "Oh, and the Oklahoma couple will need a ride to the airport at five. Can you take that, Alex?"

Alex nodded in assent, and they left.

Peace. I prayed Allen would not call and settled into work when a huge commotion erupted in the kitchen, where I found Peter giggling on the floor. The stove was on. "You'll never guess," he said. "I slipped on a banana peel." He was drunk, pans scattered on the floor and an open bottle of mezcal on the counter.

I turned off the stove, helped Peter to Bungalow Five, and put him to bed. As far as drunks go, Peter was an amiable one. No one would be in the unit until Jesse repaired the cooler, and Peter was too drunk to drive. I left him singing "A Spoonful of Sugar."

14

Ice Cream For Dinner

"And we got no cook tonight?" Glen said after I explained Peter's whereabouts. He sat at his desk facing mine, shaking his head, his hand cradling his chin. This man did not need another day of bad news.

"Yeah, yeah," I answered. "Why don't you let me cook tonight? Besides deciphering Becky's calligraphy, I can throw some barbecued chicken and biscuits together pretty fast. Peter will sleep it off; I left him singing the score from *Mary Poppins*."

"Thank you." His hoarse response caught me off guard. "I'll get Peter the hell out of here."

"Is everything OK?" I gave Glen my best smile.

"You give me the news. I'm six-hundred short from yesterday and without a cook, and then you ask, is everything OK? Listen, woman, when you're knee-deep in cow shit, you're in no condition to be smellin' roses. You get me?"

"Things will turn around."

"Tend to business, Tansy, as long as I have one, that is," and he left.

I played with my pencil, checked the mail, and concocted a list of ranch groceries. With my world reasonably organized, I opened the Accounts Receivable file and studied the figures again. My adding machine and the numbers on the page did not jive, and Becky's handwriting was illegible in places. I hoped she didn't have too many free drinks in Vegas. Consuela pushed her cleaner's cart outside, and I caught up with her to ask that she clean up the kitchen mess Peter left behind. When I returned to my desk, I found a note from Pablo asking me if I wanted to catch a movie that night. Glen returned about that time and read the message from over my shoulder.

"Honestly, Glen?" Privacy was a limited commodity at CollinCamp.

"I'll stay with the kiddos," Glen said. "You get yourself out of here for a while. Pablo's over at the stable, trimming and shoeing one of the horses. Get yourself over there."

"I'll take you up on that," I said.

When I entered the paddock, I watched as Pablo trimmed the hoof of a red-brown horse with a white mane. He peered up at me with a smile. "We have a date?" he asked.

"How about seven? Gosh, I get to ride in the '52 Chevy."

"Indeed, you do. I'll meet you at your place, OK?"

"OK," I said. "I'll be ready."

After picking Janey up from her preschool, I planned to use my kitchen to cook most of this evening's meal while she napped. Mama Cass followed my every footstep and disappeared while I washed out the pans. I wondered if she followed the dogs outside. I checked the house and found her curled in a tight circle in my closet, the place I frequented after having bad dreams. I collapsed beside her. "There you are!" I said. She meowed quietly in reply. I pulled her into my lap, all sixteen pounds of her. "I bought you some cat-nip," I said. Mama Cass wasn't sick—she was sad. Animals grieve for their loved ones, and she found where I had done most of my weeping, deep in the closet so no one would see. I started to stand, and she pawed my hand, so I stayed quiet for a few more minutes. We both needed that.

The girls and I trucked the dinner to the dining hall and put the chicken and bread in the warmers. I cut a platter of garden vegetables and made a sauce for the daring to try on the chicken. Cilantro and hot chilies tossed with olive oil and steamed with red peppers and Bermuda onions. I mashed sweet potatoes using chicken stock and orange juice.

"Thought you had a date, Missy?" I jumped at Glen's voice.

"I do," I said, turning to see Glen in the doorway to the kitchen. "Just finishing up."

"Can I have a taste?" He scooped a tablespoon of pota-toes into his mouth and closed his eyes. "You expect anyone to eat this?" He was smiling.

"I think they're good potatoes, Mommy," Janey said from her small corner table where she was coloring on a piece of butcher paper.

"Where's that other no-good kid of yours?" Glen asked.

"She's setting the tables," I said.

"Can I go help, Mommy?" Janey asked.

"Sure, honey," I said, and Janey was off to the dining room.

"Let the kids eat up here with Alex and me. Alex said he'd take 'em on a short horse ride, and we'll get 'em home for a movie. I've been watching Clea—she's all about grow-in' up, but she needs you just as much as that little sprite.

Clea's trying to take care of you and her sister. Check in on her."

How quickly I remembered my dad and me. Mother was somewhere; we never knew how or when we might see her. Sometimes happy and sometimes with dead eyes. When Dad left, I had him check in with me every hour or two, and he was never gone more than four. I was older than Clea at that time.

How could Glen see this, and I—the one who experienced the feeling and was so damn protective—missed it when it came to my daughter? "You're right, Glen. I know she's safe, and you know she's safe, and yet, for her little sister's sake, she has to pretend she feels safe and grown-up enough not to worry about me."

"What the hell you say, woman?"

"I said thank you, and I appreciate the offer." After a moment's recollection, I said, "Before you go, I made lunches for the family going to the observatory tomorrow. They're in the fridge."

"Get out of here," Glen said, "No matter how good you are, I ain't givin' you a raise."

I told Clea I'd call her before bed, hugged Janey, and left the kids with Glen and Alex. They were beginning a game of horseshoes.

With an hour left before Pablo arrived, I changed into sweats, took the dogs on a ten-minute run, swooped home, fed the crew, and saw the red light blink on my message machine. Damn. Allen's voice boomed through the recording. "Call me, Sweet T. I need to talk to you about the arrangements." He left Brette's phone number.

Sweet T—what he used to call me in college. I hated that

nickname. It took me to places I didn't want to revisit on a night when I looked forward to seeing Pablo. But, I should, I thought, I should call him back. He'd be mad otherwise. I wondered if Allen had been drinking. I picked up the phone to return the call and stopped, then hung up, picked up the receiver again, and dialed. The call went to voicemail. I hung up without leaving a message—the kids were not at home, which was the only reason he'd be calling, and I had nothing I wanted to share with him.

Finally, I shoved my hair into a high ponytail and myself into jeans that I pulled from the dryer, found my turquoise drop earrings, and stuffed my feet into my red boots. The phone rang again. I was about to pick up the call when the house erupted into barks when Pablo knocked on the door. I let the call go to message.

Pablo kissed me on the cheek, and we left the cat and dogs at the house while we rode into Tucson in his 1952 metal gray Chevy pickup. Today's newspaper lay in the middle of the saddle brown vinyl bench seat. A shiny red dash panel made me smile, and the refurbished old black steering wheel seemed original. "This is a cool buggy you have here!" I said.

"I'm glad you like Gladys."

"I love a truck with a good name."

"I have two more pieces to deliver for the show. Do you mind if we stop there first? And I didn't even ask what movie you'd like to see. Newspaper's right here." He waved it at me. "You want to check for times and choose one?"

I studied the offerings in the *Tucson Sun*. "*Jurassic Park* starts at 8:15. Everyone in the known universe has seen it but me," I said. "Sound OK?" I asked. "Or, I don't know, we could hang out at the gallery and have coffee or tea or something?"

We decided on the gallery. Pablo's work amazed me. He called the collection Ghost Town: He had wolves made from springs with jaws created from pliers and marbles for eyes. A horse with hubcap haunches came to life; its mane and tail, made from thin, narrowly cut copper and silver scraps, gave the horse a sense of flight. Screws, pistons, metal clocks, and wheels formed a buffalo. Its massive head with hair braided from thin chains, I found stunning. "Wow, wow wow!" I said after a longing look at the buffalo. "I love this guy!"

"He was fun to make."

An older couple stood by us. "Did I hear that you're the artist?" the woman asked.

Pablo answered in the affirmative, and the woman said, "When are the pieces available for sale? There will be an auction, I understand."

"Yup. The auction comes first, then sales after. Two weeks, the folks at the counter have the info."

"You are a talented young man," her partner added.

I called the house from the gallery when Clea was doing homework. She said Grandma called, and Janey was asleep.

String lights on a brick path led through the courtyard around Pablo's display. We held hands and chatted about the cat and Peter sleeping it off in Bungalow Five as we checked out the other art, giving each other our honest opinions. We both stared at a painting of large forest-green shapes of a flower's interior. "I don't think Georgia O'Keeffe has anything to worry about," I mused.

"Agree," Pablo pointed to another oil of a desert sunset with a lone horse tied to a post, a hardscrabble cabin nearby.

"That's gorgeous," I said. "Tells a story. Something about it reminds me of Monet."

"Sunset in Venice—captures the colors."

A vendor with an ice cream truck caught my attention. The friendly vendor gave us two scoops for the price of one, and we thanked him as we left. "Aw, you look like a happy couple," he said with song in his voice.

Pablo answered, "We are."

We ate the ice cream as we meandered back to the truck. On the way home, I told Pablo stories about the failed art collective and my dad, knowing how much he would have liked this man. The miles whisked by quickly. Pablo shut off the truck at my house and put his arm around me as he walked me to my door. I kissed him on the cheek good-night. "It's so easy being with you," I whispered when Pablo returned the kiss. Then the porch light went on, and Glen walked outside.

"Here you are," Glen admonished, "that ex-husband of yours called twice wonderin' where you were, and a tinny-voiced woman called, upset Clea. She said it was her grandmother. Janey went down fine, Clea read to her, and I think they're both asleep. I'll be seein' you both in the morning." And Glen left for his house.

"How old do you feel?" Pablo asked.

"Oh, about fifteen, coming home late after curfew." I tapped him on his arm. "Thank you," I said. We kissed again, and I went into the house.

The dogs and cat stared at me accusingly. "You guys are supposed to greet me, not try and make me feel guilty!" I said. "Come on into the kitchen, and I'll give you treats." Clea was awake and heard us rummaging in the kitchen.

"So, when were you going to tell me that you and Pablo were dating?"

"We've only been out twice. Does that qualify for dating? I saw the art he does tonight. Beautiful stuff. You want to split an ice cream sandwich?"

We sat at the table. The dogs were satisfied with their cookies, and Mama Cass played with her catnip mouse.

"Dad called. I heard Brette in the background. All he cared about was where you were and what you were doing. I asked him if he could come early to see us, but he said he couldn't."

"Well, honey, he'll be here in about ten days for an entire week."

"He doesn't care." Clea appeared downcast and troubled.

"I care, and he does, too. He loves you with all his heart." Clea started to turn away. "Grandma called, too? What did she have to say?"

"Oh, nothing," Clea said.

"It sounds like it was something."

"Nothing, really."

I studied my daughter's wide blue eyes. She was no poker player. "When you feel like it, we can talk about it, OK? Meanwhile, let's split another ice cream sandwich. I'm having a piece of cheese with mine."

We finished our midnight snack, and she went to bed. The slump in her shoulders told me Clea held something back. What was Agnes up to?

15

Steak Night

"**Y**ou good to barbecue steaks tonight alone?" Alex asked first thing the following day.

"Right," I said, with visions of ash floating over a sweltering barbecue. "I can do this."

"You've done it before."

"Yeah, with you," I shrugged. "I'll figure it out."

"You're not taking this so well." Alex gazed at the empty fruit basket on my desk. "Any apples left?"

"Yes—why don't you bring in some for the basket and one for the bookkeeper? She'd sure appreciate it."

Alex tipped his hat, left for the kitchen, and returned with an armload of golden delicious apples. I bit into one, and juice popped onto my chin.

"So, what did Glen want this morning?" I asked. "I saw you, two, deep in conversation on the way over from the house."

"He has me flying to Vegas this afternoon to give Becky a letter. I think he's trying to deal with her directly. You know, get rid of the lawyers. I said I would. She always liked me, so I won't be sitting with the kids tonight."

"It's OK to break our steak night tradition," I said. "Good luck with Becky!"

"I bet Pablo would help with the grill tonight," Alex rubbed an apple on his jeans and bit in. "He's handy at a barbecue; fire's his thing. I'll see if he's around—I'm on my way to my place now."

I couldn't help but smile as I returned to work.

I tried calling Allen's mother and got her voicemail. Perfect, I thought, remembering Lara's admonition. "Hi, Agnes. Tansy here. Sorry to miss your call last night. We'll catch up soon. Bye-bye."

My bookkeeping job paused at four most afternoons when I picked up Janey at preschool, and Clea got home on the bus. With the girls settled, I returned to the office, where I was greeted by a note from Glen: "Out 'til dinner," meaning that I was to cover the office and prep for dinner. I put my Ring Bell For Help sign on my desk and began marinating steaks. The office bell rang as I set out a tray of Parker House rolls to rest, and then Alex stuck his head into the kitchen. Before I could say hello, he told me that Pablo was taking him to the airport and would try to be on time to help out.

"That's great."

"You saw his work last night?"

"I loved it," I said. "You're as nosy as Glen."

After Alex left, I fell into the kitchen routine. Something nagged at me while I made a green salad with garden tomatoes, scallions, avocados, peppery radishes, green peppers, and fresh-sliced strawberries in a bed of romaine and radicchio. I divided it into two large wooden bowls and tucked them into the fridge. I shook up some fresh lemon juice, balsamic vinegar, and olive oil for the dressing, but I felt I had intentionally forgotten something. The dressing was perfect, so it wasn't that. As I pulled the rolls out of the oven and set them in the warmer, I chose one from the batch and tested it. Delicious, no butter needed.

Outside, I lit the long grill; Glen had filled it with barbecue chips, and I brought it to heat so it would be ready to go when the guests arrived and then returned to the kitchen. I was cooking for ten, and many were coffee drinkers. I filled the coffee urn with water and fresh ground coffee beans in the interior basket. It was ready to go. Man, when the coffee and yeast from the fresh rolls joined forces, it made me happy, yet something nagged at me. I debated for ten minutes whether or not I should make a blueberry and peach crisp. I decided to go for it. The blueberries unfroze while I peeled six peaches and piled the berries and peaches together, spicing them with sugar, cinnamon, and a touch of nutmeg. I tossed some oatmeal, brown sugar, flour, and butter in a separate bowl, then turned the timer on for the crisp and sat for a moment. I had baked the potatoes earlier in the day, and they were in the warming oven. We had ice cream in the freezer. Well, that's good, I thought, drumming my fingers on the table. What was I forgetting?

Clea brought Janey over to help me set up the dining room. "Mom, Mom," Clea mumbled, "Grandma called again and asked for you."

I stared blankly at the girls. That was what I was trying so hard to forget. Allen's mother. "Wow," I managed to say, "it won't be long until she and your dad are here."

Deep into service, my grease-spattered, sweaty, long-sleeved t-shirt clung to my skin under my CollinCamp apron. Hair sprung from my ponytail under a baseball cap. I was grilling steaks when Pablo rounded the corner with an apron on, holding a long-handled spatula into the air, a ready smile on his face. Glen stood in the doorway; guests chatted at the tables as I flipped two ribeyes.

"How can I help?"

I wiped my forehead with the back of my hand. "These are medium rare," I said, "Could you hand me a plate?"

Pablo handed me a small platter that I loaded with the beef. Pablo gave the steaks to Glen, who took them into the dining room. "There are four more orders to go." I stood with the metal steak flipper in my hand and waved it.

Pablo raised his spatula. "*En guarde!*"

I stepped away from the barbecue, and we fenced with our culinary tools. The battle of the beef was on! The scent of sizzling steaks personified the dude ranch cookout.

Glen came back. "I hate to interrupt, but we need two well-done and two rare. Can you handle it?"

Pablo took the remaining steaks from the kitchen platter and turned them onto the grill. "You go get a glass of water. I'll take over."

The girls had finished eating and were playing horseshoes with one of our guest's children out the far side entrance to the dining room. I drank some water and brought Pablo a glass. "The rare ones are ready," he said. "Five minutes on the well done." I delivered the beef. We plated the last steak soon after.

Pablo tended the dying grill as we chatted. I thanked him for helping out. He touched me on the cheek and moved a lock of hair around my ear. "You did great!" he said. "Is there anything you can't do?"

"I'll write you a list."

Glen joined us. "You get on home with the girls."

I was tired and hadn't eaten. I needed to get Janey to bed, and Clea also appeared sleepy. The moon rose as we opened the front door. I walked and fed the dogs after Janey fell asleep. Clea held up her novel, *Gone With the Wind*, and pointed at her room with the book. "Hey, before you go," I said. "Thanks for all your help tonight. I left a message for Grandma earlier, and I'm sorry you had to handle the call."

"You weren't mean to her, were you?"

"No, honey," I said, "sweet dreams."

I sat on the pine rollback porch swing outside my door in loose pajama bottoms and a long-sleeved, years-old shirt. I chose between eating dinner or moon gazing. I went with the latter. I was too tired to do both. In the distance, I saw a flashlight and heard footsteps approaching. I recognized Pablo as he got closer. "Can I join you?" He had a backpack and a covered plate.

"What do you have there?" I pointed to the plate. "It's a PJ party!"

"You are rocking the pajamas," Pablo said. "Glen said you hadn't eaten and fixed you a plate with his thanks. I told him I'd be happy to deliver it." With a flourish, he whisked off the cotton table napkin. "The steak is cut, and the salad dressed, and I have a fork wrapped in a paper towel in my pocket." He displayed the cutlery. "The potatoes and crisp were gone."

"This is perfect and such a treat!" I said."Have you eaten anything? We can share. I can get another fork and water."

"Actually, I have two glasses in my pack and another fork. And a bottle of wine."

"That sounds perfect."

We sat on the steps with dinner on a single plate between us. Pablo uncorked a bottle of syrah. We tapped our glasses, said cheers, and drank the robust wine. I felt my body relax as I rubbed the back of my neck and closed my eyes. "So, what happened with Peter? Did Glen say?"

"Glen took him home, packed his bag, and put him on the bus to Phoenix. He has a sister there who works at the VA hospital. Hopefully, she'll get him into a program for alcoholism. At least Glen hopes so."

"I wish him well." Pablo speared the next to the last piece of steak. "That one's yours."

"It's all yours." I turned my attention to the salad, pausing between bites. "What kind of music do you like? Are you an Elvis fan, or was it just the other night?"

"I told you—I believe you are a spell caster. I like Elvis, love Ray's work, and Coltrane when I work."

"I tend to be in that camp, too. I like my generation of girl singers, you know, like Joan Baez, Sarah McLachlan, Tina Turner, and Carole King. Always loved the Righteous Brothers and Simon And Garfunkel."

"A good list." Pablo placed the empty dinner plate on the railing above the step "You want another glass of wine?"

"Yeah, sounds nice."

Pablo poured a second glass for us. "Is this your contemplation spot? The porch step?"

I sat back and stared at the night sky. "I come out here all the time to stargaze. Listen to the coyotes. Isn't that Mars up by the moon? Pink sparkles? I know it's the red planet, and Mars is a warrior, but to me, he looks like Liberace in a top hat."

"And Venus is a Vegas showgirl," Pablo leaned toward me as he pointed to the planet.

"All shimmer and sass."

Pablo put his arm around me. "Lean into me if you like," He massaged my shoulder as he spoke.

"That feels so good," We sat quietly, finishing the wine and gawking skyward. "It's been a long day," I said, staring off into the Milky Way when the phone rang. I let it go to voicemail. It was Allen, and he sounded upset. "I better catch that." I unwrapped Pablo's arm and stood. "Thank you for dinner," and I hugged him closely. "I loved sharing the sky with you. I'll take the plates and glasses back to the kitchen tomorrow."

"I don't know if I am ready to find you yet," Pablo said. He placed his hands on my shoulders, "But you are like rain after drought."

"Is anyone ever ready?" I asked between kisses. "I don't know if I am either." I slipped into my flip-flops. "I have to warn you, I have a messy life."

"Glen told me some."

We walked to Gladys, the patient '52 Chevy. "Hey," he said and held me at arm's length. "Well, thanks for tonight." He kissed me. It was the sort of kiss that woke every pheromone in the body. He clung so tightly that my feet left the ground. His hands touched the bare skin where my shirt lifted in his embrace. He kissed me again. "I better go." The truck engine on, and Pablo was gone.

As I turned toward my door, the phone rang again, and I heard Clea pick up the call. She ran outside to the porch and yelled, "Mom, Dad's on the phone, and he wants to talk to you!"

16

Comeuppance

"Who was that out there?" Clea asked. Honeydog padded her way over to me and sat at my feet. Mama Cass eyed me from the couch back. "Pablo brought some dinner over for me," I said, picking up the phone.

"So, who's Pablo?" Allen asked before I could say hello.

I watched Clea look at the plate, wine bottle, and glasses on the porch. "You were drinking with him?" she said.

"Hold on," I said to Allen and put the phone down.

"Honey, we had dinner. We're all fine."

Clea shrugged and said, "Whatever," and called Deb and Yul. "You guys are coming with me. Then she turned toward the phone."Goodnight, Dad," she sang the words.

"Goodnight, pumpkin," Allen replied loud enough for her to hear. Clea smiled and took the dogs with her to bed.

I picked up the phone and took a breath. "Hey, Allen, sorry I missed your call. You're in Seattle?" I thought I heard change drop into the phone. "Are you calling from a phone booth?"

"I'm at a grocery." He began in a rush of complaints about what he called my unavailability. "Why are you avoiding us? Leaving voicemails to Mom? If you knew how much she cared about the kids, you'd try harder." A giant pause and exasperated sigh followed. "Try harder," Allen said for the second time as I stared out the living room window. "Where were you tonight?"

"I'm sorry your mother was not at home when I called. As for tonight, I've been home."

"I've called repeatedly—"

"I was working—from home. I was the barbecue chef tonight."

"You? Grilling steaks outside? Well, that's a hoot."

"I did alright. Got all the orders right."

"For Christ's sake, are you listening to yourself? Are you now a cook at this dude ranch? A new calling?" He laughed sarcastically at his joke. Then said, "Who's Pablo, Tans?"

"Why do you have to make fun of me? I grilled steaks at our weekly steak dinner to answer your question, and Pablo helped. He's a friend. Brought me dinner." I collapsed into my small rocker. Honeydog put her head into my lap. I petted her as I spoke. "We had a problem with the cook."

"Is this Pablo, the same guy you went to the bar with?"

"Yes, the same." I let the silence get awkward.

"Bars and late-night wine with Pablo?—"

"Allen, I don't have to report to you." His condescending tone annoyed me. Honeydog threw me a concerned look. "There's nothing wrong with a late-night glass of wine with a friend on my own front porch."

"Why are you defensive then?" Allen wasn't through.

"I'm not!" I lowered my voice. "I have a good life here."

"You left a good life in search of God knows what. You ran away."

"You and your bride lived in Japan." Allen touched a nerve. "You're the one who ran away. So, stop the BS."

"You reacted to my marriage by running away to Arizona." He scoffed. "What're you going to do now that I'm divorced? Marry a cowboy?" He laughed derisively.

"So you think everything I do is in reaction to something you've done?" I regretted the question; Allen would come up with something, so I changed tactics. "Let's move on, OK?"

I heard him depositing more phone money. "Fine."

"I have you and your mom on the schedule for next week, with Brette and Patricia flying in on Friday?"

"That's right. Lara's not coming?" He sounded hopeful.

"She's coming on Friday, too, but separate arrangements."

"Collier Camp, here we come." He sounded bored and tired the way he did after a few drinks.

"The ranch's name is CollinCamp, and we like it here." I stood, ready to hang up the phone.

"You're a babe in the woods in the real world, Tans. Lara and that lawyer in Vancouver, don't be so quick to trust either one. Or that boss of yours. Has that guy ever read a book? And you left the kids with him?"

I knew he goaded me to get a reaction, and I reacted mildly. "Well, thank you for that vote of confidence." I seethed inside but tried to keep my tone neutral.

"I'm only interested in your welfare and the kids, so don't give me that high and mighty tone, and be nicer to Mom." I heard more quarters going into the payphone. "Her intentions are good ones—"

"OK, Allen," I interrupted. I squeezed my eyes shut. "I'm going to say goodnight now. We'll see you soon."

"I'm here for you," Allen said, "but, my God, you've changed."

"Goodnight," and I hung up the phone. The dog jolted with the slam of the receiver into the cradle.

Before making breakfast, I walked all three dogs down a gully and up a trail not far from the house. I watched the kitchen lights come on at CollinCamp; Glen was the weekday breakfast cook. The brisk wind whined through a pass in the Catalina's. We turned around and went home. I showered, made coffee and the girls' lunches, and fed the birds and dogs and my dear crazy Maine Coon kitty. As the girls entered the kitchen for a pancake breakfast, I said, "Hey, you guys, your dad's coming to see us in a week. You'll have fun!"

"OK," Janey said, finishing her pancake. "Does he like horses?"

Clea said nothing. I asked her about a model of a Pueblo village she planned to build for a display at school, and she shrugged my conversation attempts off. I figured she saw Pablo as an interloper and wasn't liking it or talking about it. The three of us jammed down the path to Clea's bus stop. "Could I have a hug?" I asked Clea. She backed away from me and ran towards the bus.

Janey waved as the bus rolled down the road. On the way back, we stopped to check out the nesting wren. I wondered what she had to tell me. From the look on her beaky face, she wasn't letting anyone get too close to her chicks. I took that under advisement.

17

The Offer

I tapped a pencil on the cover of Becky's bookkeeping record book. She'd written "Charities" across the front. Alex found this notebook in a paper bag under a pile of like records inside the safe. From what I deciphered from previous tax records, the ranch sponsored many charity events and cut-rate stays. I'd been at CollinCamp for over a year with only one charitable event, a day camp for blind children, so this notebook interested me. Becky didn't seem like the generous-minded person that these records indicated. She took off thousands in tax deductions that year. Absentmindedly, I drew circles on a note Glen left me yesterday about Peter not "working out." Old news.

"Hiya, Tansy," Alex's voice startled me.

"You walk so softly, Alex; you scared the bejesus out of me." I put down my pencil. "So, how was Becky of Las Vegas?"

"She turned down Glen's proposal for a buyout."

"He tried to buy her out?

"Yeah, one hundred k annually over ten years. Becky said

she'd negotiate after discussing 'things' with her new boy-friend's lawyers. She mentioned three hundred k as I was leaving."

"Well, why are you smiling?" I asked Alex. "This doesn't sound like good news."

"Becky met some guy from Florida with money and couldn't be happier. She told me she was patient but firm, so I think we'll all be safe for a while. She likes yanking Glen's chain." He tipped his hat and turned to leave. "And I talked to Lara for two hours last night. She's one in a million."

"Glad to hear—so I'm making chicken pot pies for lunch!" I said to the back of his shirt.

"Let me know when you need me to cover when you're in the kitchen," and Alex was gone.

I opened the book and again peered at Becky's small, backhanded entries. She dotted every "I" with a circle. For 1990, she billed fourteen charity bookings at ten per-cent of the bungalow rate and nothing for horseback rides, which generally were an add-on expense at the ranch. I was missing something. I pulled up an old guest registry and matched dates with these entries. These were families mainly from the northern states looking for winter sunshine. I needed to see the canceled checks, but I smiled when I dis-covered Becky's scam.

At eleven, I went to the kitchen to prepare lunch for Glen, Alex, our writer, and the family of four. I sautéed vegetables in one pan and grilled chicken thighs with garlic and mild jalapeno peppers in the other pan. While that was working, I rolled out puff pastry and prepared it for the ramekins. I shredded the chicken, returned it to the sauté pan with stock, and brought it to a boil, adding cornstarch mixed in cold water to thicken the sauce. After removing it from the heat, I incorporated heavy cream and tossed the vegetables with fresh lemon and dill. I filled the ramekins with the mixture, topped them with the puff pastry, and socked the lot in the oven for twenty-five minutes, time enough to make a green salad.

Earlier that day, Consuela and Maria had arrived for work together, walked into the office, and asked Glen if they could work together.

I said, "Glen, that's a terrific idea. Can you help around meal times, too, ladies?"

"That'll work," Glen said. I think he visualized dollar bills floating out of his pockets.

They agreed and, indeed, helped with service. Alex rang the dinner bell, and the guests came in for lunch. I peeked out of the kitchen, wiped my hands on my apron, tossed it into the laundry, and sat next to Alex. "Did you do much charity work in 1990 at the ranch?"

"What?" Alex grinned between bites of pie. "Hell, no. We have an annual blind camp for kiddos in late June. Why?"

"According to Becky's account, you had fourteen charitable groups where Glen charged next to nothing but took off all the expenses on income tax."

"'Ninety-one was when Becky and Glen tore up the sheets right after taxes went in. I remember it because we were so busy, but Glen told me 1990 was one of the worst years he'd ever had."

"Glen never looked at his tax returns?"

"Nah. Becky took care of the taxes—Glen signed where she pointed."

"I need to get hold of the canceled checks for that year. Are they in the safe?"

"Let's get 'em after lunch." He finished his pot pie with a swallow of coffee, sighed, and said, "Jesus, woman, you can cook."

Alex and I used a table in the dining room to sort out the checks, and I found ten more "charities" in Becky's book. I imagined this was not the only year she skimmed money from the ranch. Becky was a sloppy cheater; the woman left the canceled checks from ten years ago. She had the "charity" families make the checks out to her, personally, on a bank account she once shared with her father, CollinCamp's original owner. He died fifteen years ago. I called the bank to check on the account's activity. Becky closed it before her divorce from Glen after withdrawing thousands of dollars.

Glen sat down with us to see what we were up to, and I filled him in. A smile lit up his face. He took me by the hand and led me out of the dining hall. "Alex," he called, "see to things. Missy and me are going to see that goddamn lawyer."

"Don't you think we better take the checks and Becky's book, too?" I laughed and returned to the table to collect the evidence.

Neither Glen nor I expected the response we received from Glen's lawyer when we laid out Becky's scam. He held up the copies of the checks and the book his aide had returned. "I'll keep these on file." He shook his head. "We have to tread lightly. An audit would sink you both. You signed off on these tax years, Glen. It makes you responsible, too. Don't let her know that you discovered this for now. In fact, I'm giving you back the books and checks. It's a deeper hole, I'm afraid."

Glen was quiet on the way back. "Why do you think she did that?"

A tumbleweed rolled across the highway, and the sun beat against the windshield. "I dunno," I said. "Who knows what plots were going through her head?" Emotionally, Becky broke trust, which finalized Glen's relationship with her. "Would you ever take her back?"

He shook his head.

"I'm just throwing this out, Glen, and you'll do with it what you want. My friend Lara is a really smart lawyer—she might be able to help where your guy couldn't see a path. She doesn't take crap from anyone. And she's clever. She'll be back next weekend to see me and, I think, Alex, too, by the way." Glen loved updates on our social lives. "Will you meet with her about this?"

"So, the kid's seein' a lady? I liked her," he sighed. "I thought we had a slam dunk. Yes, I'll see her."

"And I'm reminding you that my ex-husband's renting two units, full price, for his mother and him for a week. And, we have two bungalows for four days starting on Thursday—including Bungalow Five, fixed air con or not. Lara agreed to take it."

"Don't charge, Lara." He stared straight ahead as a dust devil whirled across the road outside Oracle.

"One more thing, and it's a little one. I saw a big chalkboard and boxes of chalk tucked in the chair closet in the dining room. Could we put that up over the buffet by the kitchen? We could write up the menu for the day, an easy way for people to check, and it's big enough for children to do a little art or leave messages. I think it would be fun and family-friendly."

"You keep it up?"

"Yes, of course," I answered.

"I'll get someone on it."

As we walked into the office, he started talking about being an artist. "You any good?"

"I had a show or two."

"One of them easels might look good in here. You could display your paintings. Even sell 'em. You have any that can go up and an easel? I figure you'd have an easel?"

"Yes, I have a cool easel, mahogany—my dad made it for me. I finished something a few months back and brought four paintings from Seattle."

"Pablo says there's room for you out at the barn. You can paint there if you like."

Dumbfounded. I stashed my bag under my desk. "Thank you, Glen, I'm so grateful." I covered my mouth in thought. "I haven't found a place to paint here, and I've missed it. Actual space means so much to me."

Glen took his hat off, and wiped his weatherbeaten hand through his full head of gray hair. "Don't you go get emotional on me. We'll get that board up. You good to cover the kitchen now that Peter's moved on? And this time, you hire the cook. I ran an ad in the paper this morning."

"I put one in, too."

"Two ads will bring in twice as many people; that might be good." Glen sat at his desk.

"I'll be the cook, the accountant, and hire the new cook?" I asked.

"What's the matter?" Glen answered.

"Nothing, Boss."

Glen tipped his hat, and I went to the kitchen to marinate the flank steak for a London broil in a sweet, peppery soy sauce base. We had tiny garden peas that I planned to put with globe onions and French carrots inside a creamy white sauce. I melted butter in a pan, added flour, and then a little Southwestern heat. I recruited Alex to peel five pounds of potatoes. I wondered if some kitchen time might wipe off his perpetual smile; it didn't. He was in love.

"You want to put these spuds in something?"

"Yup. It's easier to cook potatoes in a pot. Try this one."

When he finished, I started him on greens for a salad. Meanwhile, I got him up to speed about what the lawyer said and how I hoped Lara could help. "She's getting Bungalow Five for free," I added. "Of course, the air con might still be broken."

"She's a country girl at heart," Alex said. He tossed the greens with cherry tomatoes and slices of green peppers and put the container in the refrigerator. "She won't complain."

"And more news: We're going to put up that chalkboard so I can post our menus for the day, and Glen gave me studio space at Pablo's barn. Isn't that cool?"

"Pablo gave Glen the idea," Alex said.

"Glen took full credit, but I'm happy I have a place to paint."

"And Pablo?"

"Shut up!" I grinned. "That makes me happy, too." I added, "Hey, we're still on for our horse ride on Sunday?"

"We are." Alex washed his hands, put his hat on his head, and left.

As I worked quietly in the kitchen, everything seemed alright. The potatoes bubbled and did not boil over. The London broil marinated. Promising. The overhead fan pulled the air in circles, and through the windows, I studied a little spruce and white rock on sandy soil. Maybe something to draw after the wren, in charcoal. I knew at night the moon would shine down, and in the silences a coyote might yelp, or a red-tailed hawk might shriek. I loved the tremble I felt when a wild thing called.

The sense of calm changed, and panic set in as I stood over the sink. Grasping either side, I leaned into the counter for support. The sudden expanse of opportunity in the forever horizon of the Sonoran desert shifted, and it felt as if it might split open at any time. The earth rumblings ran deep: the saguaros, scorpions, spotted owls, hunter-coyotes, closet memories, paint on canvases, a mother-in-law's scowl, and Allen's impending visit merged, mixing all the colors these thoughts projected—black. The only way forward was to stay in the present.

18

Once Upon a Hammock

The ads for a ranch cook brought an immediate response. The phone didn't stop ringing all Saturday morning. I scheduled some interviews. The person I liked the best was coming late afternoon. I wore a sky blue paisley, button-down sundress, and huaraches. Semi-professional, I thought, and glad to be off from noon until I interviewed the applicant.

Clea was helping Alex with the horses before her friend, Franny, came over to ride while Maria babysat Janey, allowing me to set up my space in the red barn. Pablo cleared off two shelves for my supplies. I unrolled a canvas sheet to put under the easel. Glen gave me an extra key to the barn, and Pablo wasn't around. I intended to use charcoal and oils to paint the nesting wren. I stood back in my space; the afternoon light filtered through the open door. My sketch pad was on the paint-spattered floor covering. This works, I thought. In Seattle, I painted on an upstairs enclosed sun porch after our co-op died. Georgia O'Keeffe would paint outside, and I might, too.

The barn door creaked open. Pablo approved my setup, and I allowed him to browse my sketchbook. Seeking approval, I stared at his facial expressions. He gave nothing away. I explained what I had in mind for the desert wren.

"Yes," he said and repeated, "yes." Pablo looked up. "Who made the easel you have in the office?"

"My dad, the librarian, did. He gave it to me as a graduation present."

"I love it. I love the canvas you displayed—a red cowboy boot and red suspenders. You gave the boot age and character with the tooling. Tells a story."

"First thing I noticed coming here were Glen's red suspenders and a pair of boots in a thrift store window, and they fit me. I finished the canvas last summer. I think I need to thank you for that buzz in Glen's ear about letting me paint here, free. I appreciate it."

"You're welcome. I have some news. I moved."

Alarmed but trying not to look overly curious, I said, "What?"

"Oracle Junction. Not far. Small, but a casita on a neighboring ranch, big enough for Diamond and me. I'm going back now—I have Diamond in the truck. I had one last box to take over. You want to ride along?"

"I have some free time, but I'm interviewing a new cook at four. If you get me back by 3:30, that would be great."

"Aw, this is familiar," I said as Pablo drove into the Flores' ranch, "I drive here every day; Rena is Janey's preschool teacher. So, you have a casita here?"

"Rena is my next-door neighbor." Pablo pulled around the ranch house to what appeared to be a casita duplex. Both mud brick houses had front porches with red geraniums in white-framed windows. Inside his casita were two bedrooms. The brick-walled interior kept the place cool. Diamond, Pablo's pup, ran around us into a small kitchen in the back of the front room, with a bedroom off of it. "I have a project out back. You want to help me?"

"Of course. I'm at your service,"

"This way." Pablo held the door open for me.

A fenced yard framed a small patio. I noticed the autumn sage growing abundantly on the yard's perimeter and stopped to pick a slender branch. The scent of mint and pine mingled with the fragrance of rain. "I see why it's called a lady." I held it up for Pablo to smell.

"Nice," he said. It was as if we were posing for an artist, how still we stood, locking eyes as if nothing else mattered that day.

Self-awareness brought me back to the moment. "You struck gold—this is a cool place." Diamond ran inside the house and out as we spoke. "What's that going to be?" I pointed to what looked like a small cottage under construction.

"Miguel, Rena's son, built a one-room schoolhouse for Rena's daycare program. It's almost finished. The little ones are excited!"

"I didn't know anything about it. That's cool."

"Knowing Rena, she'll have an open house after they finish. Meanwhile, I'm finally out of my tent and Alex's hair." Pablo hefted a box containing a hammock, which he began assembling in the backyard where the fence corners met. I handed him hardware as he finished up.

"You want to try it?" Pablo said. "Are you game?"

"I'm game," and I took off my shoes. "How do you get in?"

"Let me go first, and I'll assist."

We collided in the center of the hammock and broke into laughter. "I think you hit my tooth," I said.

"Are you OK?" Pablo leaned over me.

"I'm fine." I reached up and held Pablo's face in my hands. His skin felt like sandpaper and silk under my fingertips. "You—" I said, and he kissed me. I whispered about the full moon in a few days, but there was far more kissing and touching than talking. The skirt of my dress bundled under my lower back. "We need to stop," I said, surprised by my voice's husky timbre. "I don't want to, but—"

"Yeah." Pablo shook his head. "Let me help you up."

We managed to stand and stood facing one another. I smoothed my dress down, noticing my wobbly knees. The dog had gone inside the house.

"I'm going to hug you, then make tea—I have that much unpacked, then take you back to work." He opened his arm. "You smell like autumn sage," Pablo whispered in my ear.

I scraped the chair across the old linoleum floor when I pulled it out to sit. The yellow Formica table with chrome piping fit the rose-colored walls. Pablo brought out two mugs, a tin of Mexican cinnamon cookies, and a jar of honey from a box on the small counter. The tea steeped in a brown-stone teapot between us.

"This is going to be awkward," Pablo tapped his fingers against the tabletop, "but here goes—I don't want you to think I'm the kinda guy who comes onto every woman—" he shook his head. "I feel connected to you and drawn to you." He laughed. "You get Gladys, and you like Diamond." The small beagle stared up at me, begging for a cookie. "And I respect you. And your art—that's a big deal to me."

I poured the tea. Pablo waited for me to speak. As familiar as he seemed, the scenario felt strange, as if we'd said these words before. "All I can think is that when we danced, there was an ease about it. Wasn't there?"

"Yes. I knew I was with the right woman."

"I remember thinking, this man can dance," I paused. "Can I give Diamond part of my cookie?" Diamond was doing her best to let me know she would like that.

Pablo nodded, and I broke part of my cookie and gave it to the dog.

"I bet you like chocolate milkshakes and french fries," I said.

"Yes, ma'am," Pablo answered. "So many things about you feel familiar. You know, life hands us experiences and sometimes people without consulting about the right timing."

"I've noticed." I tested the tea, and it was still too hot to drink. "If I told you that I thought maybe we knew each other in another life, I don't think you'd think I was crazy."

"I keep thinking I know you like we've made love before. That's what I mean, an awkward conversation."

"Whatever goes on between us," I said, "let's treat it as a gift. And go with it. But you must remember I have kids, and they have to be my top priority. Their dad will be here in the next few days, and he doesn't like the girls living at the ranch."

"I wondered about him. Are you worried about his visit?"

I let my worry spill. "Allen can be difficult when he's in the mood. His mother's going to be here, too. She's clueless about him. He appears princely to her. Allen owes back support, and if I know him like I think I do, he'll try to get out of paying it by claiming what a lousy parent I am and then threaten to take me to court about leaving Seattle without notifying him. Or something like that. His mother's stirring the custody pot, too—hates the idea of the kids living in what she sees as the wilderness. And thinks I might be a little crazy." I stopped. Pablo hadn't heard this much of my story before and appeared somewhat alarmed as he sipped his tea.

"When you say 'difficult,' what do you mean?" he asked.

I shrugged. The word "scary" crossed my mind, and I dismissed it as overly dramatic. "It was always easiest if I went along with whatever Allen wanted, he'll no doubt turn on the charm offensive when he's here to make me look bad in front of his mom." I shook my head. "I'm known for over worrying and overthinking. So there is that." I added quickly, "Lara will be here. So it might go OK. I think he's scared of her." I laughed a little, realizing the truth in that last sentence. "Honestly, I worry about everything. Right now, I'm worried about getting back to the ranch to interview the cook. I want to impress her because, God, we need a cook." It was an awkward change of subject.

Pablo squeezed my hand, "Lady, you have it together. One more question: When does Allen get here?"

"Wednesday afternoon. I think they're renting a car."

"Could we plan something Tuesday night?" Pablo asked. "Sometimes, I take Gladys up for a spin to a special place above the ranch. I camp out sometimes in the truck bed up there. Moon's supposed to be full. And solar storms might make the sky pretty if the predictions are right."

"That sounds tempting."

"I want to make it clear: nothing has to happen between us, physically, I mean, because I think something is happening between us, but—"

"—You're an overthinker, too! I feel more at home. I trust you. Come around nine. I'll get Maria to stay with the girls, but I can only be out a couple of hours."

Pablo took the cups and the teapot to the sink, and I sat at the table with my hand curled under my chin, watching.

"You look thoughtful," he said.

"I don't know why you're in my life, but I'm glad you are," I said.

He nodded. "I feel the same. Let's get you back to work."

Pablo dropped me off at my place. Before I closed the truck door, Clea and her friend, Franny, walked out of the house. Crestfallen— the only way I could describe the look Clea gave me. Pablo drove off, and I stood facing both girls.

"I was at the office looking for you," Clea said, "and then we came here, but I see you were busy." Her cheeks pinkened. "You told me you were going to be at work."

"Hi, Franny," I said, then turned my attention to Clea. "Pablo moved into the Flores' place, and I helped him with a few things. Did you need me for something?"

Franny gave a half-wave and put her arm down at her side.

"I wanted to say hi. We're going riding now. Alex is waiting." With that, she turned around and left.

19

Cooking with Dina

Maria watched from the porch. Her broad jaw and set mouth showed disapproval, her long black hair pulled neatly into a chignon. "At her age," Maria said, foregoing a hello, "they need their moms to be their moms. Clea's proud of you. Took her little friend to show her your painting in the office. She worried about you when you weren't there." She stared at me as if to ask, what didn't I get about this situation?

"I guess I should've told her, but it was spontaneous with Pablo, and I knew she was with Alex, and then the girls would ride. You were here," I took a breath and sighed. "I blew it. Right?"

"She'll be OK, but talk to her when things are quiet." Maria relaxed her posture.

"I'll do that. Speaking of going out, Pablo asked me out for a few hours on Tuesday night. He'll come after me at nine. Can you stay with the girls—and believe me, Clea will know well beforehand, and I'll be home by eleven."

Janey napped while Maria and I chatted. Maria agreed

to come over on Tuesday night. When I got Janey up, we returned to the kitchen, where I planned to create enchiladas, a fresh fruit salad bar, and refried beans. Overnight, I'd soaked the dry pinto beans, and they were ready to be boiled. I decided to interview while I cooked; if the woman I interviewed volunteered, she might get the job. Janey played a sorting game with a bag of mixed fruit and veggies at her small window-side table.

Dina Noyse rang the office bell as I cut up cascabel peppers for the enchilada sauce. I stuck my head into the office and invited her into the kitchen. Sturdily built, Dina topped six feet. She wore neatly pressed jeans and a checked, cotton western-style shirt tucked inside by a silver buckle. Her application informed me she was fifty; indeed, fine lines were resident around her deep brown eyes. Such soulful eyes, I thought as she surveyed the work counter and Janey at play at the little table. Running opposite to her large appearance was her voice, softer than rainwater. "It looks like you have your hands full," she said.

"I've been filling in since the cook left," I said. "I'm happy to meet you. Please call me Tansy, Ms. Noyse."

"Only if you call me Dina," she replied."I don't want to be forward here, but can I put on an apron and show you what I can do? I see it's enchiladas and refried beans." She pointed to the taped dinner menu I posted to the fridge. "You can ask me anything you want while I work."

I wasted no time. "This is where we keep aprons and kitchen towels." I opened the pantry door and retrieved an apron.

Dina rolled up her sleeves, put on the apron, washed her hands, and rearranged the workspace. "This will do for now, but we need to clean this area up, meaning no disrespect."

"None taken," I said. Dina, you are hired, I thought. However, I didn't want to act too excited, fearing I might scare her off. I backed away and let her work. "Tell me," I said, "I want daily menus posted on the chalkboard so guests can see what is in store for mealtimes. You willing to do that?"

As she chopped onions with the precision of Julia Child, she answered, "Certainly."

"Peter, our cook, had a drinking problem that grossly interfered with his performance—"

Dina interrupted, "I had a husband whose drinking and gambling grossly interfered with our marriage. My drink of choice is Pepsi." She eyed the pans hung above the multi-burner stove. "We need to do some reorganizing here. Have you marinated the meat?"

"Yeah, It's in the fridge."

"Mommy, I made a picture of a frog," Janey said.

I admired the frog picture, supplied Dina with the marinated meat, and asked if she wanted me to begin making the tortillas.

"Why don't you take that little one for a walk before the stove gets fired up too high, and I'll finish up in here. To finish up your questions: I don't drink, can work weekends, and odd schedules are OK. I'm here because I love the outdoors, have no children, and I love horses. I don't like high-pressure, high-maintenance people, and I'm a dang good cook. Oh, if you give me the budget and menus, I'll shop."

"Dina Noyse, you are hired. I'll get out of your way. We'll take care of the dining room setup and breakdown. Janey and I will go find her big sister, Clea. We'll talk salary later, OK?"

Dina was massaging the meat mixture in a large bowl I supplied. "Thank you, Tansy. I'd shake your hand, but—" she waved her large meat-enveloped paw at me.

Janey and I nearly collided with Glen and Clea as we headed to the stable. I held up my hand in front of them. "Stop! We were going over to get you," I said to Clea. "And Glen, wait 'til you hear!" Excitedly, I rolled out the news: a new cook, and "she's making dinner now—I hired her."

"You might have consulted me," Glen puffed.

"You gave me full authority. And it's a done deal. Her name's Dina Noyse, and she loves horses."

"Her references check out?"

"Well, of course, that's something," I said, "but you know," I tried to shmooze, "her organizational skills and how she handled the kitchen was like watching an artist paint."

Glen dug into the ground with his boot and whistled under his breath. "Check her references." He shook his head and smirked, "If they're fine, she's hired."

"That sounds fair."

"Glen hired me after Franny's mom picked her up," Clea said. "I'm going to help in the dining room at dinner." She sounded overly polite and still pissed off.

"I think your references will check out," I mused. "Come on, you guys," let's go home and get ready. I'm helping, too."

Before leaving the house, I braided Janey's hair and mine. I gave Clea an apron in the ranch kitchen before she began refreshing water glasses and coffee cups. The aroma of cheese and beef in a deeply spiced marinade filled the dining room. I opened the windows and watched happy diners eat. Glen made several trips into the kitchen and told me to get "on home" when guests were leaving. Maybe it was my romantic viewpoint at the moment, but I thought he might have found Dina to his liking. We took enchiladas, refried beans, leftover fried chicken, a fresh fruit salad, biscuits, and rice pudding topped with whipped cream on our way out of the dining room.

"Tomorrow, you guys get your way with me," I said. "To horse!"

20

The Talk

"Why are you laughing, honey? Janey, we don't feed the dogs at the dinner table; they don't like enchiladas. Janey, please." I watched Honeydog let the spicy goop fall from her open mouth. I turned to Clea. "Why are you laughing?"

"You on a horse, boy, I can hardly wait. You're scared of big dogs."

"It's just a little outing in the desert." The thought of mounting a horse sent a chill down my leg, but pride determined that I would not admit this.

"I mean, it's great and all, you know, I've begged you to go riding, but where's Janey going to ride?"

I hadn't thought of that either. I saw myself—one arm around Janey and one arm around the horse—as it took off to join its brothers, the wild ponies, in the hills, and never to be heard from again—of course, it would buck off its human cargo first. It's no big deal, I thought. I'll get out of the whole thing, call Alex—

"Earth to Mother, come in, please." Clea giggled again.

"I can see it, Mom: a chicken on a horse."

"You're right," I said.

Then Clea laughed harder, a warm, mellow sound emanating deep inside. "There's nothing to be scared about—really, Mom." It was good to hear her laugh.

I laughed, too. "I wonder why it never occurred to me that I was actually going to get on a horse? Well, I guess every twenty-five or six years, I should give it a try." I shook my head. "I think Janey will ride with Alex."

Janey nodded. "Alex knows what to do."

"Janey, don't throw chicken bones to the dogs." I picked up the drumstick before Honeydog made her assault. "You know, Clea, you did a great job serving today. And you helped Janey be a good assistant." Janey nodded proudly.

"It was so busy for a while. Did you see that guy try to tip me?"

"Who did that?" I asked.

"I don't know. It must have been someone from town or something. Anyway, Glen came up to him and told him to put his money away. The man kinda got flushed and said, 'Sorry, guy.'"

"I don't know if I like the idea of you growing up."

"Oh, Mom, I knew if I said anything, you'd react like that."

"Which reminds me, honey. After I put Janey to bed, Clea, we will talk."

"I'm really tired, Mom, and I really don't want to talk."

"Well, we are going to. Now, Janey, you help me take the dishes into the kitchen, and then we're getting ready for bed."

"Why do we have to talk?" Clea whined wistfully, "I mean, oh, never mind. I'm not mad at you now."

She started to say something, and I cut her off. "Honey, we will do this, and it won't take long." I had no idea what I was going to say. I only knew I missed the openness of her laugh, and I was damned if I was going to consign it to memory.

Janey was asleep in fifteen minutes. A full belly worked like a natural tranquilizer. I lay by her in the still of her room, wondering what I would say to Clea. She poked her head in the door. "It's Pablo on the phone. Do you want me to tell him you're asleep?"

"No, honey. I'm up."

"Now, you'll talk all night to him."

"You go watch TV," I said. "I'll catch up to you in a very few minutes."

Clea shrugged, handed me the phone, and returned to the living room.

"Is Clea OK?" Pablo asked.

"I think everything's fine."

"Clea avoided me at the stable when she and her friend were gearing up to ride," Pablo said, "not her usual bubbly self."

"Thanks for the call," I said. "Clea and I are going to hang out tonight, but we're still on for Tuesday night?"

"I'd love it, but I don't want to mess with your family time."

"I don't think that's what's happening," Mama Cass weaved herself between my legs, then bee-lined it to where Clea lay on the floor with her elbows propping up her chin. Sitting on Clea's back, Mama Cass began grooming her toes.

Clea turned her head toward me. "Do you see that, Mom? I think she likes me."

I said a quick goodbye to Pablo and replaced the receiver

to its cradle. "Of course, Mama Cass likes you!"

"What did he want?" Clea asked as I sat down beside her. "You want some popcorn?"

"We talked about going out for two hours on Tuesday night, and I told him that'd be OK—and, yeah, I'd love some popcorn. Let's go in the kitchen while I make it."

"You're not going to make me?" Clea asked.

"No. You were in service long enough today. You know, I thought about the guy who wanted to tip you. That means you were doing a professional job. I think that's terrific."

"That's what I thought, but Glen embarrassed me. I like him, but he makes me feel like a baby."

"He does the same to me." The oil was hot in the pan, and I added the popcorn and put on the lid. "He considers us family." I moved the pan back and forth over the burner as we waited for the kernels to pop.

"You looked pretty tonight, Mom. With your hair up and makeup—boy, I hope I look that good when I'm pushing forty."

"Oh, yeah, I'm a beauty queen." I laughed. "Melt the butter, will you, sweetie?" I emptied the popcorn into a bowl. "Do you know why you're so mad at me?"

"I meant it about how you look." Clea melted the butter, and then we sat in the kitchen at a small chrome dinette with the popcorn bowl between us.

"I know you did." I tried to keep the conversation focused on her feelings. "Is it me seeing Pablo and your dad coming back?"

"I just got used to us being here on our own, and now this guy comes along. He's got a cool horse, but it's like you don't care about us anymore. Dad's coming in four days, and you hate him." She stopped talking and started crying. I stood up and removed the popcorn; I didn't want her to choke. The good thing was the cries cut through the stuttering angry crap. She sounded like a captured whale, simultaneously distressed and uncertain and knowing. I moved my chair to her side of the table and put my arm around her. She wept into my shoulder.

"I don't hate your dad, honey. He loves you to bits. Are you counting the hours 'til he gets here?"

She hiccoughed. "Last Thursday was Dad's Night at school."

"I didn't know."

"I didn't take the paper home." Clea wiped her nose on a paper towel. "It didn't seem like you cared if I had a dad or not."

"Did the kids talk about it at school yesterday?"

"Well, sure. Our class made decorations for it, and we made invitations. I knew Dad couldn't go, but I saved his invitation for him, you know, for when he gets here."

"Can I see it?"

Clea jumped up and went to her backpack by the backdoor. She fished out the invitation for Allen. It had a star and a horse in ink and gold acrylic on the front.

"God, that's good, honey. He'll love it. Isn't that Jeremy?"

"Yeah, I used him because he's the perfect palomino. He does tricks for Pablo, you know?"

"Like what?"

"Like go up on his hind legs. And he can count."

"The horse can count."

"Yeah, Pablo asks him to 'give me three,' and Jeremy pounds his hoof three times, and then he gives him another random number up to six, and Jeremy pounds whatever Pablo asks."

"He sounds like a smart horse. I loved how you used the gold in your drawing."

"Do you think Dad will like the card?"

"Like?—he'll love it." And I took another paper towel from the roll to wipe my eyes. "I'm so sorry about not knowing about Dad's night, sweetie. I love you twenty-four, seven."

"Don't cry, Mom."

"I'm—"

"Mom, you can't be Dad, so don't try."

She appeared so young to me right then, yet her words were grown-up-wise. I held her tightly. "Glen would have gone, you know. Of course, you would never be able to return to that school again."

"Why wouldn't I be able to go back?"

He would have told every boy the other side of twelve to keep his gun in his holster, or he'd have nothing to shoot with."

"God, Mom, that is so gross."

"I heard him say that once when talking to some kid from town doing work on the ranch."

She laughed. "There's something else," she said, "something that Grandma said the other night." She studied my face.

"What'd she say?"

"Grandma says Dad wants us all to move back to Seattle. She said they're worried about you— that taking care of Janey and me is too much for you." Clea held the invitation in her hand. "She said that Dad wants to take care of us, that he needs us. And—" Clea studied her hands, "Grandma said when I got ready for high school, I could go to the same one Dad went to in San Francisco. But Mom, I'm not sure I want to do that."

Mama Cass hopped into my lap. "Wow," I said. Mama Cass reached her long body over to Clea and tapped her paw on my daughter's arm. "The cat thinks we do OK," I said. "How do you feel about Arizona? And living on the ranch?"

"I love horses, and Alex teaches me all the basics. I wish we could use the pool, and Franny is like my best friend. It was hard changing schools. But you know, my teacher's an astronomer, and she's super cool."

"You like it here?"

"I do."

"One of the reasons I thought the ranch was good for us is that I can work and be at home. It's family-style here, and the guests come in and go out, but we are in a place where we can have our pets and time together. I like it here, too."

Cass moved over to Clea's lap. "But what about Dad?"

"We can work that out. Your dad can come here whenever he likes," I said. "You and your sister are the center of my universe. I promised you and Janey a long time ago that I would raise you and love you the best way I can, and I always will. Not always perfectly."

"Would you ever go back to Dad?"

"No," I said. "I'll be glad to see him, and I know he's excited to see you. But you must accept that Dad and I live separate lives now."

Clea put the invitation face down on the table. "So, you'd never go back to him?"

"It took a lot of courage for me to come here on my

own with Janey and you. I was scared a lot of the time, but I wasn't going to let fear make my decisions—a new job, house, and schools for you and Janey. I decided a lot of things. I prayed it would work out. Now, I even have a place to paint. I like being on my own with you two. You will always have your dad. Nothing takes that away from you. Do you understand?"

Clea dislodged Mama Cass from her lap, poured herself a glass of apple juice, and sat back down. "Dad's going to buy us a big new house in Seattle, and he said I could take riding lessons. Grandma said so, and she said if you wanted to stay in Arizona, that would be OK."

I shook my head and sat back. "As for Grandma, my goodness, she's full of ideas about what's best for us." I peered straight into my daughter's eyes and pressed my hand to my chest. "I intend to see you grow up and not miss any part of it. I love you and your sister to the moon and back, and you'll stay with me."

"Can I visit Dad?"

"Of course, but let's let him get settled," I said, then switched subjects. "Boy, won't Dad be surprised when he sees Janey?"

"He's hardly seen her at all." Clea's eyes softened. "At least I can remember who he is. Janey's still a toddler."

"Well, honey, she won't have to hurt so much about it."

"I don't mind that so much 'cause I remember him. I wish he'd write more often like he did after he married Julie." She eyed the telephone. "Can I call him to see if he's OK?"

"Not tonight, sweetie. It's late. You can call him tomorrow."

She stood and stretched. "I'm going to bed. Are you?"

"Yes, I am." Astounding, I thought, the amount of manipulative moves Allen and his mother had made over the last week, promising a private school in San Francisco and riding lessons in Seattle, couched in some harebrained notion that taking care of Clea and Janey was "too much" for me. Ridiculous. I tucked my conversation with Clea in my back pocket, grateful to understand what dynamic was coming with Allen and his mother's arrival at the ranch. They wanted control of my children.

21

Horse Ride Interlude

It was a sunny mid-October day in the desert.

The wind blew slightly, and I managed fine on a wide-shouldered, dappled horse that Alex promised me was fifteen years old and not much interested in her wild pony cousins in the hills. Janey giggled, and the absolute smile of delight had not left her face since I handed her to Alex, who rode Thief. Clea rode behind me and occasionally caught up with me, expressing amazement that I appeared to be enjoying myself. I was. The desert air, my cowboy buddy, and the unrehearsed exuberance of my children combined for a mighty high, and I sucked it in hungrily.

Janey fell asleep on the way back to the ranch. Alex dismounted with her in tow and helped me down without waking her. Clea and I were both impressed.

"You act like you've done this before," Clea said.

"It's not the first time," Alex answered.

"You have any kids?" Clea patted her ride while the horse drank water from a communal trough.

"Clea," I said, "is that any of your business?"

"No," she peered over at Alex. "I was just curious."

As he spoke, he rocked Janey gently in his arms. "I don't mind," he said. "A long time ago, I had a little girl whose hair was like sunshine. We called her Sunni. She and her mom live in Hawaii now, but when she was this size, she always fell asleep on the way home."

"How long have you been divorced?" Clea asked.

I didn't interrupt her inquisitiveness this time—I was curious, too. Lara would be interested.

"Seven years."

"Do you ever see her?" Clea asked.

Alex reddened slightly and handed Janey to me.

"Clea," I said, pretending I had control over what came out of my daughter's mouth. "Enough. You have the pertinent facts."

The four of us returned to my place, and I put Janey down to continue her nap. Clea retreated to call Franny. I brought two beers to the porch for Alex and me.

"Thanks," Alex said.

"Thank you. I had a wonderful time. Angel Foot was so well mannered as if she knew I was a rookie."

"That's why I put you on her. You're going to love riding. Pablo will make sure of that."

"Maybe so." I changed the direction of the conversation. "Clea rides well, but maybe she's a little nosy?" I sipped my beer. "I didn't know you'd been married and had a daughter. Talk to me, cowboy!"

"My wife hated the ranch and split one day when I was on some mission or another for Glen. Her family lives on Maui. Her auntie is in San Francisco, so I see Sunni and Kristin when they come over. Saw them last month."

"Kristin remarried?"

"You're as nosy as your daughter," Alex chuckled and drank more beer. "She remarried and, by all accounts, happy." He finished the beer and crushed the can in his hand.

"I'll take that," I said, and Alex handed me the crumpled can.

"Did it change you? The divorce and disruption. Not seeing Sunni?"

"It sure as hell sobered me up. I used to drink a lot. Spent time with the boys, you know? Card games. Tavern crawls—that kind of nonsense. The fact that Glen sided with Kristin burned, too. He told me straight up, 'You earn a place in a kid's life—in a woman's life.' And Glen's right. I cleaned up too late to save the marriage, but as it turned out, I became a good dad."

"I know my kids love you," I said. "You're patient and kind." I peered into his eyes. "And I think you like Lara."

"You're amazing, don't get me wrong, but Lara ..."

"She rings all the bells?"

"At once!" Alex said. "I can't explain it. "Has she said anything to you about me?"

"From what I can tell," I said. "I think you're pretty much a bell ringer, too."

22

Auroras Over Oracle Hill

The girls and I shopped for a welcome home gift for Allen, a photo album with pictures of the children from the last year. We made another for his mother. Clea designed the covers from heavy white construction paper and Janey helped color it in, and then Clea edged the covers in gold. We made handprints of the girls for each.

I scoured every inch of the house, including the baseboards and oven. As I finished cleaning the birdcages Tuesday evening, the phone rang. I imagined a call from Allen or Agnes postponing the trip as I had grown used to explaining why Daddy couldn't be here. Clea answered. She raced to where I stood on the household ladder, inserting the cage tray for the last cage. "It's a long-distance call from Canada, Mom," Clea said.

That had to be Mother's lawyer. He'd said he wanted to stay in touch and he had. "Good to hear from you, Charlie," I said. At first, Charlie Trucker apologized for sending my mother's cat without calling me first. I assured him he'd done the right thing. When he asked how the cat was adjusting, I replied, "Right now, she's sitting across from me on the sofa with her new friend, Honeydog. I swear she talks to me. Thank you for sending her to me."

"Tansy," Charlie's voice tinged toward the serious, "I need to tell you about something. Might be nothing. Might be something."

"Well, now I'm curious," I said.

"Your ex-husband is Allen Daniels, correct?"

"Right," I answered.

"He came to my office, and I saw him. He wanted to know about your inheritance."

I froze. What the hell was Allen doing? "I'm so sorry—"

"His visit didn't bother me, but his, well, his manner did. He reeked of charm. And I mean reeks like cheap aftershave. He seems so different than you. I didn't tell him anything—he left empty-handed. But something about him wasn't right."

"I'm sorry," I said again, uncertain what I was apologizing for or why my skin crawled. "Allen always took care of things," my voice softened and disappeared.

"I'm an old man who tends to pick up on details," Charlie said. "You mean 'controlled' everything?"

"I guess so." My words stumbled out.

"He said you may want to contest your mother's will."

"That's not happening," I said. "I have the cat. I'm happy." I may have laughed to lighten the exchange.

"I told Allen that I could not help him, advise him, or advise you unless you hired me. I showed him the door. His last words betrayed a less kindly person. 'Well, this was a wasted day,' and he was gone."

"His mother probably sent him," I said. "He's spoiled. I'm sorry you had to put up with him."

"I don't trust him. And I know this comes out of the blue, but be careful around him."

"I try to be," I tugged on a strand of hair. "You're not the first person to tell me that about Allen, but we're all OK. And, like I said, he was probably annoyed with his mother."

"Was that guy talking about Dad?" Clea asked when I hung up the phone.

"Yes."

"Why?"

"Your dad had a meeting with him, and Mr. Trucker wanted to let me know.

Maria came over to stay with the girls on Tuesday evening, and Pablo arrived promptly at nine. I waved at him from the door and turned to Clea, "I'll be back by eleven, just like I said." Truly, I wanted to stay where life was familiar, and all my energy into cleaning, straightening, mother-daughter talking, and even the cat compelled me homeward. It was cold for an October night, and thinking about making out in the back of a pickup truck tanked the attraction; I wasn't sixteen. Allen was coming the next day, and I had a headache. I wondered if real intimacy scared me because the soft whine of my thoughts did not dispel how attracted I was to Pablo.

I hopped into the truck cab and sat back. We said hello, but if I was reading the room right, this gazing-at-the-stars event felt weird to Pablo, too. "Can we go somewhere for fries and chocolate milkshakes?" I blurted as Pablo turned off the property onto the main road.

"Trust me on this," Pablo said. "You heard about the solar storms Sunday night into Monday?"

Apparently, I was reading the room all wrong. "Yeah," I answered. "Clea's teacher is an astronomer and said there was an outside chance we might see an aurora this far south—"

"The observatory up at Mt. Lemmon was pretty excited, too," Pablo said. "It's possible, I can't promise, but hang on—"

I hardly heard the last of Pablo's words because the sky directly over the Catalinas moved in violets. "The northern lights," I said half aloud. "Wow."

"Let's go up to my lookout. By the way, I brought lawn chairs. The whole star-gazing in the truck bed felt weird."

"Felt weird to me, too." We both oohed and awed at the violet and pink moving skies. Stars blinked through the luminous heavens. Cars parked along the road where Pablo turned Gladys up a gravel road that curved around Oracle Hill, then another short jaunt upward, and we were both pointing at the ever-changing sky. Pablo brought his camera and shot one photo after another. He had one of me pointing at the Milky Way. I took a couple of him.

We sat back in the lawn chairs, eyes steady on the skies. I put my hand over Pablo's. "You're cold." He turned my hand around, stroking each finger.

"That feels good."

Pablo kissed my hand and dropped it, then stood. "Why don't we let Gladys warm us up?"

In the truck, Pablo turned on the heat while the engine hummed. I took off my puffy jacket and sat beside him on the bench seat. All that magnificent pulsating with colorful flashes dancing sky had its effect. The heavens tuned into us. The lovemaking surprised us both, but it was as if the solar storms conspired and urged us on. Deep in afterglow, I rolled off of his lap and giggled. "We are good," I said. We opened the doors, I stepped outside and dressed quickly.

The sky lightened to pale gold with lavender touches. Back inside my yellow bubble coat and fully dressed, our thighs touching, Pablo took me home. "My show opens on Saturday. Any chance you can be there?" he asked.

"Maybe we can double with Lara and Alex?" I said. At the thought of making Saturday plans, my heart navigated to the days ahead and plummeted. "I don't know what it'll be like after Allen gets here, but Lara arrives on Friday."

"I will take a maybe," Pablo said. He wrapped his free arm around me as we drove down the road.

23

Flu Prelude

It was 10:45 p.m. when we arrived at my house. Maria must have heard Gladys as Pablo parked because she came outside, her index finger pressed against her lips. Pablo did not turn the engine off. I scooted over to the passenger door. Good night, I mouthed, and he whispered, "I already miss you."

"Clea might still be awake; the little one felt warm to me. She said her tummy hurt." Maria looked me up and down. "He's a good man, Pablo." She smiled. "I better be going." We entered the house; Maria retrieved her sweater and bag, then left.

I realized I hadn't paid her, so I chased out the door and caught her before she drove off. "Thank you, my friend," I said. "It was a magical night."

I checked the girls, walked the pups around the house, returned, and gave the canine crew fresh water. Mama Cass looked annoyed until I gave her a late-night snack. My thoughts floated under a hot shower; Pablo and I managed a nearly perfect evening. One for the memory book, no matter what else should happen. Dressed in a twenty-year-old t-shirt and ready for bed, I opened the bathroom door when Janey screamed. I ran to her room and found her throwing up.

"Poor baby," I said and raced her to the bathroom and pulled off her pajamas as I ran a warm bath. An hour later, she was asleep in my bed; I crawled in beside her. She emanated hot, dry heat, so I sneaked out of my room to grab a cup of apple juice and liquid Tylenol. Clea yawned as she came into the kitchen.

"What's going on, Mom?"

"Didn't you hear your sister throwing up?"

"Yeah. I thought it was a car horn at first. Does she have a fever, too?"

"A car horn? God, Clea. Yes, she feels like the quintessential hot potato." I poured her a glass of apple juice. "Are you feeling OK?" I put the palm of my hand against her forehead, and she felt cool.

Clear shrugged off my question. "What'd you and Pablo do?"

"You know what? We saw the northern lights from those solar storms Mrs. Ramos told you about. Pablo took some pictures. Wait 'til you see!"

Clea followed me to my room. "I wish I could have seen that." She drank some juice. "My throat stings a little."

Janey still slept, so we went back to the kitchen. "Let me check it out—open wide." Under the kitchen ceiling light, Clea's throat appeared normal. "I think you're OK. Better get back to bed. What you need is sleep. I know you're excited about seeing your dad—it's going to be a big day."

"I think I'm getting sick," Clea said.

"I think you need sleep."

"Aren't you excited at all to see Dad?"

I pointed to her bedroom door.

"If Janey gets sick, it's poor baby, but me? 'You're just tired, Clea.' It's not fair."

"So little in life is." I sighed dramatically.

"You're just trying to get rid of me."

"Mama!" Janey screamed from my bed. Clea and I ran to my room to assess the damages. Janey had vomited again.

Clea said, "Well, maybe I better get some sleep," and left the room quickly.

"Turncoat!" I shouted at her retreat. From a distance, I heard her laughing.

"Well, sweetheart, what'll we do about you?" I carried her into the bathroom and peeled off her PJs. "Are you done throwing up?"

"I think I'm done throwing up." Her cheeks reddened, and tears popped from her big blue eyes.

"It's scary, isn't it, honey? That's alright. You let those cries out." I held my bathrobe around her while running a cool bath. She felt hot; hopefully, the tepid water would help bring her fever down. After dressing her in the last clean set of pajamas, I gave her some Tylenol and prayed it would stay down. Before stripping the mattress cover and blankets from my futon, I bundled Janey in an afghan on the floor, then tended to my bed. The mattress was untouched, but I turned it over for good measure and piled the sheets and anything vomitus in the washer. After making the bed and tucking Janey in, I climbed in beside her. I peered at my clock: four in the morning. As I listened to the washing machine chug on, I fell asleep.

24

Like A Bad Penny

Clea and I agreed that she might as well go to school because her dad wasn't going to arrive until the late afternoon, and I made a deal with her that if he should appear earlier than we thought, we'd send him to release her from school for the entire week. Even so, she was reluctant to leave. Janey's fever still hadn't broken, so we said goodbye to Clea at the front door.

I called the ranch office to tell Glen I would not be in because of Janey's flu. "Hey, Alex, is the Man in?" Alex sounded a little off. I usually arrived well before nine, and it was half past the hour.

Glen picked up the call. "What's up?" he asked, his voice drained of emotion.

"Janey is sick, and I'm functioning without sleep. If Alex kindly brings over the books I have out on my desk, I can continue where I left off yesterday. I'm unable to work in the office today."

"You need a doctor?"

"There's a bug going around. I think she's OK, but I have to get her fever down."

"Alex'll bring over the books, and we'll figure out the phone. You alright for food?"

"We're good. My ex-husband and his mother are checking in this afternoon. Agnes said they're renting a car, so you don't need to send anyone to meet them."

"That woman called after nine. Guess she expected to speak to you. They're comin' in early this mornin' sometime—same plan with the car an' all—their flight got rescheduled or some goddamned thing."

"Well, fine," I muttered. My body ached with the need to rest. What would I do with Allen and his mother all week? A vanishing aurora moved like liquid through my thoughts. If last night was an illusion, perhaps today is an illusion, too—the best I could come up with while wishing to hang onto one and not the other. Does life work that way?

"Dina officially starts today at eleven. She'll post the menus in the dining room on the chalkboard we put up. I left a big box of chalk for the guest kids to draw with. I shopped Dina's list, but she suggested she'd like to do the shopping—I think you can trust her with that. For now, she can give us receipts, and we can reimburse if that's OK with you. It's all on the list, but I believe there'll be six for lunch, not counting you guys. And if my party comes in early, you better plan on two more. Please let Dina know, and be nice to her! Anyway, the list with anything else I can't remember right now is next to my calendar on my desk."

Glen paused. "Did we settle on pay for Dina?"

"Yeah. She comes experienced, so I offered what you told me, eleven an hour. She's new to the area, so she's trying to find a place close to the ranch."

"She seems like a nice gal," Glen said.

"Jimmy Andrews from the Tourist Bureau may be coming out to the ranch today. Today or tomorrow—I have it on my list."

We said goodbye, and I was taken aback because he didn't argue about paying more than the minimum. I smiled. I thought he liked Dina, which was one in the plus column. Twenty minutes later, Alex knocked at the door. Janey sat in my lap while we watched a tape featuring Winnie the Pooh. Alex poked his head inside. "Hi," he said. "Here are the books from yesterday." He held them up.

"Put them on the table," I said, "and thanks."

He leaned over the couch and patted Janey's head. "And how are you, little one?"

Janey snuggled close to me.

"Her fever's still high, but we hope it'll be down by lunchtime."

"Glen said to send Clea up to the office and help with the new cook after school if it works best for you."

"Well, that's really sweet, and Clea would love that job, but her dad's due anytime. Thank Glen for me. Janey's about ready for a nap, and then I'll get out of this chenille robe, brush my teeth, and work on the books."

Alex took the dogs out for a walk before leaving. Janey felt a tad cooler after a dose of Tylenol, and I read to her. She fell into a calm sleep, so I tucked her into her bed and tiptoed from her room.

I tapped my fingers on top of the ranch books and stared outside. Honeydog came over to me and then put her head in my lap. "Aw, you sweet dog," I said, ruffling her furry head. "Mama's got to get to work." Not to be outdone, Mama Cass jumped on the table and began playing with a pencil, knocking it off. My head hurt, and I was deeply distracted. I rose from my chair to get a dose of Tylenol and a glass of water, but the phone rang midway to the kitchen.

It was Clea's school. Clea had thrown up all over the Seever's kid and ran a slight fever. Could I come to get her?"

"Oh, that poor boy," I said, "And poor Clea. "Yes, we'll be right over. Her little sister has the same flu, but someone from the ranch will pick her up."

The school secretary told me that she felt fairly rotten herself, and almost half the staff had one bug or another. She sneezed and began coughing as we hung up.

I called Alex, who assured me he would pick up Clea, but Clea's dad was standing in the office with his mom. They had arrived. He handed me the phone.

"You did get here early," I said.

"Mom's here, too. Just got in."

"Janey has some kind of bug, and the school called. Clea's sick, too. I was going to have Alex pick her up. I think she'd be thrilled if you went along, too."

He sounded like he was in a good mood. I hung up the phone and felt Janey tugging on my robe. Awake and feverish, she told me that she was hungry. Instead of brushing my hair, I boiled an egg for Janey. She ate some of it and drank a little apple juice and water. She played with her building bricks while I washed my face. I heard Clea slam Alex's truck door as I left the bathroom. I opened the front door to greet her; Allen was a few steps behind. Alex tipped his hat from the truck and drove away. A shot of adrenaline coursed from my knee to my brain. Holy shit, I was still in my bathrobe, and I couldn't remember brushing my teeth.

Then I heard Clea's bell-like voice, "—then Mom said—"

Her laughter and joy were a simple restorative. She might be sick, but the child had her father.

Allen wrapped his arm around Clea and followed me inside. The dogs wagged their tails and greeted Clea. I motioned for Allen to take my chair, but he remained standing. I sat with Janey on the couch. "Welcome to CollinCamp," I said to Allen. Clea stood between us. "How ya doing, dolly?" I asked her.

"Not very good, but you should see Robby."

"So, how'd he make out?" I asked.

She sat as close to me as the laws of science allowed. "My stomach started to do twirlies, but I thought I'd be fine until break."

I peered up at Allen, who stood back. We exchanged proud parent looks—something I suddenly became aware I could share with no one else.

Clea continued with her story. "We were going to correct social studies papers when—"

Allen's bright hazel eyes rested on me; he wore creased khakis and a short-sleeved red and blue checkered shirt. He stood tall and lean, with black, metal-framed specs perched on his slender nose. The details of his stance and what he wore stuck with me. They framed the man I wanted him to be, easy-going and self-assured, not the arrogant asshole I dealt with a couple of nights ago on the phone.

"And then!" Clea said with a giggle, "Rob turned around to give me his, and I gave him my breakfast. Boy, was Robby surprised! Kids started yelling, 'Robby got slimed,' and everyone started making retching noises. I was so embarrassed, but the look on his face, Mom."

I touched Clea's forehead, and she was feverish.

"Mrs. Ramos got me out of there. She was pretty calm. She told the secretary to call you. The secretary said, 'Everyone's sick.' She told me to take a chair cause it would be a while. Mrs. Ramos said, 'Oh, for Pete's sake, this girl needs to go home; please call her mother! Then call Mrs. Seever. Robby's in the bathroom cleaning up. I have a class to tend to—I want the janitor immediately.' The secretary says, 'Well, what do you want me to do first?' Mrs. Ramos pointed to the phone. 'Call,' she said.' "

Clea stared up at her dad and then at me. "Well, the rest, you know. "I think I'm going to put on my nightgown. Sorry, Dad, that I'm sick. The little toddler on the couch—I guess you know that's Janey. Mom, would you tuck me in when I call you?"

"Sure, sweetheart. I'll bring you some 7-up, too. Rinse your mouth out, and get into bed."

"I need some Tylenol, Mom."

"Of course."

Clea left the room, and I felt like a team without a cheerleader. Janey wanted back on my lap. "The little toddler on my lap is Janey," and I played with her toes.

"Mom, Mom," Clea returned to the living room in a burst. "We forgot Dad's present." In her hand was the album the girls and I made for him.

"Oh my gosh, this is wonderful," Allen said.

"We have one for Grandma, too!"

"You can show Dad all the pictures in a little while, sweetie pie. Why don't you get your nightgown on now?"

"When you're all comfy, I want to see all the photos," Allen said.

Allen placed the album on the end table and Clea left for her room.

"You want to say hello to Daddy?" I kissed Janey's head. "You can show some photos to Daddy, too." I hugged her. "Can you say, 'Hi, Daddy.'"

"Of course, I can. I don't want to."

"You know, Janey, you couldn't say a word the last time I saw you. Now, Clea tells me that you talk all the time. I brought special surprises for you and your sister, too. But, we'll wait 'til later for that." He reached into his pocket and grabbed something. "Well, I do have a surprise for you right in my pocket. Do you want to see what it is?"

Janey nodded yes.

Allen pulled out an airline pack of playing cards.

"Hi, Daddy. Mommy, can you play cards with me?"

"Mom!" Clea yelled from her room.

"I have to go see what your sister wants. Daddy will play with you." I left Allen unwrapping the cards for Janey, who sat very still beside him.

"What did he give Janey?" Clea sipped her soda after taking the Tylenol.

"Playing cards from the airline," I tucked her blankets around her. "Quit eavesdropping. You have a fever of 101 and books to read."

"She doesn't even know how to play," Clea said.

"Your dad and Grandma will have very nice presents for you—they always do. If you need anything, let me know. Right now, I'm going to see how your dad and Janey are getting along."

"Mom, you look awful."

"Thank you, my dear—I call it bathrobe-chic."

In the living room, the three of us played a matching game with no rules and watched Barney be very, very nice to all his television friends. Janey fell asleep, and I put her to bed. Clea slept, too. Now it was good ol' dad and me.

Allen turned off the television and stared at me as I sat in my small rocker across from the couch. I folded my hands in my lap, and a wave of tired sickness went through me. "I'm not looking my best," I said, as if I needed to explain.

"Did you get flu shots?" Humor softened his voice.

"No, but it's fall. They said lots of kids and staff were out at school." I played with the polyester fringe on my bathrobe sleeve.

"Mom and I got flu shots before coming here."

"Wise," I said. "I'm going to get a 7-Up. Would you like anything?"

Allen trailed behind me as I entered the kitchen. "Let me get it." I didn't think he wanted to risk getting whatever the flu shot didn't cover. "Hey, can I have a beer?"

"Sure!" I pointed to the cupboard where I stored glassware.

"First, you. You have a bottle opener?"

"Yeah, somewhere," I opened the junk drawer and started piling through assorted extra batteries, pens, menus, notepads, last year's calendar, and stray rubber bands.

Allen held up a hand. "I got it. Allen pulled a Swiss Army knife from his pocket and opened the bottle with one of its attached tools. "No ice, right?"

"You remembered." Allen handed me the glass, then extracted a beer mug with the old Rainier sign on its bowl. "We got these as wedding presents," he sighed. "You still have them?"

I nodded. This moment felt natural in the kitchen. I watched Allen fill his glass, and I led the way back to the living room. I plunked my aching body on the sofa. He sat across from me in my chair.

"Why is everyone so tight-lipped about your mother's will?"

Wow, it didn't take Allen long to get to business. "Yeah, I heard that you went to see Charlie. He wasn't being tight-lipped, but it wasn't his place to explain the terms of the will to you. It's all public record, anyway."

"Did he call you after I left? How'd you find out I paid him a visit?"

"Yeah, Charlie called. So, here's the deal: Mother left me four thousand the rest of the trust fund, about fifty grand, went to a charity for cats and a community project for a nonprofit she was involved in—seed money for a community center for street kids." Mama Cass jumped into my lap as if cued. "Well, I got another grand and her, too," I said, "as it turns out. Meet Mama Cass Elliot." She swished her tail toward Allen and hopped onto the sofa back.

"You can contest that," Allen said. "You deserve more than a friggin' cat rescue and as far as a community center? From the looks of things," he peered around the room, "you could put money away for the kids' education, a house, or something. You are no lady of leisure anymore. No more Mrs. Housewife."

"I'm fine with it," I said.

"You're going to let him roll over you? And why the hell didn't Lara object?"

I shrugged. My mouth felt gummy, and sweat popped on my neck. The last thing I wanted was this conversation. But, damn, Allen's accusations angered me. *Mrs. Housewife, lady of leisure,* what freaking planet did he live on? With my tongue against the rough of my mouth, I pressed on, with a slight change in subject. "I liked Mother's lawyer—apparently, he was a friend, too. Originally, Charlie was going to take care of Cassie, but—"

Allen sipped his beer. "Well, funny how that worked." He was not interested in my adoption story of the cat. He was all about the money. "Seriously, how do you expect to support yourself and the kids?" Mama Cass hissed at him, which tickled me. Honeydog joined us; she lay down at my feet while Yul and Deb formed an outer boundary. Deb was stationed between Honeydog and Allen, within reach of Yul. I got the feeling that none of them trusted Allen. We all had our reasons.

"And you took that four thousand and partied it away."

"When was that exactly?"

"From what Clea said, you have a new boyfriend and had a party weekend with Lara. Paid for her trip, no doubt."

I took a breath to slow down my response, and a wave of nausea caused me to pause. "If you are curious about who I see and where I go, please ask me, not Clea."

"I would have if you ever answered my call or had longer than five minutes to speak. These are my kids, Tansy, and I care how they are raised." The conversational tone in his voice belied his words.

My hands went cold. "There is nothing more important to me than the children," I said. I swallowed some soda and began to cough. I covered my mouth and peered over at Allen through my rheumy eyes. "I'm not at my best today," I said.

"Are you making even minimum wage at this guest ranch?" Allen stared back at me. "I'm hurt, Tansy. It hurt that you didn't come to me when you wanted to move to this place. You didn't have to uproot the girls."

I studied my hands. "We like it here."

"Well, this is getting us nowhere," Allen sighed audibly. "I'm sorry if I came on too strong. I'm hurt," he sighed again. "When Vivian lay dying, you called me in tears, and then I heard crickets when you promised to keep in touch. We guessed it was all 'ding-dong the wicked witch is dead' and party-on."

Lara told me to keep things light. Allen had no idea that Lara was waiting for me to green light another court date about support. "Allen, the kids love you, and they are excited to share the album with you. I have one for your mom, too. You sound upset about the will, and frankly, I'm sick. I have to rest before one of the kids wakes up." I forced calm into my voice that I did't feel. I wanted him out of my house. "You might want to go horseback riding or something. Lots of good hiking, too."

Before he responded, a knock at the door interrupted, and Agnes waltzed in. Allen's demeanor instantly changed.

"Agnes, I'm not going to hug you. I don't want to give you whatever bug we have. But good to see you. Are you all settled?"

"You're the color of flour paste. Why on earth are you up?" Agnes asked.

"Go, find your bed," Allen crooned, "and we'll look after you and the girls for a change." Good Dad had returned.

I protested for a moment, and then the room began spinning. "OK. OK." I shuffled off to the bathroom and then to my bedroom. Honeydog trailed behind me and the cat. Allen came in with a fresh glass of soda. "Dogs need to be fed around around five. Can you do that?" I asked.

"I'll take care of everything," Allen said. "Everything."

I closed my eyes and fell into a deep sleep.

25

Table Talk

I awakened in a pool of sweat; chills riveted my arms and legs, and I couldn't tell what time it was, but I thought my fever had broken. Someone had closed the curtains across my windows, and I thought I heard Honeydog from far away. I gotta feed the dogs, I thought. Then I remembered Janey. Janey, my baby—she's sick. Clea's sick, too. I tried getting up and fell back on the damp pillows, then rolled over and called: "I'm coming, girls; I'll be right there." My voice was a hoarse whisper. The hell with this, I thought and mustered what reserve I had and forced myself up. The room danced around, but I stood quietly and prayed that the nausea would abate. I stared down at myself. Who dressed me in my running sweats and plaid pajama top. Allen? The thought turned my stomach. I walked down the hall, seeing Allen and Agnes in the living room. They both turned to see me at the same time. I surprised them. I don't think they wanted me to hear anything they discussed.

"Agnes, sorry, I missed you—God, I hope you guys don't get this."

"Allen and I had our flu shots—I guess you didn't. Oh my Lord, dear, you look miserable."

Allen nodded wisely.

"How's Janey? Where's Clea?" I asked. "What time is it? Is it still Wednesday? Did I tell Glen that I'm sick? Is there any ginger ale?" I didn't wait for answers but turned to check the girls.

"Where do you think you're going," Allen asked.

"To the girls. I have to see how they are—if they need anything." I peered at mother and son, who gazed at me. I never realized how much they resembled one another. "Your names should rhyme. Do you know that?"

"Tansy," Allen said, "both kiddos are asleep. It's 11:30, Thursday night. Glen called a doctor who looked in on all of you. Do you remember?"

"That seems so long ago, the guy in a hat. Glen's the only guy I know who could get a doctor to make a house call."

"He said this flu is fast and dirty—Beijing strain. Comes on quickly and leaves the same. You should be a little weak, but basically, fine by late tomorrow. I called Lara and Brette, and they'll be coming next week instead. Glen's been kind of a jerk, but we insisted he rearrange everything. So why not go back to bed? Janey's fever broke about an hour ago, and she's feeling much better. Clea is still pretty sick, but she's been asleep for about an hour now." He tapped me on the shoulder and pointed to the couch. "You better sit down before you fall down. You look like shit." His eyes teased. Helpful, companionable Allen presided.

"That's not a nice thing to say, Allen," I said. "Not nice a bit."

"I was teasing."

"I know, and I'll check the kiddos before going back to bed. Thanks for your help."

I peeked into Janey's room, and she was asleep. She had a new stuffed bear propped in her arms. Agnes was behind me.

"The bear was from us," she whispered. She backed slightly and pointed to my bedroom.

"I'm going to check on Clea, then I will."

She was awake. "Mommy?" Clea said. "I feel awful—I think I got a fever. Will you check me?"

"Yeah, baby, I'm right here." Agnes started to say something, and I shook my head at her. "Can you get me the thermometer strip, Agnes? It's in the top cupboard above the microwave." She left. I checked Clea's forehead; I didn't need anything else. She was hot.

"My nightshirt's all wet, so I think my fever might have gone down some."

"How do you feel?"

"Really bad, Mom, and Janey's been crying."

"I checked her, sweetie, and she's asleep. Now for you— do you know when you had Tylenol last?"

"Three hours ago," Agnes checked her watch. She handed me the thermometer strip, and I placed it on Clea's forehead.

"One hundred and three," I said. "You feeling a little dizzy?"

"When I try to sit up, I do," Clea answered.

"Honey, I'm going to walk you to the bathroom and run a coolish bath for you. OK?"

"OK."

"I don't think that's necessary," Agnes countered.

"Her fevers run high, Agnes." I helped Clea get up and walked her to the doorway. Agnes moved reluctantly. "Agnes?" I asked. "Would you please change Clea's sheets while she's in the bath?"

"Where are they?"

"In the bathroom cupboard. Follow me." We all went into the bathroom. My pale daughter sat on the tub's edge while I ran her bath. I handed Agnes the sheets, and all three of us pondered each other in distaste.

"Flu's ugly, isn't it, darlin'?"

"You think I'm going to strip for you—you have something else coming." Clea sounded firm and assured me she wouldn't faint in the bathtub. Her protest was a good sign, I thought. I agreed to wait outside.

"Mom?" Clea called a few minutes later. I opened the door slightly and leaned against the wall. "You can come in." She pulled the shower curtain shut so that she could maintain her privacy. "Can I get out now?"

"You've been in about five minutes. I know it's hard, but let's try for five more. I'll get your nightie. Your sheets will feel good, and it will almost be time for more Tylenol."

"Will you stay with me when I'm back in bed?"

"Sure, honey."

"Dad gave me a TV with a built-in VCR, exactly like Patricia's. Do you think he'd set it up?"

Allen set up the television in her room as Clea finished up in the bathroom. She emerged with her hair brushed.

"You appear about a million times better," I told her in the hall.

"I want to look good for my dreams," she said.

"Your eyes are droopy, and," I placed my hand on her

forehead, "you're still a hot potato but cooling, I think." I motioned her toward her room. "Want some ginger ale?"

"I might throw it up," she answered.

"Why not try little sips? Let's get you in bed."

Allen put *Gone with the Wind* into the machine, and I lay beside her. Clea sipped her ginger ale, and I stayed until it was time for her Tylenol, then kissed her goodnight. She was sleepy, and I knew it wouldn't be long until she slept in earnest.

I checked Janey. It bothered me that Clea said she had heard her little sister cry. All the activity had disturbed Janey's sleep, and she saw me from the doorway.

"Mommy?" she said.

"Baby, I'm right here," I answered.

"Can you lay with me?"

"Yeah," I said and smiled. "I can." Her skin felt cooler but not wholly without fever. Before lying down, I gave her some apple juice and water with a dose of Tylenol.

"Where were you, Mommy?" She asked when I had my arm around her tummy, and she nestled safely in my arms.

"I was sleeping because I have the same thing you and your sister have."

"Oh, you poor thing," she whispered and nodded off. Sometimes, I believed Janey was an old soul.

I found Allen and Agnes playing gin rummy in the living room. "They're all set," I said. "Thanks so much for standing in."

"I think it's time we put you to bed," Allen said. "Mom changed your sheets, and you have some ginger ale waiting for you."

"Thanks," I said. "Where are the dogs?" I asked, finally noting that they were missing. "I thought I heard Honeydog a while ago. Where's the cat?"

"Outside," mother and son chorused.

"They have to come in—they're house dogs. And I don't know if Mama Cass has ever been outside." I opened the front door, and all three lunged inside. "Honeydog never goes out alone, and Deb and Yul don't know the first thing about camping." I shut the door. "Are they fed? And what about the cat?"

"They are fed," Agnes said, irritated. "I don't know where the cat is. I believe I'll go to my cabana."

My heart skipped a beat. I had to find Mama Cass. I needn't worry. She was on the porch swing, and she immediately came inside. Agnes was behind me, ready to leave. "Agnes, thank you for everything. I appreciate your help." I was grateful, but my voice wobbled. "If you need a flashlight, there's one—"

"I have a flashlight," Agnes turned to her son. "I order you to put this woman to bed and sit on her until she gets better." A beam of light penetrated the night as Agnes left the house.

Allen walked me to my bedroom door. "I'm staying here. Don't even think about protesting, so stop shaking your head, Tans. You're sick." He took my wrist. "Your pulse is rapid, and you have a fever. Mom will help tomorrow, but I'm sleeping on the couch. And I love you. Goodnight."

He was a contradiction; now, he was kind and loving, and I knew better than to trust him, but I only wanted to sleep. "Whatever," I whispered half-aloud. Mama Cass sat on my bed, and my bedroom door was closed. Ginger ale shone pale by my bedside lamp in the otherwise darkened room. I stretched and shut my eyes, then the door opened, and Honeydog jumped to her spot at the end of my bed. "Thank you, Allen," I said. I heard him go down the hallway. Mama Cass jumped onto my pillow and nestled into my side.

I was too sick to care about Allen's sincerity level, but he seemed sincere enough. He cared about the girls—I trusted that part. The remainder of that night and the next day became a blur of faces. By afternoon, I felt better. I told Agnes where Janey's favorite pony's t-shirt was. Clea and I bunked together, watched the end of *Gone with the Wind,* and read.

Agnes's face shone with a Mother Teresa aura each time she delivered juice or Tylenol. Clea rolled her eyes whenever Agnes turned away from us. It got so the sight of her with the tray lined with a white paper towel set us off in giggles. The flu hung onto Clea and me a day longer than Janey's.

26

Unraveling

I was back at work by Monday morning while the girls played hooky with their dad. At eight, I turned on the office lights and viewed my desk with alarm. It had become a veritable dumping ground of unopened mail, receipts, and notes, some taped to my desk lamp. I tossed my bag under my desk and began unraveling the mess. I cleared everything off my desk and sorted the mail and messages into three piles: guests and reservations, bills payment due, and bills payment delay. Three neat piles later, I looked at our accounts receivable and decided to catch up on the daily reports from the week past. Before anyone could be paid, I had to see what we had to pay with.

Consuela and Maria burst into the office, speaking rapid Spanish, turned to me, and in heated English said, "That man," Consuela shook the cleaning rag she held in her hand, "he burnt a pan black, then leaves the stove on this morning. Tequila bottles empty in the trash and a pile of his clothing for me to wash? He leaves this note." Consuela dug into her pocket for the paper the guest left and handed it to me.

That man had to be Allen. "I am so sorry, Maria. I'll take care of the laundry."

"And his mother's, too?" Consuela asked. "She leaves a bag, too."

I noticed two trash bags on the cleaner's cart on the patio. "Is that their clothes?" I asked.

"Yes," Consuela said.

"Leave it with me, and I'll run it at home. I am so sorry for the disrespect they showed you."

"You are not their maid, Tansy," Consuela said. "They have a car, and there's a laundromat in Oracle." Her cheeks blushed with anger. "*Plancharle los pantalones*? No!"

Maria patted Consuela's shoulder to calm her cousin's temper.

"What does that mean?" I asked.

Maria made an ironing gesture. "Mrs. Daniels me *preguntó—*"

"She asked you to iron her pants?" Now, I was getting mad. "Ridiculous. No one irons on vacation!" Or at all.

The door opened and in sashayed Agnes. "I have a headache," she announced, stepping in front of both maids, who backed away.

I rose from my desk, walked around my former mother-in-law, and spoke to Consuela and Maria. "Thank you for all the hard work you do. Would you be so kind to leave the laundry on my porch? I'd sure appreciate it."

"Sí, yes, of course," Maria said. Consuela opened her mouth to speak, and Maria patted her shoulder. They both left through the open slider.

Agnes stood frozen, staring at my vacant chair behind my desk, then slowly turned to face me. "Ha! You're the laundry service? You do have washers here! Certainly, I didn't overburden them." Her imperial tone was slick with arrogance. "How impertinent—"

I interrupted. "Stop. Please, I'll do your laundry when I get home. I have to get back to work now. As for ironing anyone's clothes? I'll see if I packed mine."

"I have a headache, and I don't appreciate your tone. I want my lunch sent over to my cabana and," she locked eyes with me, "another set of towels."

"I'll take care of it," I said. "I'll be over around 1 p.m." I paused, "Do you need any aspirin? Or Tylenol? I have some at home—the door is open."

Agnes abruptly turned away from me and left the office. Her nose was so high I thought she might fall backward.

I sat back, took a deep breath, and continued on last Friday's daily report. It was then I noticed an envelope with LAST WEEK'S CHECKS scrolled across it. I needed to make a deposit before paying bills. I glanced at the reservations and wondered why someone, hey, anyone? hadn't matched the checks confirming reservations with the calendar noting guests' arrivals and bungalow assignments.

At midnight, I tossed Agnes and Allen's washed and dried laundry into a basket, unearthed my iron and ironing board, and headed to the lit front porch. I plugged in the iron and stared into the motionless sky, vivid with stars. My lavender fleece over my pajamas kept me warm as I sorted and folded Agnes's clothes. After tackling Allen's, I began to iron slacks and shirts as I reviewed the day. Dina delivered Agnes's lunch, so I had no further interaction with her. Allen dropped the kids off at the office when I was preparing to leave. He said, offhandedly, that he and Agnes were eating in town. I was pleased that I didn't have to speak to him. I was getting good at nodding and smiling in response to what he had to say. I hated confrontation and counted the days until they left.

I pressed into Agnes's long-sleeved white, Calvin Klein blouse' sleeve, and the steam poured from the iron. After finishing the other sleeve, I tackled the collar. "You are a pain in the neck," I whispered in the shadowy light and turned the collar over to press the other side. That struck me funny. I hung the shirt up and continued with her Saint Laurent sage slacks. "And you are a pain in the butt—" I murmured as I moved the iron on around the rear of the pants. My shoulders ached, tired, I guessed, from the long day. In the distant moonlight, I wondered how Pablo was and how his show opening went. The Biosphere in Oracle came to mind—that ill-fated, quasi-scientific ballyhooed universe built to contain a crew of eight for two years. They harvested what they planted and lived off the grid. Some called them latter-day hippies. The purpose was to learn about ecosystems, generally speaking. They nearly starved and fought, formed camps, mimicking the least attractive elements they left when they entered the massive bubble.

I left Agnes and Allen's world for a desert view at midnight. Two worlds as separate as the Biosphere and Oracle, except I ruminated the CollinCamp world had more love and simple goodness than anything I discovered in the Allen world. The ironing board creaked as I folded it. I carried the laundry inside and retrieved the hanging shirts and slacks I had laid out on the porch swing.

Mama Cass and Honeydog viewed me with what looked to be concern, then followed me into my room, where I got ready for bed. The last thought from the day: what the hell am I doing ironing their clothes?

The first thought of the new day: here we go again. I sat inside the closet on my pile of clothes that I never moved. My knees shook. I hoped the kids hadn't heard me scream. The damn knife dream was back. I woke to visions of Allen standing over me with a Swiss Army knife—me tangled in the iron cord wrapped around my wrists. He cut the cord. This won't hurt a bit. Muttered words and blood oozing from my wrists.

Well, the good news is, I thought, as I waited for the panic attack to leave and for calm to return to my brain, the good news is the knife morphed from a boning blade to a Swiss Army knife. The closet door moved slightly, and Mama Cass squeezed inside and sat by me. Honeydog guarded the door from the other side. I knew she was there as she always was when nightmares landed me inside the closet. I felt safe with the dog and cat. Finally, when the panic eased and my mind quieted, I picked up my alarm clock,and looked at the time. "Forty-five minutes on the nose," I sighed and went back to bed.

27

Disneyland

"**D**addy's going to take us to Disneyland!" Clea scrambled into the office with the news midmorning the next day. In her wake were Janey and Allen, followed by Agnes. They flanked my desk.

"Disneyland, Mommy!" Janey said.

I put down my pen and shut the ranch's checkbook. "What?" I asked.

Allen gave a sly shrug in my direction, then smiled. "Brette suggested it last night on the phone, and Mom thought it was a great idea," he said. "Brette decided to take Patricia to Disneyland before coming to this place—so we'll meet up. The girls are excited! You're busy here with work and all." His voice faded. "Oh," he added, "thanks for doing the laundry."

Pleading eyes from both girls met mine. "I guess I can't argue with those eyes," I said.

"We booked the flights about an hour ago," Agnes added, "I'm glad you are OK with it. We're going to have a grand time."

"Mommy, you're going, right?" Janey said.

"This will be a surprise adventure with Daddy," I said, "Mommy has to work, but Allen," I added, "I need to talk to you right now about the arrangements. Girls, why don't you take Grandma over to the gardens and see what they're harvesting today?"

Agnes cocked her head toward her son and said to Clea, "That sounds fine." She opened her ring-studded fingers for Janey to hold. Janey appeared confused but took her grandmother's hand, and they were off. Allen pulled a chair up facing my desk.

Glen ambled in from the kitchen with a cup of coffee. "Say, Tansy, Jimmy Andrews is coming out with his camera this afternoon. Around 2 p.m., he said."

"I will add that to today's calendar, too," I snapped. "Sorry, Glen. It's great that Jimmy's on track to make a new brochure for CollinCamp." I held up my hand. "I'm going for my coffee break. I'll be back in a bit." I stood, fed up by Allen's unannounced events laid at my feet. "Allen, let's take a walk, OK?" He gamely opened the slider for me to pass through.

Glen sighed his way into his desk chair, "Take your time," he hummed.

"The kids are really excited," Allen said as we crossed by the saguaro.

"This is the last time this happens this way," I said.

"What do you mean?"

"The rule is," I waved to Dina as she headed over to the kitchen, "that you ask me first before informing the kids. I am the custodial parent."

"For now, you are," Allen said, "but that can change."

My nostrils flared. "That's not happening today or, I think, ever. We walked past my place and followed the dry riverbed leading to the pasturing horses. The hills were blanketed in sunshine while heat waffled the air. "And, no matter what any judge says, now or ever," I emphasized, "we have to co-parent and at least, for the girls' sakes, appear to get along and respect each other."

"Why don't you relax a little? You are tightly high-strung—high drama. Give it a break."

"And, by the way, Clea does not get along with Patricia," I added, ignoring his taunt.

"There you go, creating drama where there is zilch. Nada, nothing."

I shook my head as Alex and Pablo rode over on horseback in our direction. I hadn't seen Pablo since the night we watched the aurora, the night we made love. They broke to a trot as they met us. I felt obliged to introduce Allen to Pablo, which I did matter-of-factly. "How was the opening?" I asked Pablo.

He smiled broadly and gave me a thumbs-up. "Are you free tonight?" Pablo asked.

"I will be. Maybe we can go to Ringo's?" I asked. "Come by my place at seven?"

Pablo nodded. They turned to resume their ride, and then Alex turned back, "Hey, Tans, I have some jeans and work clothes—could use some washing," he said with an impish grin. "Say, maybe—"

"You get the hell outta here," I laughed. Alex doffed his hat in Allen's direction, and they were off.

"So you made a joke out of doing our laundry?" Allen sniffed the air while raising his chin.

"I didn't say anything," I said. "We're a close community. Word gets around."

"And that's the boyfriend?"

"What's with your tone, Allen? Yes, that is Pablo. And he's not 'my boyfriend,' but we do like to hang out."

"What's wrong with my tone?" Allen's voice sounded more pinched than before.

"Nevermind. Let's get back. I'll have the kids packed and ready to go by noon. Is that OK?" As we retraced our steps, I added, "I want to hear from them every night by 6:30. You got that? I want arrival and departure times and where you will be staying."

Allen nodded. "Mom has the details. I'll have her give them to you," and he left me by the open office door.

Dina had bacon lettuce and tomato sandwiches for lunch alongside a pasta salad dressed in light vinegar and olive oil. Allen, the girls, his mother, and I ate together and then walked the kids home, where I packed their bags. "You call me whenever you want," I said to Clea. You know how to call from the hotel. You put the long distance on the room number."

"It'd be perfect if Brette and Patricia weren't coming," Clea said. "Why does Patricia have to be there?"

I shrugged. "You'll have a great time at the park. Your dad is fun on vacation."

"I want Mommy to go," Janey said.

"You'll have amazing stories to tell me, sweetie. You're going to have so much fun!"

Allen and Agnes arrived shortly after. I wore sunglasses as I hugged the girls goodbye. I asked Agnes about the itinerary, and she muttered, "Whoops—I forgot."

Allen peered over his shoulder at me, "We'll be at the Disneyland Hotel, right girls?" They laughed and Clea gave me a thumb's up.

I returned the gesture. My voice was tight with emotion, and my eyes were wet with tears, but I held back until Allen loaded the kids' bags into the car rental, and the entire family, without me, rolled out of CollinCamp.

Lara called while Jimmy Andrews waited in the office for Glen to return from the barns. Jimmy, dark-skinned with a sleek afro and wide smile, pivoted in a full circle, taking in the office. "It looks the same," he mused, "as when I was here." His thumbs were in his pockets, a new Canon camera around his neck, and his tripod folded and attached to his backpack. "I took some of the original photos in the old brochure."

I peered over the phone receiver and smiled at Jimmy. "I can't talk right now," I said to an agitated Lara, "but I'll get back within the hour, OK?"

Lara understood that my professional tone indicated a busy office. "Do that, Tansy," she responded and hung up.

"I swear I should leash Glen," I said to Jimmy, who looked at his watch. "Tell me about your time here. Where did Glen find you?"

"I was panhandling outside the feed store—a trucker picked me up in a place called Wilcox, Arizona, and dropped me off at Oracle Country Store. I was fifteen, a runaway from Texas. I lied to that dude. Told him I was eighteen and in the Army. Truth is, my dad died while serving in 'Nam, and my grandmother raised me 'cause my mother was sick. At least, that was the story told to me. Grandma had a heart attack and landed in the hospital. I took care of her afterward, but she didn't get better. She died." Tears formed in Jimmy's eyes.

"And you were so young," I said.

He pressed his lips together and raised his eyebrows. "Yes, ma'am. A teacher told me I was too young to be on my own, so they were going to put me in foster care. Instead of going to Grandma's funeral, I took off from our house in El Paso and got rides off of Interstate 10. Grandma would've understood."

"You landed on your feet. I think your Grandma would be proud." I eyed my digital desk clock and said. "Sorry about Glen being late, but go on with your story. Is that where Glen found you at Oracle?"

"Alex and Glen. Glen was in the store, and Alex came over and chatted me up. I told him I was in the Army. So Glen comes out, and Alex introduces me as Private Jimmy Andrews."

"What'd Glen say?" I asked.

"He knew I was full of BS. He gave me that laugh, you know when he figures the shit meter needs more change?"

"I'm familiar with the look," I smiled.

"They took me home, fed me lunch, and somehow worked it out with the State of Texas to have me stay on his ranch—where I finished school, fed pigs, and learned all about cameras from a ranch guest, who gave me an old one of his. Got a degree in Hospitality. Glen, he saved me." Jimmy wrinkled his forehead. "You hear that?"

The sound of a siren, first faint, now boomed. EMTs rushed into the office, followed by Alex. "He's this way," Alex said, and the medics left with him.

What a weird set of circumstances—Jimmy had no more than told me about his grandma's heart attack when Glen suffered one.

After the ambulance left with Glen, Alex came into the office. He told us Glen mended fences with him in the morning but began complaining about a headache and his shoulder acting up. Glen wanted to rest in the cow barn and "fell asleep in a cubby we have out there for breaks. I woke him up," Alex said, "and he was stiff with pain. Got on the phone and called in the EMTs." Alex's face was pale, and his words were direct. "Pablo and I are heading into the hospital. You and Dina are holding down the fort. OK?"

"I'll follow you in," Jimmy said. "Nice meeting you, Tansy."

"Call me when you know anything. I mean it," I said and hugged Alex. I hugged Jimmy, too.

The aching loneliness and fear that somehow Allen would take off with the girls made room for the worry about Glen's wellbeing. Marty Chicago appeared after everyone had left, and I told him what had happened. "What hospital?" he asked.

"I don't know. Probably Banner. It's where he goes for check-ups." I sucked in a breath. "He has to be OK."

"Let me know when you hear anything," he said and left.

Lara called as quiet filled the office. Before she began to speak, I told her about Glen. "I'm so, so sorry," she said. "I wanted you to know that Allen's lawyer contacted me this morning. He's going to petition for a reduction in support and change in custody."

Custody was the only word I heard. "I have sole legal custody. Allen's unreliable. No way is he—"

"Hold on. Allen and his lawyer want to file before we do. I showed Max how much Allen was in arrears with support and told him I think we should talk before going back to court. Max agreed when he saw the figures.

"Agnes wants more control of the kids and money. I bet Allen's gone to her to dig him out of debt, and she has some stipulations. Joint custody, one of them. I'm sure he's not coming out of divorce number two, a wealthier man."

Lara paused, then asked, "How's it going with them? Is Allen laying on the charm?"

"He and Agnes took the kids to Disneyland. Brette and Patricia are meeting them there."

"Well," Lara said, "we know why Brette's packed for Disneyland. I have news on that front, but that'll wait 'til I get to CollinCamp."

"It's a small world, after all." I heard Dina come through from the kitchen to the office. "I have to go, Lara. Dina and I are running the show today."

"Call me when you hear anything about Glen. I'll see if I can get out of here tomorrow. I should be there for Alex and can help in the office and otherwise." Lara paused. "It's good the kids are away a few days. We'll figure this out."

28

Matters of the Heart

Dina and I worked in tandem all afternoon. I did a grocery run, and Dina managed the office while I was gone and when I went to the barns to relay to our work crew about Glen's hospitalization.

Uncle Jay, an old cowhand whom I'd only seen in passing, offered to guide the horseback riding scheduled for late afternoon. Glen had told me that Uncle Jay, with his signature Eagle feather in the band around his weathered Stetson, was hired as a young man by Becky's father. Uncle Jay claimed his people used to camp here in what Glen referred to as the "before times." He had said hello and goodbye to age eighty years, some time back. The crew listened to him, and Pablo mentioned that Uncle Jay told stories about the Hohokam people. Uncle Jay and Pablo shared some of the same heritage.

I spoke to him first. His shoulders were slightly bent, and his legs bowed; suspenders held up his old denim jeans. His crinkled face was a map of the times he lived, and his demeanor calmed me. He nodded as I spoke. I eagerly accepted his help with the horse riders, and Uncle Jay said he'd make sure the animals were tended and fed.

"Any word from Alex?" I asked Dina as I entered the office.

She shook her head. "Not yet."

The news came soon. "Glen's artery was eighty percent clogged—that's what the doc said." Alex's tone was light as we spoke. "They're putting in a stent right now and want to keep him a few days. He was badly dehydrated, too. As you might imagine," Alex went on, "Glen's not the easiest patient." Alex told me that Pablo and he'd be back at the ranch around suppertime.

"Uncle Jay's taking care of the critters and subbing as horse guide," I said, deeply relieved that Glen was feeling his cantankerous self. "The hay guy delivered. Uncle Jay came by with the receipt." I continued to fill Alex in on the day's activities. "The well-guy from the State measured our water depth today, too," I sighed. "Everything has to happen today?"

"Way it goes," Alex sighed.

"Jim Andrews at the hospital, too?"

"Yup. The three of us shared old times and played three-handed bridge when they were looking after Glen. Jimmy always has a deck of cards with him."

"I'll go in to see Glen after you guys get back," and continued, "I forgot to tell you, Lara's on her way down. A night flight. She called and left a message with Dina. I can meet her, or?"

"What time's her flight in?"

"Arrives at 10:30."

"I'll get her."

"She's in Bungalow Five."

"I think we're good, Tans," Alex chuckled.

I let Dina know about Glen. She immediately asked who would look after him when he returned to the ranch. "Someone's going to have to lean on him 'til his ticker heals," she crooned. Her willow voice was so soft. She returned to her pan of chicken, turning the pieces as a flume of flame rose from the gas burner. "I'm still looking for a place—I could stay out here. Easy for me to keep my eyes on the kitchen and sit on the boss." A slight blush colored her cheeks. "I didn't mean—"

I smiled. "I know what you meant. I'll talk to Glen tonight, and we'll work something out. You will get paid, so track your hours."

I closed the office around five and headed home. Guests' voices swelled in the quiet evening from the games' room. Mama Cass waited for me. I waved to her as she sat on the window sill looking out onto the porch. The dogs sat side by side on the couch. It looked in order, but my world was in disarray: the banter, the teasing laughter, and the playful hugs—all of it was missing. I kept busy trying to fill the gnawing emptiness inside me. I walked and fed the four-legged crew and began to clean the birdcages while waiting to hear from the kids. The phone rang as I hauled away the stepladder after finishing the cages. I dropped the ladder and tripped over it as I ran for the phone. "Mommy, I talked to Micky," Janey chirped. Clea told me about the Disney characters in the hotel lobby and how lucky they were to see them.

"I can hardly wait to see what happens tomorrow!" Tears streamed down my face.

"Mom? Are you crying?" Clea must have heard the strain in my voice.

"No," I said as tears dripped from my chin.

Allen took the phone. "Hey, Tans, we'll call you when we return from the park tomorrow. We're going to try to stay for the fireworks, so it might be later."

"Good," I muttered. "Very good." The kids are OK, I thought, but the emptiness remained.

29

Bad Dreams About Old Times

Alex and Pablo returned to the ranch shortly after I got off the phone with the girls. They brought a pizza for the three of us to share. We sat around my table and strategized how to handle Glen, whom they informed was ready to pull the IV from his arm and head home. The discharge plan was for Glen to have convalescent care for two weeks, and he fought that notion tooth and nail.

We decided that Pablo and I would return to the hospital that evening. He would play bad cop, and I would play good cop.

"I don't need no one lookin' after me," Glen said after I explained that Dina offered to stay at his place while he healed from the procedure. He was getting fluids by way of an IV, and I noticed they had him on a catheter. Glen squirmed in his bed. His larger-than-life presence shrunk by simple exhaustion from the day's activities. His lips appeared salty.

I picked up a paper cup filled with melting ice chips and offered it to Glen. He shook his head and gave us both a defiant look. "I want out of here."

"Boss," Pablo said, "you heard the doc. You're getting extra help at home or in a convalescent home. Alex checked a few places, and hell, man, no one wants you." Pablo smiled broadly. "A convalescent home, if we can find one, and they're expensive or Dina. Those are the terms of your discharge from the hospital."

"You can keep an eye on things at the ranch." I held up the cup of ice chips. "Sure you don't want any?" He shook his head. We'd been going in circles with Glen for the past half hour. He was hellbent on getting his way. He wanted to go home and put this entire day in the rear view mirror. "Like Pablo said, for a week or so, you need to rest, and Dina's a great cook. You get catered meals at home and in a convalescent place, a crapshoot, right?"

"The doctor's not budging, Boss. If you want to recover at home, let us know. Come on, Tans," Pablo checked his watch, "visiting hours are almost over and—"

"You get Dina set up proper then," Glen said. "Have Maria and Consuela see to the house and the extra bedroom." He looked as if he had eaten something sour. "I hate company," he whined, "and damn, I hurt."

"You won't see her that much," I said, "she'll be in the kitchen, too."

"In a convalescent home," Pablo drew out home, "you'd have lots of company."

"Damn ticker," Glen muttered. "OK."

We high-fived in the elevator upon leaving Glen for the evening. "We were good," I said.

"At a lot of things." Pablo gave me a side hug.

Diamond waited for us in Pablo's '52 Chevy. She sat on my lap as we pulled out of the hospital parking lot. "I'm glad he's going to be OK." I rolled down the window for Diamond to stick out her head and enjoy the evening breeze. Pablo drove slowly through the darkening twilight, the desert at ease. "Can you stay a while?" I asked as we parked at my house. We hadn't talked much on the way home. "How's Diamond with cats?"

"She ignores cats," Pablo said. "My ex-girlfriend had three of them."

"We could bring her in and see how she does. Mama Cass is the chief negotiator—if Diamond can deal with that, there won't be a problem."

"It'll be good," Pablo said.

And it was.

Mama Cass reigned over the meet and greet. She sat on the sofa back, my three dogs lined up on the sofa, each claiming a cushion. Pablo got on the floor with Diamond, who sat stalk-still beside him. I balanced myself on the armrest. Mama Cass walked across the back of the couch and gently tapped my hand. Honeydog jumped to the floor, nudged Diamond, and left for my room. The cat yawned.

Pablo and I took this opportunity to stargaze from the porch steps. The weirdness of the moment lingered. I loved having time alone with Pablo, but I missed my kids.

"You're quiet," he said.

"Why don't you kiss me, then let's lay out under the stars. Didn't you say you had a futon in your truck? You think Gladys would mine if we, hmm—"

"You want to?"

"Hell, yeah. It's mathematics."

"Math?"

"The way I see it is I miss my kids, and you are here."
I touched the side of his face with my index finger and
brought my finger to his lips. Pablo put his hand over mine.
"I'm attracted to you, as if I needed to say. And I repeat, you
are here. No one can ever substitute in my life equation for
my girls. No one, not ever. You are a notably sexy addition
and a friend. We have fun, don't we?"

"OK, I get it—addition without substituting. The girls are
not an X factor, so I become another term in the equation."

"Oh, you are so sexy when you talk math to me."

"Aw, shucks," he said. "After the day we've had, I like
your proposal."

We set out for Gladys, the truck. Pablo unwound the futon and laid it in the truck bed. I ran into the house, left my
clothes in a lump on my bed, and wrapped myself in my old
serape. I brought out a sheet to lay over Pablo's sleeping bag.

Pablo peeked over the side of the truck as I approached.
"Hey," he said, "I have a joint and my lighter in my jacket
pocket. I left it inside Gladys. You want to grab it?"

I opened the truck door, retrieved the weed and lighter,
and smiled. I liked how carefully Pablo folded his shirt and
jeans. Pablo took care of things. I thought about the pile of
clothes that I left on my bed. I could learn from this man,
although I knew Mama Cass appreciated my casual effort
and that I would later find her nestled inside my messy pile
of clothes, which I did.

I crawled in beside Pablo. His rock-hard body met the
soft contours of mine. I remember hearing the coyotes howl,

but Pablo said it was me. I laughed at that. "Could be," I whispered. "I feel like a wild thing."

We smoked the joint and made love again, and then we went back inside the house. Pablo gathered Diamond, a sleepy beagle, and we kissed goodnight or good morning. It was three a.m.

30

Full House

I fielded calls the next day. Clea called twice, complaining about Patricia. Pablo and Alex went back and forth to the hospital. I kept Diamond in the office for a while, then took her to my house to stay with my dogs.

Lara took over Glen's desk. When Alex dropped her off at the office, he was all smiles. It was the first time I had seen him being his good-natured, easygoing self since Glen's heart attack. While I tended to the telephone and guests, Lara reviewed the extra set of books Becky kept while pilfering money from the ranch.

"And, let me get this straight," Lara asked again, "Glen's lawyer told him to sit on this to avoid an audit from the IRS?"

"Basically," I sighed. "He said Glen was as liable as Becky because the ranch was community property."

"She scammed the ranch for nearly a hundred grand, and that is the advice he gave?"

I nodded. A guest interrupted with questions about nightlife in Oracle. I advised them to go to Ringo's. When they were on the other side of the slider, I said to Lara, "The lawyer said that Glen'd be liable for all the back taxes on the money Becky stole."

Lara tapped the eraser end of her pencil against the opened accounting book kept by Becky. "It's nuts that she didn't destroy this. She recorded all the deposits over ten years. Put the money into a private account she once had with her father. And before the divorce, withdrew every cent and closed the account."

"I was shocked that the bank handed over the old checks." I shook my head.

"I think that was an error on their part," Lara said.

"What do you think? I asked. "I sure would like to give Glen good news."

"You're sure Glen knew nothing about what Becky was doing?"

"Yes, Glen makes me feel like a bookkeeping genius. And you know my track record. Becky took care of the money. And Glen let her."

"I think this is the best path forward. Get a tax attorney, and I'll bet they'll advise Glen to turn everything over to the feds. You have all the evidence that Glen knew nothing of the scam, and the money went into an account that started before he married Becky. The only person who has benefited is Becky. The IRS may go after her separately, but who knows? If they fine Glen, he could sue her for any damages brought against him. He could sue her civilly. The best thing is all this lawyering and IRS goings-on will tie up anything Becky threatens."

"Can you find a tax lawyer?" I asked. "I don't want to say anything to Glen while he's recovering. And talk to Alex.

Explain this all to him. I think this is brilliant, but he knows Glen best. They both have to be clearly on board."

"I can do both, and we can get things underway, but let's not forget your problem. We need to talk about Allen and Brette, and I need a key to my unit. I stayed with Alex last night.

"Oh, you did?"

"It's a little soon for—you know?" She smiled. "I don't want to rush things."

"Maria and Consuela will have you all set up in Number Five. I don't know if the cooler's working. Jesse, Maria's husband, has the parts and may be out tomorrow to fix it."

"I'd love to take a walk. I can grab my backpack at Alex's. You think Maria and Consuela will be finished with my unit in an hour, or do they need longer?"

"That's perfect. Why don't you drop by here," and I'll give you the tour and the key."

She waved at me, turned toward the slider, and let a group of new arrivals pass inside as she left. They wanted to know if they were too late to sign up for a horse ride due to leave in fifteen minutes. The four women were from a small town in western Oregon and wrote together. Besides horseback riding, they were enthused about the desert as a muse and asked if it was really Marty Chicago they passed on the way to breakfast.

"The very one," I said.

"Does he ever give talks?" A pert blonde bespeckled woman said.

"No, he doesn't," I said. "He's here, like you, to write, and we do our best to let him. Now, let's get you over to the horse barn to check with Uncle Jay about the ride." I put up our Back in Five sign on my desk and grabbed my camera because I kept thinking Uncle Jay should have his picture in the new CollinCamp brochure.

Uncle Jay whittled on a camp chair as riders gathered around. When he saw me, he motioned me over, and I asked if these women could join the ride. He nodded yes.

Alex came out of the barn, and I pointed to the women. "We have four more riders—Uncle Jay okayed it."

Diego, Maria's son, followed Alex, leading two horses. "Aren't you supposed to be in school?" I asked.

He kicked a little dirt. "It's a teacher workday for high school," he said.

"And?" Alex quizzed.

"And I may have gotten a three-day suspension." He gave me his most charming smile.

"I imagine you and Alex have had a little talk about that," I said.

"First my mother, then my aunt, she has a fiery temper, by the way, and now Alex, and now you?"

"Well, it's a good day to be here," I said. "These ladies need horses." The quartet of Oregon women fanned around me.

Uncle Jay took the reins from the spotted saddle horse tied to the corral railing by the water trough. Alex directed Diego to bring out horses for the writers. I snapped photos of the group on their mounts as Uncle Jay led them out of the corral. Uncle Jay looked gallant on his pony, Maxine.

Back at the office, I called Jimmy Andrews and told him I photographed Uncle Jay leading a horse riding group, and I thought it should be on the cover of the new brochure. I offered to do the layout and text to allay costs, which had been my plan all along. Jimmy asked about my experience, and I told him I was an artist and good at conceptualizing design. Plus, it was cheaper than fielding the work to someone outside. Jimmy laughed. "You're beginning to sound like the boss." I caught Jimmy up on Glen's prognosis and scheduled a day the following week when Glen could give him the official tour. We both hoped that Glen would be up for it.

Alex came into the office with Lara on his arm. "That's a great idea," Alex said after I told him about Jimmy's upcoming visit and my role in doing the brochure. "That'll chuff Glen up."

"But get your name as a designer or some such on the brochure somewhere. You deserve the accolade," Lara added.

Alex babysat the office while I walked Lara over to her unit. Lara was most interested in Brette and Patricia being at Disneyland with Allen, Agnes, and the kids. "There is not a spontaneous bone in Brette's body," Lara said.

"With what's been happening at the ranch, I haven't given the Brette drama too much room in my brain. Let's get you settled."

"How's Clea doing?" Lara popped her backpack on the overstuffed loveseat. The flouncy, floral couch contrasted with the white birch desk under the window and the art on the wall of a steer skull on a desert dune. Overall, the design had no cohesion, but the room felt inviting.

"She's annoyed with Patricia, as usual. Patricia stole her doll furniture when they were small. Brette denied it, but Clea saw the furniture at Brette's, and she's not forgiven her."

"Patricia's had a lonely life growing up." Lara sat on the edge of the bed and bounced. "This feels like a decent mattress," she said. "Aren't you curious why Brette and Allen have been in daily—I have it on good authority—contact?"

I shrugged. "I want my kids home. I gave up on Brette a long time ago. I don't trust Allen or Agnes. Do you have any news about what Allen's lawyer said he would file?"

"Well, that goes back to Allen and Brette's daily updates."

"How do you know about the phone calls?"

"I took her out for happy hour and fed her martinis. She told me. She and Allen are looking for houses. She claims they've always been in love, but some obstacle, you, mostly, always got in their way. And," Lara said, "I had the mother of all hangovers the next day to prove it. I had a mini recorder in my bag and got the whole conversation for you, not court."

"They're buying a fucking house?" I asked. "Fuck," I added.

"I talked to Max, about the arrears in child support. He told me he's putting a petition into the court for a change in custody and support. The basics of Allen's petition are this: Allen wants to end spousal support altogether and wants primary custody with you getting the kids over vacation with supervised visitation. Max told me that's his wish list."

"Max, the ever-faithful lawyer." I sat on the loveseat. "We're in a good position to counter it, right?"

"Allen's going to say that your moving the kids to the ranch is tantamount to emotional abuse and neglect. That he was only informed after you accepted the job at CollinCamp about leaving Seattle. According to the divorce decree, Allen claims, you had to get approval first to remove the kids from the family home. We can fight that, but technically, he's correct." Lara stood and stretched. "Put it together—he's buying a new house, Brette's providing the down for, so he'll appear squeaky clean at the hearing," Lara said. "We'll have documented years of missing spousal and child support. And the court record."

"And the Disneyland trip?" I asked.

"Allen and Brette's coming out party as a couple, according to Brette. She wants your life, the one you left in Seattle, anyway. They booked to Anaheim the same day they booked to Tucson. And more evidence for the hearing that Brette is a capable, loving step-parent." Lara began unpacking. "This is a sweet dresser," she said as she deposited her folded tees and sweaters. "Pine, right? This bungalow features many different styles—makes it feel homey."

"Every bungalow has a different sort of character, so to speak. We go to a lot of garage sales!" I stood. "When do you think we should file, and should I be worried?"

"I told Max—"

"Good ol' Max, Allen's legal eye, ha. I never liked that guy."

"I told Max that we were going back to court on support arrears—seriously, Allen's track record of downright desertion and adultery during your pregnancy and his residency with a second wife in Japan follows him. He can't get away from what he did versus what he wishes. Any judge with anything more than crackers for brains will weigh that on any order issued. But—" Lara looked me squarely in the face, "Justice is not always fair, and there are good 'ol boy judges who might look at your move and job with jaundiced eyes. I plan to load up on evidence and beat the bastards."

"Allen's been so goddamn cocky," I said. "He thinks he holds all the cards."

"Well, we'll see about that."

A knock at the door interrupted our chat. It was Alex who wanted to take Lara on a horse ride. She gave me a toothy grin and turned her attention to Alex.

"I better catch up with Dina. See you guys later," I said and left.

31

Panic

Diamond, Honeydog, Deborah Carr, and Yul Brenner set up their camps inside my bedroom. Honeydog and Mama Cass slept on my bed with Pablo and me. Diamond slept on a rug by my bed; the other two guarded the outer perimeters. As I closed my eyes to sleep with Pablo's arms wrapped around me, I believed I would sleep without any dreams. I woke with my hand over my mouth. I hadn't screamed, but the dream scared me. Mother chased me with the boning knife up a green hill, and the hill melted into a courtroom where I sat facing the back of Mother's head. I peered up at the judge's bench to discover Allen sneering at me. Instead of a gavel, he pointed at Mother with the boning knife.

I was moments from a panic attack. Cold sweat dripped from the base of my neck down my spine. My knees shook. I eased out of Pablo's arms and crawled down the length of the bed. Gratefully, he didn't wake up. I tiptoed around the dogs with Mama Cass behind me. As I collapsed onto my closet nest, I wept into my hands, gasping in gulps for air.

Mama Cass sat by me. *Nothing changes*, the words screamed in my mind. I fought to keep myself from shouting aloud. My body shook, and my heart raced.

"Hey babe, what's going on?"

I opened my eyes, and Pablo crouched beside me.

"A panic attack—it'll go away—it'll be OK." My words stuttered out between breaths. I wanted to tell him my panic attacks, the rides from hell, lasted forty-five minutes. I've timed them. I wanted to say that my closet is a little messy. I wanted to tell him I had lost something and remembered it was in the closet, so I got up. I wanted to lie. I wanted all this scary shit to go away.

"Let's go back to bed," Pablo said.

"I," I sucked in a breath and let it out, "I can't stand."

Pablo held me firmly under my arms and lifted me to my feet. The dogs made way as he led me back to bed. We sat side-by-side. He didn't say a word but wrapped me in a blanket and held me closely. "Breathe with me," he said.

The attack was over sooner than usual. "I think I'm OK now," I said. "I'm sorry you had to see me like this. I have bad dreams about old times."

"Tell me about it," Pablo said.

And, so, I did. About Mother and the boning knife and about Allen saving me and how I can't get away from them in my dreams, which went away for a while but have come back. "I'm such a mess," I said. "I'm sorry."

Pablo hugged me closer. "You're poor brain's on over-drive."

Mama Cass tapped my arm with her paw. I petted her and told Pablo, "The cat and I share the closet." I studied Pablo's face. "You don't think I'm crazy, do you?"

"No, not at all. You have PTSD like a bunch of 'Nam vets and like Peter and probably Glen."

"If Allen knew, he'd call me crazy. He says I'm like my mother. He'd bring my panic attacks to court, and I'd lose custody." Tears rolled down my face. "I'm sorry—I shouldn't go into all this."

"Lara won't let that happen," Pablo said. "You're safe, and we need to get a little sleep."

32

Landing

I met Pablo at Glen's to welcome him home. Dina was in the kitchen, and the smells of chicken soup and gingerbread filled the space. She'd been here for the past hour since finishing up her duties in the ranch kitchen. Maria and Consuela thoroughly cleaned the house, which Glen would not abide by if he had his say. Maria told me that Dina spent a few hours of decluttering, too. Paintings of indigenous people and horses decorated his walls, and beautifully detailed ceramic ponies lined his shelves. I noticed a metal-worked pickup truck in a prize position across from the broad couch covered in a wool Navajo blanket. Its vibrant Native design was perfect for the room. "Amazing," I said to Pablo, "I've been in this room too many times to count, but it's the first time I've seen it without the piles of magazines and stacks of books. It always felt like the whole walls collapsed in a heap of stuff on every conceivable surface. Now, the bookshelves are filled, and that dusty blanket is clean. God, it's beautiful."

"We'll see how long that lasts," Pablo grinned.

"The pickup is Gladys, right?"

"I did that for Glen when I headed to Toronto."

Dina joined us, carrying a plate of warm gingerbread that she put on the birch and glass-topped coffee table. "Finally, they released him! He'll be happy to be home."

"Gosh, that looks yummy," I said. "Glen might be a tad grouchy. He's a bit of a hermit. Don't take anything he says personally."

Dina shrugged. "I went in to see him at the hospital. He's OK with me being here. I checked." The woman blushed. I nudged Pablo.

I heard Alex park in the circular drive outside. The boss was home. Glen was quiet. He sat on the couch with a har-rumph and gathered the blanket around himself. I kissed him on the cheek and said how good it was to see him, then hustled back to work. Pablo and Alex stayed longer.

Glen was not the only one coming back to CollinCamp that day. Allen, the kids, Brette, Patricia, and Agnes were due anytime. We had assigned Brette and Patricia their own bungalow. I didn't know the sleeping arrangements at the Disneyland Hotel, and I wasn't asking. Checkout here was Sunday. My stomach tightened every time I heard a vehicle arrive outside—I was anxious to see the girls and have them home and anticipated the worst about Allen and whatever plans he cooked up.

Deep in thought, I caught up on some paperwork when Lara popped unexpectedly into the office. I jerked to attention.

"I didn't mean to scare you," Lara said.

"I thought you might be Allen," I answered. "Did you have a good ride?"

"Uncle Jay told me stories the entire ride."

"Glen is home, and I think there might be a little romance blooming between Dina and the boss."

"That makes me smile," Lara said.

The sound of a car horn broke our conversation. The family had returned in the minivan.

Clea hung back while Janey jumped into my arms. "I want to go home, Mommy," she said, pushing her head into my shoulder.

"That's what we're going to do," I turned to view Clea. "I want a hug, too!" I said to her. She felt damp holding her. The word "wilted" came to mind. She wiped her eyes with the back of her hand and fell back a pace, locking eyes with me.

Brette and Patricia stood next to Allen at the front of the vehicle. He wore a baseball cap backward. His face appeared flushed. Agnes was yet to emerge from the van. I noticed she rode in front. Her head faced forward.

"Mom, can Janey and I go home?" Clea said.

"I'll stick around the office," Lara said. I hadn't noticed her behind me. "Alex was going to meet me here. So, if you want to walk the kids over—" Lara waved to Brette; she ignored her.

"That's perfect," I answered. "Hey, kiddos, can you grab your bags?"

Allen strode around the minivan and unlatched the rear partition. Patricia lagged behind and hung her head.

"Patricia, you're going to stay with your mom," I said. "And you have your own parking spot next to your bungalow. So you're Allen's next stop."

"That's not what my mom said," Patricia uttered.

"Huh?" I said as I gathered Janey's backpack and small duffle. Brette joined us while Clea slung her backpack over her shoulder.

Brette smoothed her white jeans and fitted Minnie Mouse t-shirt. "We thought it would be fun if the older kids had their own bungalow, and then the grownups had theirs."

I swallowed words I wanted to say, like in your fucking dreams. I took a breath. Keep it professional. "Clea, do you have all your stuff?" I asked before turning to Brette. "You and Patricia are in Bungalow Ten, right between Agnes and Allen. As for the three of us, we're going home. Dinner's at six. Games and horseshoes after. Hope to see you then."

Everyone quieted, waiting for Brette to speak. Allen shut the van's gate. "Come on, you guys, let's take Grandma home," he said tight-lipped.

Brette tapped her foot and opened the side door to the van. "I think we need keys," her voice a flat monotone.

"I'll be right back with them." I set Janey's gear next to the patio door and got all three of them their keys."

Allen had started up the van as I handed him the keys. "Hi, Agnes!" I said. She turned her head and nodded an acknowledgment. From the circles under her eyes, I judged she had aged ten years.

"See you at dinner, kiddos," Allen said. "We need to talk," he directed to me.

Allen slowly backed the rental around and eased out to the short drive to their bungalows.

A cloud hung over Clea, or so it felt. Janey bopped along ahead of us. "Clea, honey, I cleaned your room. I hope you don't mind. You have clean sheets, and I swept." She showed no reaction. Clea's room was her sanctuary; she was a lot like Glen in that, I mused, so I was surprised by how quiet she was. I patted Janey on her back. "I cleaned your room, too. I missed you guys so much."

"Why'd you make us go?" Clea asked.

"A trip to Disneyland—I thought it was something you'd love."

We were home. The dogs bounced and greeted the girls. Yul Brenner was attentive to Clea. I think he saw that cloud over her head, too. Dina left a plate of gingerbread on the table. The girls ate that while I poured apple juice.

While Janey watched a Winnie video tucked inside her favorite blanket with Mama Cass close by, Clea and I talked in the kitchen.

"Grandma was OK, but Brette was mean to Janey. When Janey cried in the Haunted House, she told her to grow up. Mom, Janey's only four." Clea shook her head slowly. "All Patricia did was whine and complain about being allergic to milk. She's not. She ate a ton of ice cream. But everything she doesn't like, she's allergic to. When she got tired at Disneyland, she said she sprained her ankle. And her mom's all smiles and little private conversations."

"I'm sorry," I said.

"Brette hogged up all Dad's time. They stayed together and held hands and junk."

"Did you stay with Grandma?"

"It got all mixed up the first night," Clea said.

"What do you mean?"

"Brette said that Patricia wanted to stay with me. Dad had a bedroom, and I had the bed in the main room—it was cool. It looked like a cupboard with bookcases on both sides. You open the cupboard, and the bed comes down."

"That's called a wall bed," I said. "Did Janey sleep with you?"

"She slept across from me in another one of those beds, except it was smaller."

"That sounds like a nice setup," I said. "But we're not to the mixed up part, yet."

"The very first night, Brette and Patricia came over to our room because Brette and Dad were going for a walk. Brette said Patricia could stay overnight with us. Patricia started to yell about how 'it's not fair' that we had two wall beds, and she didn't have any. And she wanted Janey's bed. Hers was toddler-sized. So Patricia got in bed with me.

"How'd that go?"

Patricia ate chips in bed and got crumbs all over everything. I kept waiting for Dad to get back, and it got later and later. Janey wanted a story, and Patricia complained about how hard the bed was. Then Patricia wanted to go back to her room, and Janey cried.

"When did Dad get back?"

"I don't know. I read to Janey, but she wanted you to read. Patricia started to tell ghost stories she had heard from camp, and I told her to stop. Janey got really scared and crawled into bed with us. Then, there was a knock on the door, and we all jumped. Grandma yelled loudly to let her in. She told us that Daddy had called her and that he was going to be late, so Grandma stayed with us until he got back. Patricia started complaining about the bed, and Grandma told her to be quiet. And then she read Janey a story and sang her a song. That's the last I remember."

"You don't remember Daddy coming in, then?" I kept my voice light as the fullness of the scenario played in my brain.

"I remember the light from the hallway, and Daddy shut his bedroom door, then I went back to sleep."

"Did you guys stay together like that the whole time at Disneyland?"

"No. Grandma made sure. She told everyone the next day at breakfast that this was a family vacation—and that there would be no more sleepovers."

33

Skirmish

I heard the front door open, and Allen yelled, "You-hoo."

"Why don't you call Franny and see what's new at school, and I will talk to Dad, OK?"

Allen came into the kitchen. He high-fived Clea on the way out, then straddled a chair backward, like his ball cap. "I guess I should have told you about Brette," he offered in a breezy way.

"You don't, ah, I mean, I was surprised," I stuttered. "I mean, whatever, but not in a snarky way, but—" All the while, I fiddled with the dishes in the drainer.

"Will you sit down, for Christ's sake? What are you doing, counting your plates and forks?"

"Sure, sure," I took a chair across from Allen.

He moved his chair around to confront me directly. "Can you show my mother and Brette more respect? Is it inside you to do that?"

"What is this about?" I asked. "I said hello to your mom and Brette."

"The kids thought it would be fun to share a bungalow,

all grown up. Patricia is super disappointed. You shut Brette down without considering Patricia's feelings."

"Good Lord, the girls are twelve, and in my world, that is too young to stay by themselves. Ever," I emphasized. "Besides, Clea has her room. If you or Brette made promises, that's on you. No one asked me or consulted Clea."

"We are trying to blend families, but it will take all the adults acting like adults." Allen's face puffed, and the artery in his neck pulsated. "Drop your fucking agenda."

"What agenda are you talking about?"

"You are so dense. We all have to tiptoe around you—have you noticed?" He tapped his fingers across the table.

"What do you want?" I asked, reigning in my agitation.

"I think an apology to Mom, for starters."

"You're kidding—are you talking about the laundry? I ironed her fricking clothes."

"You left a burn mark on the sleeve. She's sure you did it on purpose."

"I did it on the porch at midnight. The light was dim. Good Lord."

"And, an apology to Brette," Allen said, "in front of Patricia."

"I'll talk to Agnes. I never meant to burn her blouse. But I'm not apologizing to Brette. Not a chance."

"Keep your voice down!" The tapping changed to a closed fist-pounding lightly on the table.

Clea came into the kitchen. "I can hear you guys from my room," she said. "Maybe Patricia can stay over here. Would that be OK, Mom?"

I was pale with anger—how dare Allen bring Clea into this. "If that's OK with you, honey," I said, somewhere between a whisper and a hiss.

"Why don't you and Janey walk over, and you can ask her," Allen said. "You're more grown up than some grownups I know."

I pondered Allen's white knuckled-fist and said, "Let's all go together."

The four of us followed the path that circled to the second row of bungalows. Brette's door was open, and the air conditioner on. Patricia lay on the floor, sprawled on a throw rug, an opened jigsaw puzzle spread out on the wood-planked floor. She turned her head toward us, yawned, and yelled. "Mom, someone's here."

"Hi, Patricia," I said. "You making any progress on the puzzle?"

Patricia shrugged and turned away.

Brette came from the bathroom with a halo of hairspray floating around her. She side-hugged Allen, giving him a generous smile. "So, to what do we owe the pleasure?" The words oozed like syrup.

"Patricia," I said, "we'd like you to stay with us tonight. I've got to go back to work, and Maria is coming to my house to take care of this little munchkin," I picked up a giggling Janey. "But Clea can introduce you to the horses and other fun stuff at the ranch. What do you say?"

"I don' know." Patricia sat up, eying her mother, Allen, and me.

"We'll see you at dinner," Brette said. "And if you don't want to stay at Clea's house, we can talk about it then."

"'K," Patricia muttered. She stood, leaving the puzzle pieces scattered on the floor.

"Let's go." I patted her on the shoulder and turned to leave with all the girls.

"Wait, a minute," Brette said. "You forgot your bag."

In slow motion, Patricia went over to the couch where she had left her bag, still unpacked from the Disney trip. "Where are you going to be?" she asked her mom.

"We're going to a place called Ringo's." She wrapped a manicured hand around her daughter's shoulder and squeezed.

"Patricia," I said, "should we scoop all these puzzle pieces in the box? Maybe you and Clea can work on it in the activity room before you see the horses."

"Good idea," Allen opened his mouth for the first time. He stood closest to the door but moved quickly to the puzzle pieces and put them into the box. "There, you're set."

Clearly, Patricia was outnumbered, so she acquiesced and followed the kids and me outside. We walked to the turn in the path which led to my house. I took Patricia's bag and Janey back to my place while the older girls headed for the activity room with the puzzle.

Another skirmish averted, I thought, but the look in Allen's eyes sent a chill through a hot Arizona afternoon.

34

A Strange Alliance

I needed to be in the office while Dina and Consuela laid out dinner. Supervision of ranch duties fell solely on Alex while Glen recovered. Janey and I waited for Maria at home; Maria planned to stay with Janey when I returned to work. While we waited for Maria, we cuddled on the couch. I didn't want to leave Janey's warm, small being, but there was the job, and gratefully, it was within a few minutes walk away. Maria arrived with carrots to feed the horses after Janey napped. Janey loved Maria, who hugged her generously. "Go," she told me, and I was out the door.

I had an hour or so left in the workday, time enough to do the books and check on our scheduling. The beckoning smell of cornbread teased my senses. I threw my bag in its usual place under my desk and sat still. Dina's chili wafted through from the kitchen, and I thought I detected an apple cobbler from the cinnamon in the air. We closed the office at 5:30. If any emergency or guest's need came up outside the hours, Glen made himself available by phone, listed in our guest paperwork in each bungalow. We supplied each unit with Alex's phone number earlier in the week should an emergency arrive. I missed Glen sitting across from me; everything seemed out of kilter.

I forced my attention on the books and away from the visiting thoughts. I remembered dancing with Pablo at Ringo's. I pictured Brette and Allen there and shook my head. *Let It Be* —Paul McCartney, I need you right now. I laughed, continued with my adding machine and task at hand, and finished the bookwork for the deposit.

My mind drifted back to Brette. How dare she sweep into my life and sweep me out of it? And scorching Agnes's blouse? Who in their right mind would think I had done that on purpose? But then, I did it, intentionally or not. I must apologize. As for having Patricia at the house? God help me, I begged myself to remember—she was only a child, a spoiled one, and the poor kid had her mother to deal with full-time. Be kind. Bear with it, I counseled as I opened the mail. Two more days.

I stared through the slider as I tossed the junk mail aside. Well, great, I thought as Agnes approached the doorway. Terrific. I motioned her in with a smile. "Are you settled?" I asked.

She shrugged. "I don't know," she said. "Isn't this office missing its cowboy?"

"Sit down," I said. "Glen had a heart attack, or a near one anyway. An artery was clogged, and a stent inserted. He got back today."

"I'm sorry to hear that," she offered with nary a snarl. Was she sincere?

"I know you have Alex's number in case of an emergency, but you can call me if anything—"

Agnes held up her hand to stop me from continuing. "Did you burn my blouse on purpose?"

"Allen told me about the blouse. Never, Agnes, would I do that. I ironed by porch light after the kids were asleep, and I didn't notice it the next morning. You know, usual morning rush. I will replace it."

"I didn't believe it for a minute. You don't have a vindictive bone in your body." Agnes sounded nearly warm-blooded. "I've known you since you were fifteen. The lake house. I blamed you for the divorce, a feminist hippie ignoring my boy. That's what I thought." Agnes was direct.

"Yes, we go back," I said.

"Accidents happen, and don't worry about the blouse. I do have a question." She fingered a gold bangle on her thin wrist as she spoke. "I wouldn't put it past that woman, though."

Baffled by what Agnes said and, frankly, her whole demeanor, I asked, "Are you talking about Brette?"

"None other." She pushed her chin forward and stared straight at me. "I wondered why she and her daughter were with Allen and the girls. Didn't you?"

From my side view, I saw Lara on the porch. She stalled at the doorway. "Knock, knock," she said, "am I interrupting?"

"You should hear this too. But shut the door, dear."

Lara did as Agnes directed and sat in Glen's chair.

"I met Brette from time to time in Seattle when you were with Allen and setting up the art cooperative. I thought she was classless, then. And I saw you let her walk all over you. I wanted to see more backbone from you and better styling." Agnes took a breath and slowly exhaled. "And now? Well, now, Brette is still boorish and dead-set on marrying Allen."

"That part we figured," I said.

"Then, you know the rest?" Agnes searched both our faces and laughed. "I guess you don't. Allen told me not to say anything. I didn't actually say I wouldn't." A wry smile crossed her face. "Patricia is his child."

"What?"I said. But it all made sense.

"He told me before they arrived. In Anaheim."

"The pieces come together," Lara said.

"I'm mad as hell at my son," Agnes said, "and I will love him until my last mortal breath and beyond, but I couldn't let this be a secret. She wants my money, my social standing, and I'll be damned if that will happen."

I started to stand and then sat. "Poor Patricia," I said, "does she know?"

"Allen says she doesn't know." Agnes pointed to Lara. "I will not testify against him in a custody fight. But you," Agnes turned to me, "need to get some backbone. I'll see you at dinner." And with that, she strode out of the office.

35

The Redirector

"You got your walking orders," Lara threw a paperclip at me from Glen's desk. "You think about Patricia and the timing of her birth."

I nodded. "The girls are five months apart." I pushed my chair out; it was time to close the office. "We now know who that boyfriend was she met out of town—you know, the one we suspected was married?" I shook my head and chortled.

"She bragged about it," Lara said.

"I gave her a baby shower and lent her Clea's clothes. Think about it! Brette must've cheated on both her husbands with Allen."

"Home base, I guess, for her," Lara said, "and him. We'll insist on a paternity test."

I closed the office and walked Lara to her bungalow. When I returned home, Maria greeted me. Clea and Patricia were at the horse barn and would come for dinner from there. Janey told me the horses ate all the carrots. Maria had taped Janey's latest painting of what she claimed to be the

Tiki Room at Disneyland to the fridge. I oohed and awed over the joyful primary colors and fat birds with enlarged beaks. Janey giggled in response. Maria sailed to the dining room to help Consuela set up dinner service. That woman was a jewel.

The family would gather around a table opposite the kitchen entrance in the dining room. Consuela and Maria filled the sideboard with kettles of chili, meat or vegetarian, and salad bowls with greens, sliced peppers, heritage tomatoes, and scallions. A pasta salad with olives and artichokes looked inviting. Popular with our youngster guests, potato soup and mac and cheese were also on the menu. Cornbread and baskets of white and whole wheat bread with jam and honey centered the display.

Janey and I came to dinner early. I snapped photos of the lovely spread of food for the brochure. Janey drew pictures on the children's chalkboard as I photographed the sideboard from different angles. I worked hard at distracting myself from the dinner ahead. Anxiety bubbled each time I heard a door open. Everything I believed about my marriage was a lie. I had no idea what lay ahead.

Clea and Patricia entered the dining room before family and ranch guests arrived. Clea led, and Patricia lagged a few steps behind, studying the floor. Patricia's blonde hair needed washing. Her Minnie Mouse t-shirt looked to be a size too small, and her blue shorts clung to her hips. Clea's step was light.

"How were the horses?" I asked.

"They're mean," Patricia said.

"I love the horses, but I'm new to riding. Sometimes, because they're so big, they scare me," I said. "But they're very gentle."

"I'm allergic to horses," Patricia said.

"I brushed out Jeremy for Pablo," Clea said.

"Nice of you!" I said. "Did Jeremy do any of his tricks?"

"He only does them for Pablo," Clea said. Patricia remained downcast.

I pointed to our table with the reserved sign. "Take your places there." Janey skipped over, and a trace of a smile crossed Patricia's face.

The dinner bell rang out, and guests entered the dining room. Brette, Agnes, and Allen waved to us from the door and joined us. "OK, kids," Allen said, "You get a plate and fill it up. Let's go."

Janey hung onto my leg. "I'll take care of hers," I said.

"Daddy will." Allen lifted Janey up and waved me off.

Janey's mouth formed a perfect square, and her body visibly stiffened. She let out a wail and then screamed. "Mommy!"

People turned toward my unhappy child. "Come on, Janey. Let's get some soup." As I retrieved Janey from Allen's arms, I smelled gin, which explained Allen's slightly glassy eyes. He glared at me and said nothing but fell back in line with Brette, who was talking to Marty Chicago.

Ever watchful, Maria saw my dilemma. When Janey and I got to the sideboard, Maria had Janey's dinner ready: Potato soup, mac and cheese, and cornbread. I quickly loaded a bowl of chili and green salad onto my tray, and Maria guided Janey and me to the table. "I'll get the booster seat," Maria said, patting Janey on the head.

The room was awash with voices and guests. We had service for twenty that night. As I sat, Marty Chicago tapped me on the shoulder. "How's Glen doing?"

I gave Marty the update. Brette, with a tray in hand, butted into the conversation. "It was great talking to you, Mr. Chicago. I love your writing. I write, too. Short stories, mostly. I'm working on something now, as a matter of fact, and I wondered—"

Oh, Lord, I thought, she's going to ask him to read one of her stories. Marty rarely mingled with guests because he relished his solitude and writing time and did not like disappointing fans. Marty called me "the redirector" because, as I had earlier in the day, I changed the direction of the request. I interjected to Brette. "Gosh, I didn't know you wrote."

"CollinCamp's a great place for artists and writers," Marty added quickly. "I wish you well." And then to me, he said, "Dina is the best cook west of the Mississippi. "I'm going to grab some of that chili and disappear. My best to Glen. Nice to meet you, Brette. Tell Glen I'll be over for a game of rummy if he'll have me." And with a good-natured wink, he was gone.

"Who's Glen?" Brette asked.

"He owns CollinCamp," I answered. "He had a heart attack."

"That's too bad," she said, waved to Allen seated on the other side of the table, and blew him a kiss. "I think I'm wanted," she smirked as she left to join him.

Clea and Patricia took up seats near them. Agnes placed herself at the head of the table.

The whole room was a bevy of activity and voices and laughter. Folks were on vacation except for me, and I felt weird vertigo as I listened to Brette praise Marty's last novel from across the table to a bored-looking Allen.

Alex and Lara had eaten earlier with Glen, so I was surprised to see them coming in from the kitchen. Lara leaned over and whispered, "How's it going?"

"Like a boxful of birds," I smiled through clenched teeth.

"All feathers and shit," she whispered; We knuckle-bumped before she left.

After apple crisp, the girls played horseshoes with Allen and Brette for a while. I set up a Monopoly game with Janey and called Clea and Patricia inside to play; that went OK until Patricia claimed her eyes hurt and wanted to see her mom. Her announcement concluded the game. We walked her to Brette's bungalow to say goodnight.

I should have known—should have figured this scenario out, but I skipped the obvious signs: drawn blinds and no answer as we stood on the porch knocking on the door. "Mom said she'd be at home if I needed anything." Patricia pounded harder. Agnes's bungalow was a hair's breadth from Brette's, and she was returning from a walk while we waited for someone to answer Brette's door.

36

When the Bough Breaks

Agnes watched the drama unfold from her porch. It dawned on me then. Brette and Allen were inside and otherly engaged. "Why don't we," I began to say when the door opened wide enough for Brette to stick out her head. Smeared lipstick, tousled hair, and the strong scent of Chanel No. 5 fueled the air. She cast a look at me that melted stone.

I wrapped an arm around Patricia and said, "We stopped by to say goodnight." Patricia blushed and scraped her foot against the porch floor.

Brette raised an eyebrow. "We said goodnight after playing horseshoes, but goodnight again, Pattycakes," and began to shut the door.

"Mom!" Patricia yelled, "I want to stay here! Clea hates me. They make fun of me." Agnes quietly joined us on the porch while this back-and-forth occurred. When Brette saw her, she tried to close the door and would have if her daughter's foot wasn't blocking the move. Brette grabbed her sheer silk robe together across her ample chest and allowed Patricia entry. I had time enough to notice a shiny ring on her left hand before she banged the door in our faces. We all stood on the sidewalk facing Agnes's unit.

"Clea?" Agnes asked, "Have you ever told Patricia that you hate her? Or, made fun of her?"

"No," Clea said.

"Have you ever told a lie?" Agnes asked.

"No. I don't tell lies," Clea said and added, "ever!"

"I believe you," Agnes said. "Always be truthful, even when it hurts." Agnes turned to me. "Let this go," she said, and we parted for the evening.

On the way home, I told Clea about Glen's heart attack. "Maybe you and Janey can make cards for him. I'm sure he'd like that." We agreed that we would do the card-making tomorrow. At that point, I felt relief. We averted a confrontation and blessings to whatever entity looked over us because no one asked where Allen was. The quiet of the evening refreshed me.

We returned home, where I cared for the canine and feline crew. Patricia had her pink stay-over bag at our house. Clea asked if she should leave it on Brette's porch. Janey rounded the hall corner, saying, "I set up the barn and all the ponies. Come play with me, Clea. You said you would."

"Are you using my shoes for barns again?"

"I used Mommy's," Janey said with a problem-solved attitude. They took off, and I was about to collapse into my small rocker when there was a loud knock at our door. Brette and Allen appeared with Patricia, whose tear-stained face told its own story.

"Are you going to stay over?" I asked. "Clea's playing ponies with Janey in her room, and your pink bag is on Clea's bed."

Patricia shrugged and held back.

"You owe us an apology." Brette pointed her manicured index finger at me.

"Patricia, Janey's room is right next to Clea's. Why don't you see what's happening with them while I talk to your mom and Allen."

"Go," Brette said. Patricia skirted by her mother and disappeared down the hall.

"Patricia wanted to see you, to say goodnight when we stopped by earlier," I began, "I'm sorry we interrupted—"

"Clea said you didn't like her and wanted her to go home. Patricia blurted that out after I coaxed her—through her tears."

"That's not what happened," I answered.

"It's what my daughter said!" Brette replied. All the while, our voices were low. "You're just jealous as hell—"

I stared at her, then shook my head. "Wow. Jealous of you?" And I laughed. You pretentious bitch, zipped through my mind. "There is nothing you have that I want." I glanced in Allen's direction.

Brette flashed her bejeweled left hand. "Are you sure?"

"Absolutely," I answered. "Why don't you kids run along," I continued. No one misunderstood my sarcasm, especially Allen.

"Brette, take the flashlight and go back to our cabin. I want to talk to Tansy before things get out of hand. You're a lady and shouldn't be involved with this." He spit the words out.

"Allen, I think you need to leave, too. We'll talk tomorrow when you're sober," and I motioned for them to go.

Allen put his hand across my arm and pushed down. "We're talking now."

Brette took the flashlight Allen offered and left.

We stood like boxers, ready for the bout, sizing each other up. It was the moment before, the minute that stretches into the length of a marriage gone soulfully wrong. The time when both know what happens next is unavoidable: a mountain emitting slow streams of molten lava before the eruption that goes thirty thousand feet and sends a tsunami's killer wave onto a distant shore. The time comes. The minute passes.

"What do you want to tell me?" I said. He was drunk. "Better yet, just leave."

Allen took me by the shoulders and pushed me back. "You've poisoned the well. You turned my own mother on me. Mom told me about your little conversation today."

"Yeah, Allen, I know that Patricia is your child. And you are a dirty, lying, weak jerk. By the way, Lara knows, too. And the court will know. You owe me past support, and I will get it. Now, get the hell out of my house!"

Anger registered in the pulsing vein in Allen's neck. So mad.

He turned away and then around to confront me; the whites of his eyes were bloodshot. Allen balled his hand into a fist and opened it slowly, partway, and shut it tight. He hit me across the face. I felt the sting of the punch across my open eye. The room turned black, and I lost my balance and fell against the side table next to my small rocker. The table edge cut my forehead. The table lay in pieces. Allen fled.

As I stood, regaining my balance, I tasted blood.

"Mom, are you alright?" Clea said. "We heard everything."

Janey and Patricia gaped at me, open-mouthed.

"You're lying. You're lying," Patricia wailed and began hitting me on the chest.

I took her hands into my trembling grip and stared at her. "Look at me," I said. Patricia locked eyes with me. "Patricia, honey. This is a terrible way for you to find out that Allen is your father. But he is. That means," blood dripped onto my shirt from my wounded head. "That means you and Clea and Janey are half-sisters."

"I want my mom." Patricia pushed me backward and out of her way—adrenaline shot like stars through my veins.

"You stay here," I yelled at Clea. "Call Alex. I think he's at Lara's. Tell him what happened. I'll go after her."

I ran toward Brette's. "Patricia," I yelled. I rounded the walkway toward the bungalows and found her in a heap of defeat along the path. I thought about when Mama Cass jolted from her carrier and how I sat with the cat while she settled down. My heart raced, and I imagined Patricia's heart raced too. So I sat down beside this child and waited. In a minute or two, I eased my arm around her, and she cried into my arms. I held her. I don't know how much time passed. All I could think to say, and I said it like a mantra, was, "You are loved. No matter what. You are loved."

Alex and Lara found us, followed by Brette.

Brette shined a flashlight on her daughter and screamed. Blood had fallen on Patricia's shirt. Patricia skinned her knee when she tripped, running toward her mom's. When Patricia stood, her mother turned to me. "What did you do?"

I felt dizzy, and Brette blurred in front of me. Lara turned a flashlight on me. "What happened?" I heard Alex's voice.

"I'm calling the cops," Brette said.

And I fainted.

37

Silent Sirens

Alex grabbed me before I hit the ground, and it took me a moment to refocus and regain my balance. While the cut on my head made a bloody mess, I didn't think I was badly injured.

"I'm OK," I said.

Brette stared at Patricia. "Where are you hurt?" she asked. "Did she hurt you?"

Patricia shook her head and squeezed my hand, then let go. "It's not Tansy's fault," she yelled. "It's not."

Brette stood in the center of the path, unmoved by simple gestures. "Tell me what happened tonight. Where's Allen?"

"I don't know," I said. "I need to get cleaned up and check on the girls."

"I'll go with you," Lara said. "Alex, maybe you take Brette and Patricia back to their place. We'll see about Allen later." Lara wrapped an arm around me, and we walked home. I hadn't realized I was barefoot until I felt gravel against the soles of my feet. "I hate the taste of blood," I said. My left eye felt hot and oozy.

"What were you doing out here without shoes?" Lara asked.

"Chasing Patricia. Didn't have time," I said.

We neared my porch, and the light gave Lara the first real look at my face. "Dear God, Tans, let's get you inside."

"That bad?" I asked as Lara opened the door.

"Mom," Clea yelled. Her shocked look scared me.

"Let's get your mom cleaned up," Lara said.

"Where's Janey?" I trailed Lara to the bathroom.

"She crawled under her bed," Clea said. "She told me she won't come out 'til you come home. The cat's with her."

I began to follow Clea to Janey's room, but Lara interrupted. "No. We need to wash your face. Maybe, Clea, honey, can you tell her Mommy's back?"

Clea left for Janey's room, and Lara and I went to wash up. I glanced at myself in the bathroom mirror, and the reflection horrified me. The cut on my right temple bled like tears down my face. My left eye swelled nearly shut, the eyelid black from Allen's blow, and my split lip leaked blood and drool. "Did you hear that? Is someone at the door?"

"Let me check." Lara stood back in thought for only a moment. "Where's your camera?" she asked.

"On the kitchen table. Why?" I sucked in a breath and turned on the sink water.

"Evidence," Lara said and left me.

I leaned over the sink and ran cool water over and over my face. Lara returned with the camera and Agnes. "Alex sent me," she said. "What on earth?"

I stared open-mouthed at my former mother-in-law. "Could you take the kids? I need to," I stopped, unable to speak, "I need to get myself together."

"Oh, dear God, Allen did this?" Agnes brought herself up, shoulders back. "I had it out with him tonight. Cut him off financially when I saw that ring on Brette's finger. I paid for it. And then he came here—"

"I want to take some pictures," Lara interrupted.

"Mom," Clea said from the other side of the door. "Mom, are you OK?"

"Let me get the girls," and Agnes left.

"That bastard is not getting away with this," Lara whispered. "I'm glad you have a flash."

I leaned against the sink, facing Lara as she snapped photo after photo. The world turned red, and stars like fireworks shot with each flash from the camera.

The cut on my forehead needed closure. I handed Lara the box of butterfly bandages I kept supplied in my first aid kit. I remembered packing it in Seattle and stowing it in the car for our trip south. Little did I ever dream I'd be using it to repair my face from a brawl with Allen. "You want to do the honors?" I hiccoughed and took in a breath. "My hands are shaking, and I feel a little weird." What I felt was a panic attack building. Blood dripped into the sink.

"Mom? Janey wants to say good night," Clea said from the other side of the bathroom door.

"Go with Grandma, sweetie," I said. "I'll see you really soon." I put my hand over my chest to keep my heart from heaving out. Agnes had them out the door before another word.

"Where's the antibiotic ointment?" Lara asked.

I pointed to the kit and sat on the toilet while Lara applied the ointment and the butterfly bandage.

"You should have this looked at, I think," Lara said. "It's deep."

"No, no, I'm OK. No hospital." I tried to smile. "I'm better than it looks," I whispered.

"Sit on the couch, Tans," Lara said. Honeydog roped herself around my legs. The cat perched on the sofa back and gently tapped my head with her large furry paw. Yul and Deb lay by the front door. "Your entire four-legged family is guarding you. I'm getting you some water." While she was gone, I heard her talk to Alex on the phone. She returned with a new butterfly bandage and cleaned up my forehead again. I sipped the water as Lara tended to the injury. "Alex called the sheriff's office," Lara said.

I jerked away from her. "No, Lara. I feel so awful, and I'm not badly hurt. Allen was super drunk."

"The cops just got here. Alex is talking to them now."

"I didn't hear any sirens," I said.

"Alex had them turn them off to not scare the bejesus out of the guests."

"This is just so humiliating," I said. "I'm not going to talk to them. I'm not."

"Your head is kind of rattled right now. They will be over, and you will talk. I'll be right here.

The grandfather clock chimed once for the half hour, and then eight chimes as the hour struck. Finally, there was a rap at the door. "Hold on," Lara called. "We're getting the dogs situated." She hustled the dogs and the cat into my bedroom. While she did that, I rose from the couch with a firm desire to show everyone I was in control of the situation.

The men appeared big, giant-size, as I opened the front door. Alex was with them. The sheriff's officer looked at me and the broken table not far from where he stood and said, "Let's get some pressure on that head wound. That bandage is not going to hold. Ma'am," he said softly to Lara, "can you get me a clean towel, please."

Lara quickly left and returned with a towel. She handed it to the officer. He told me, "Let's get you sitting down," and ordered his subordinate, "Call in an ambulance, Jerry. Head injury," And back to me, "Ms. Daniels, I want you to lean your head back against the couch; I was a medic in 'Nam." He put on latex gloves and gently held a towel against my forehead. "I'm Captain Renn Walker, and Deputy Sheriff Jerry Carrol is the fellow by the door. Most folks call me Renn. Can I call you Tansy?"

"Yeah, good," I muttered. The towel draped over half my face so I couldn't see the deputy sheriff. I focused on the silver engraved button on Renn's shirt.

"How are you feeling, Tansy?"

"I'm OK," I said.

"Can you answer a few questions?

"I'll try," I said.

"We had quite a talk with Brette—Alex was with us— talked to Agnes Daniels, too. She speaks quite highly of you. I want you to tell me about the children. I understand y'all ate together?"

"We had dinner and played games in the activities room. Patricia, Brette's daughter, was going to stay with us but wanted to see her mom. We walked her to Brette's bunga- low. Patricia raised a fuss and wanted to stay with Brette, so the kids and I came home." I took a breath and wiped my mouth off with the hem of the towel. "Then Brette, Patricia, and Allen knocked at the door. Allen was drunk. I smelled gin on him at dinner, and he slurred his words."

"Slow down. You're doing really well, Tansy. So why do you suppose they came over?"

"Allen insisted he wanted to talk to me, and Brette yelled at me about how I treated Patricia."

"Didn't you find out today that Allen is Patricia's father?"

"Yes," I answered. "His mom told me. No one was surprised."

"And Brette told us that you used to be business partners. So, you've known her for years. Is that correct? Like, Lara, here, a friend?"

"Not a close friendship, but yes, a friend." What was he getting at? Lara was out of eyesight. I hoped she was taking notes.

"Was Allen mad about anything else?"

"I don't know. He owes a lot in back support. He's mad that we're taking him to court about that. And mad that his mom told me about him being Patricia's father."

"So, the three of them are at the door; what happened next?

"I told Patricia to go play with the girls, out of earshot. She went to find the kids and I told Allen we'd talk tomorrow. He insisted we talk right then. I kept asking for them to leave."

"Brette tells us Patricia was in tears after dinner because you told her you didn't like her. And Clea, your daughter, teased Patrica. Called her names. Any truth in that?" the captain asked.

"I never said anything like that," I answered.

"Did you think Patricia wanted to stay over after what happened earlier?"

"Patricia was set to stay over—that was the original plan. Her things were here. I thought everything would be OK if Brette and Allen left."

"And you had no hard feelings against Allen, just calmly told him to leave?"

"More scared than angry. Allen was drunk. I didn't want to talk to him drunk. I wanted him to leave. I hate talking to people out of control."

"Have you ever had a violent confrontation before with Allen?" Renn asked.

"Not with Allen, exactly, but with my mom a long time ago. Allen saved me from her. She had a knife," I stopped. "I don't want to talk about it." The horror of that day made my skin crawl.

"OK, that's fine. Ms. Daniels told us about that incident." He tapped me on my hand. "Let's get back to this evening. Brette and Allen are at the door and not budging. What happens next?"

I peered away from the silver button on the pressed tan shirt and glanced upward at Renn. He smelled like Old Spice, and his chin was squared with a dimple. The gentle pressure on my forehead never wavered, nor did his calm tone.

"Allen sent Brette away, and he said ugly things to me. He pushed me. I think I hit the door frame, I don't know. Ugly words. Accused me of having a grudge against Patricia." I took a breath and swallowed hard, the taste of blood in my mouth. "I did get mad because he wouldn't stop, and I finally yelled, 'I know you're Patricia's father,' and called him a jerk. That's when he slugged me, and I fell against the table." My heart sped up, and I hiccoughed.

"Closed fist?"

"So odd. I watched him close his fist. Oh, God, I knew it was coming."

Renn said, "I know this is hard. You got beaten up tonight, and none of it was your making. So take a breath. The ambulance should be here anytime. What happened after you fell to the floor? Were the kids watching?"

"I don't know when the kids came out of Janey's room. But they heard us—heard me. Allen ran off. I got up, and Patricia ran over to me and started pounding on me, saying, 'It's a lie. You're lying,' and then, she ran off. I told Clea to call Alex and chased after Patricia. I found her on the ground where she tripped over something. Held her. Told her she was loved. That's when Brette and Alex discovered us." I was forgetting something. "Lara, you were there too, right?"

Lara patted me on my shoulder. I thought she was on the other side of the room. "Yes, I was watching a movie with Alex in my bungalow when Clea called. We ran to Brette's first and found Tansy and Patricia nearby."

"That must have been mighty hard on Patricia."

"I deeply regret that—that she heard the truth from me and not her mom."

The captain's radio went off. He handed Lara a pair of gloves, told her to put them on and exactly how to put pressure on my bleeding head, and then left to speak to someone on the porch. She did as he advised.

The door was slightly open. Three, maybe four, cops were on the porch. "Why are there so many people here?" I turned to Alex.

"Hang in there, Tans," Alex avoided my question. "We'll get you through this."

The officer came back inside. "Tansy," Renn said, "this young man is Kim Layman. He's going to take some pictures of your injuries." The camera clicked while the officer's flash went off over and over.

"I want some photos of the table, too. Check for blood." Officer Kim did as Renn directed.

I started to hyperventilate and began crying. "I don't want to go the hospital. I'm OK. The cut's not serious. I don't want to make a report." With every sentence, I took in a breath. My voice sounded foreign to me.

"She's in shock," Lara said. "I took photos, too."

"Very good. If we need them, we'll ask," Renn said and resumed with a gentle pressure on my head.

Blaring sirens and three EMTs came into my living room. The three of them worked on me quickly and had me on a gurney and into the back of the ambulance.

38

Gloria

Everything whirled. The EMT who fed an intravenous line of fluids into my arm swayed with the road as the ambulance peeled through the desert to the hospital. I had this feeling of time swirling like desert winds, blurring my field of vision in waves of sand and uncertainty. I squinted because of the diffused bright lights inside the ambulance, and as I looked around, I couldn't make out one person from another. I felt the pokes in my arm and listened to voices, but I could not distinguish words. Except for one person. She pressed her hands gently against my shoulders and said, "Hello, Tansy, how are you feeling?" She wore a petal green jumpsuit, and unlike the other EMTs, she did not wear a mask or gloves. Her deeply colored ebony skin framed large honey-brown eyes. "Tansy," she said, "you are safe. Your children are safe. My name is Gloria." She offered her hand to hold, and I grabbed it.

My mind spun with the wheels of the vehicle. "Are you real?"

She laughed. "Well, you had quite a knock on the head,

but you're not seeing things."

"Did I faint again? I vaguely remember getting into the ambulance."

"Your blood pressure dropped, and you left us for a few minutes."

"I remember everything that happened, and I don't think I have a concussion. I have low blood pressure and panic attacks. So don't give me oxygen."

"Renn told us," Gloria said. "He told me your story."

"The captain?"

"The same," Gloria said. "He told us about you hyperventilating, and Tansy, you don't necessarily lose your memory with a concussion. No one's going to hurt you. We want to make sure you're OK."

"How come I can see you but the others?" I glanced at someone taking my pulse. "I can't make them out very well."

"Everyone is here to help. I'm staying with you."

"Are you an angel?"

She laughed and shook her head. "Well, not according to my son." She paused and continued. "You know, when a chick cracks through its egg, the first being it sees, it takes as its mother. And that baby hen does not see or care about any other being, cannot even see them at first. Sometimes, when a person is injured and passes out when they first wake up, they can focus only on one person. Intuitively, they know this is the person who can help them."

"Or kill them?" My voice fell flat.

"Aw, yes. Like your husband. Married him. Forgave him."

"An old story?"

"It's written in your eyes." Gloria quietly chuckled. "And in Renn's report." I clung to her hand.

"Can I ask you something else?"

"Of course."

"Is Patricia OK? I don't think anyone told me how she is." The ambulance weaved around cars and blared its siren. "I guess there's a reason they strap you on the cart," I squeezed Gloria's hand. "I know my kids are OK, but Patricia, no one has said how she is. You see, it was my fault she ran off."

"She's with Ms. Daniels—with your girls."

"Then everyone's alright," I sighed.

"Not so quick," Gloria said. "Let's get you better and hold Allen accountable. Close your eyes. These lights are pretty bright."

"Don't go," I whispered.

"I'm right here," she said. "Nothing that happened to you is your fault."

"But I knew Allen was drunk, and he gets mean when he drinks, but I yelled at him anyway. I knew better."

"Allen could have walked away. Don't make excuses for that boy—it won't help him or your kids."

Another EMT checked my IV and pulse.

"You're so kind." I opened my eyes, and it appeared to me that a rainbow haloed Gloria. "Are you real?"

"As real as sunshine," Gloria said.

"I might be hallucinating," I said.

"Does it matter?" Gloria said. "Right now, Tansy, I want you to breathe with me." And so we breathed together, doing counts of four for intake, held for four counts, and exhaled four counts. After a few minutes, someone took my blood pressure.

They wheeled me into the ER, and then Gloria disappeared.

A doctor sewed up my head, and someone took an x-ray of my foot and neck. Aides wheeled me one place and then another, and I finally ended up in a room hours later. I slept. I may have been sedated—I didn't mind.

39

Captain Renn Walker

Captain Renn Walker showed up after morning rounds with the doctor. Lara was with him. He led me through the evening again. He asked me why I had panic attacks. I deferred because I didn't want to talk about my mother. "They have nothing to do with what happened," I said. But he pressed me to answer, and I finally responded, "It was a long time ago." He asked questions about the incident that happened "a long time ago," and he appeared content to keep asking me about it until I peered squarely at him through my black eye and sewn-up forehead and said, "My mother held a knife on me, and Allen saved my life." And then I cried in a small voice that lived somewhere deep inside me. "But Allen wasn't there last night to save me." I sucked in a hungry breath and continued, "I have panic attacks because I've been so afraid. He gets so mad."

Renn kept writing in his notebook, then paused. "None of your injuries are your fault." He tapped my finger with his pen as I gazed off. "You don't get a black eye all by yourself."

I stared blankly at Renn. I could write a script about a woman like me and what good, caring people tell her. But their well-meaning words were void of the memories, the nuances. Allen took care of me after Mother left the scene. Even when I knew she was in Canada, I wouldn't answer the door or the telephone. Dad couldn't reach me; I'd gone so deeply into myself. Allen wrapped me into his arms, and I was safe. Agnes called him Saint Allen. Well, Saint Allen fell off his pedestal when he left me pregnant with Janey and seven-year-old Clea. Agnes told me he deserved to have a life with a woman, his equal, and advised me to grow up and stop living in the past. And she repeated Allen's new refrain, "If you don't change, you'll be just like your mother."

"I don't know where you are, Tansy Daniels, but I want you to listen to me."

"I'm sorry. I'm listening," I told Renn.

"This is my take, and I've seen too many women in your situation. It's a pattern guys like Allen follow. Allen likes control. He wants what he wants. He divorced you but had you live in a house his family owned. Then you left—made the move to Arizona. Got yourself a job and a boyfriend. Stood up to him about back child support. You haven't played by his rules. Then, his mother called him on the carpet. Cut him off, and Allen blamed you. So he got himself good and drunk, fired up, and whacked you across the head. And he could have killed you."

"But he saved my life," I said half-aloud. "At one point in my life, he was all I needed to feel safe."

"Eye roll," Lara said from across the room. "Renn's right. Allen dug the control, and you took that from him. You felt safe because he pulled you away from your mother. Full stop. One time. Don't go memory blind."

"Gloria said something like that." I closed my aching eyes and opened them.

"You like Gloria—she's a peach," Renn said.

"She was the only EMT without a mask. We had a long talk. I thought she was an angel."

Renn stood. "Gloria works for us—and rides along on domestics. She's not an EMT, but an advocate for domestic violence victims, and she's been in your shoes. Well, we found you without shoes, but she understands better than most about how hard this is for you. I chatted with her for a moment before they left. I thought you'd get along." Renn put away his notebook inside a messenger bag. "We're preparing a statement for you to sign so we can ask the prosecutor to file charges against Allen for assault." He raised an eyebrow at Lara. "I'll be back this afternoon before you're discharged with the papers. And by the way, I've heard word-for-word from women who didn't press charges and ended up dead." He tapped me on the hand again. "You will press charges?"

"Yes, yeah, I guess." I knew they wanted a firm "yes," but that spinning sensation had not stopped; none of this seemed real. Except Gloria, and I thought she was an angel.

Renn tipped his Stetson and added, "Good day, ladies. "Oh, and Lara, let Tansy know what Allen was up to last night after he assaulted her."

"I can tell when you are waffling. Now is not the time." Lara fiddled in her bag, brought out a mirror, and sat in the chair Renn vacated. "I want you to take a long look, Tans, and don't forget who did this."

"Oh, God," I said. "I don't want to look." I turned the mirror over on my hospital tray.

"Honey, I want you to think about what Allen is capable of and why Captain Renn is so pissed off. You hear me?" Lara minced no words.

I nodded. "What happened to Allen? No one said."

"He couldn't run to Mommy—she just cut him off. So he ran home to Brette. Pablo was there to greet him."

"Pablo?" Oh, God, Pablo. I imagined he never wanted to see me again. That dance at Ringo's felt like it belonged in someone else's life, someone who deserved to be with Pablo. Not me. "How did Pablo get involved in all this?"

"Of all movies, Alex, Pablo, and I were watching *The Shining* when Clea called. I nearly jumped out of my skin when the phone rang." Lara pulled a chair close to my bed. "From what we could tell from Clea, you were hurt, Allen was gone, and Patricia ran outside in the dark. The three of us checked with Brette first, and Pablo stayed behind in case Allen showed up. When Brette and Alex returned with Patricia, Pablo and Allen were sitting on Brette's porch.

I interrupted. "You're telling me that Pablo and Allen sat peacefully on the steps?"

"Not exactly peacefully," Lara said.

"What happened?" I asked.

"When Allen saw Pablo, he took off for his mom's, and Pablo caught up to him, dragged him by his collar to Brette's, and sat him down pretty efficiently." Lara smiled and shrugged. "Alex and Brette, with Patricia, arrived minutes after. I don't know how Allen broke his nose, no one would say."

"Pablo beat him up?"

Lara shrugged. "It wasn't over for Allen. When Patricia saw him, she started screaming and hitting him. Pablo peeled her away and took that poor kid to Agnes's. He stayed with Patricia when Agnes came over to get the kids, but that was after the sheriff arrived. Later on, Pablo and his little dog, Diamond, helped Agnes out—didn't leave until the kids went to bed."

"Pablo did all that?"

"Yes."

"Was Pablo questioned about Allen's nose?"

"Yeah, the cops wanted to make sure you didn't do it." Lara shook her head. "Allen blamed Pablo straight up, said Pablo was going to kill him, and how he dragged him in the dirt—"

"But Pablo?"

"The cops called Allen a flight risk. Let Pablo go."

"And Allen?"

"An officer put him in the back of a cruiser and waited until Renn talked to you. He was at the ER, too, getting his nose fixed, then they hauled his ass to jail. But—"

"But what?"

"Brette bailed him out, and they are at the Lasater Inn. She's standing by her man. Brette went to Agnes for bail money. Agnes said no, but she would take care of Patricia at the ranch while things got sorted."

After Lara left, I grew restless. I wondered what on earth Glen would make out of all this—if I had a job to return to. I worried about my kids and where I could take them next. And Pablo? Lara brought *Clan of the Cave Bears*, a novel I intended to read, but my head hurt too much to concentrate. The tectonic plates had shifted, and it was the day after.

40

Nobility on a Bookmark

Gloria handed me a pen and paperwork. I read through my statement. "I'll sign it later, "I said. "Lara will take it to the sheriff's office, probably tomorrow."

"My next stop is the sheriff's office—I'm happy to hand the statement to Renn."

"There might be some words I want to change," I said. "Take a line or two out."

Gloria raised an eyebrow, and we left the papers on the bed tray. "I'll stay with you until your friend, Lara, gets here," she said. "Let's talk."

I searched for something to say. "I want it to be springtime," I told Gloria. "Everything's dying this time of year." My heart raced because I knew I should sign the papers. Gloria wanted me to. "I'm sorry, I'm not much of a conversationalist. I don't want to drag this thing out. I don't mean to do that. Some of the statement sounds over the top. He hit me once, and he ran after decades of knowing him. It was only once. I know everyone means well."

"Certain things have to be said," Gloria paused, then pointed around the room with her index finger. "You are in the hospital. The whole side of your head is swollen. You have stitches on your scalp. You could be dead. No matter what you think about him, he did this."

"What am I going to tell my kids?" I shook my head.

Gloria opened her folder. Inside was a clipboard from which she took a bookmark. "Take this," she said. "It's directions. It'll tell you what you need to say and do."

"Noble Eightfold Path" in script ran along the outer edge. Under it in italics in slightly smaller script, they were listed in a single line. *Right View, Right Thought, Right Speech, Right Behavior, Right Effort, Right Mindfulness, Right Livelihood, Right Concentration.* A picture of Buddha bled through the background.

How was this supposed to help me? I appreciated Gloria, but I felt confused. "You're a Buddhist?" I asked. She didn't get me like I thought she did. She only wanted me to sign the papers.

"I haven't decided," Gloria smiled. "When my husband beat me up, and I was in the hospital, the chaplain was a Buddhist. I felt pretty bad for myself and my son. He told me, this chaplain, to look at each marker, like signs along a highway, to sort through bad times. It's so easy, Tansy, to fall into the grip of pity and see the world through a string of regrets and excuses. And scare yourself shitless, meanwhile, with everything that might go wrong. Ask yourself, what is the right view about pressing charges against Allen? And I don't mean, particularly, your view. None of the answers are easy ones and it takes practice. Act on the right thing to do—it's a hell of a lot easier to explain to yourself and to your kids. Think about it. Keep the bookmark with you."

I tucked the bookmark inside my novel. "Thank you, and I'm sorry your husband hurt you." I tried to redirect the conversation away from the unsigned statement on the bed tray.

"I didn't sign a statement either—the first time. Couldn't believe Virgil would hit me again. He only slammed my hand in the door." Gloria picked up the papers and put them down. "I made an excuse and told the officer I wanted to wait a few days for my hand to heal enough so that I could properly sign my statement." Gloria laughed. "The officer was onto me but couldn't do anything more for me without a signed statement." She peered straight into my eyes.

"What happened?"

"I went home. Virgil was out of jail. On a Saturday about a month later, Virgil was back. Upset again. I was washing dishes. He told me to stop, to listen to him. His list of grievances was the very same—repeated over time. His voice got louder, so I concentrated on the dishes. The sudsy bath in the sink—bubbles are so innocent, you know? The more scared I got, the louder Virgil got. I kept my head down, staring into the sink, and ran a plate under hot water. All the while, Virgil stood behind me. He grabbed my hair, and pushed my face into the water, and held it there. All the commotion woke up Wesley. He was eight.

"We had one of those small fire extinguishers in the kitchen. Funny thing, Virgil installed it a few months before. He's a fireman. Interested in safety first, right?" Gloria rolled her shoulders and continued. "Wesley's a curious boy, and I was worried that he might set it off by accident someday, so I explained to him exactly how a fire extinguisher works and why we only use it in emergencies." Gloria took an audible breath. "So there's Wesley in the kitchen and his dad pressing my head into a sinkful of steamy suds. That boy turned the fire extinguisher on his dad. Virgil released me and started wailing.

Wesley and I ran to the neighbors and called the cops."

"Oh, my God," I said. "You know, I had the same thing happen with Allen. He'd been drinking and in the kitchen with me while the kids played. I was drying the dishes and locked eyes with the silverware while Allen ranted, mad as hell, that I wasn't listening to him. Said something about me counting the forks. Clea came in—broke up the mood. She was protecting me, and it should've been the other way around. Allen is the kind of guy who helped people—that's why I can't wrap my mind around any of this."

"My ex-husband was a firefighter committed to helping people in danger. People called him a gentle giant. And he was until he wasn't. Now, Tansy, you have more protection than I had. Allen has an order to stay away from the ranch— part of his bail release. If he breaks those rules, he goes back to jail for disorderly conduct and public drunkenness. Your boss filed those charges. But that doesn't touch the abuse or protect you, and that is why you must sign the papers."

She handed me a pen. I signed the damn papers. "What happened to Virgil?" I asked.

"He got married again and moved to Delaware after serving time for felony assault.

"Not any of us know what to say or do in every instance, but if we cut through the crap, we can see clearer. It takes guts, and it gets easier as you go along. Anyway, you have great friends and sweet kids. Start there. I've got to scoot.

My son's soccer match starts in thirty minutes, and Renn's waiting for these." She waved the signed paperwork. "You can have the life you want anytime you're ready for it."

Lara handed me a new pair of Jackie O sunglasses and a crocheted floppy-brimmed hat. "Thank you," I breathed, "I feel more like Greta Garbo than Jackie Kennedy, but this will do nicely."

"I love the hat," Lara said. "When I saw it, I knew it would look good on you."

The discharge nurse sighed, shook her head, and pointed to the wheelchair. "Oh, you girls," she sighed, "no partying for you!" It was her job to roll me out of the hospital. "If I were you, I would get into a program. Have you tried AA or church, maybe? Nice fellas at church, not bars."

"Clearly, you're not me," I said.

"I'm a square, oh I know, but girls, you don't want to end up here again, my dear."

"This didn't happen at a bar," I put my bag over my shoulder. "I don't need the chair."

"Hospital rules," the nurse said as she fingered the cross around her neck; her stern expression stayed stark. Her gray hair matched her sallow cheeks.

Lara, the nurse, and I arrived at my car. I was silent for a few miles. The whole hospital scene hung on me—brought my shoulders down. This world that buzzed by under Lara's heavy foot was the reality.

"Don't take that nurse seriously," Lara said.

"I know. But for a minute, after Gloria left, I felt a little human, then you came with the hat and glasses, and that damn woman sucked all the joy out of the room."

"Get really pissed off and let it go. Thank God you're not married to her."

"Point taken. I guess that's taking the right view of things." We both laughed. "I can have the life I want, can't I?"

"Damn straight," Lara said.

41

No Matter What

When Lara turned off the Nova's engine, I sat still. Here we were at home. It felt like I'd been gone a month. Mama Cass appeared inside on the window sill, her nose pressed against the glass. I opened the car door and heard the birds bursting with song, well, song to me; others called it a high-pitched racket. The dogs barked, the front door opened, and Agnes and my canine crew greeted us. Agnes hugged me, then gently touched my face beneath my black eye and sunglasses. My head wound hid behind the sun hat. "I'm so sorry," she said, "none of this makes sense."

"You didn't do this," I said, "so you—"

"I encouraged you to grow a backbone—I think I actually said that," she interrupted. "My God—"

"Let's get inside," Lara said.

The dogs raced through the door. "Where are the girls?" I asked.

"Glen took them on a horseback ride—they should be back soon," Agnes pointed to the couch. "Sit," she told me. My pup, Yul, took her seriously and immediately sat.

"You're a very good boy, Yul." He walked over to me and softly put his head in my lap. "A very good boy—and it's good to be home."

My head buzzed with the household sounds. My eye throbbed. Honeydog sat in front of me and pawed my arm. I leaned over her soft brown head, and she nuzzled into my shoulder. She was my heart dog, and she knew it.

"Take off your glasses and the hat. I want to see your face."

I sighed. "Jesus, I hate this part," but did as Agnes asked. "I keep wondering how I can run the front office with this face going on. People will ask. I can hear them, "How'd you get that?""

"Tell 'em you don't want to talk about it," Agnes answered.

"Make up something." Lara carried my bag to my bedroom door and put it inside. "You know," she continued, "like after the bear attacked you, you crawled on top of it and beat him senseless with your face. And the bear is doing fine, by the way."

I laughed. "I might use that one." Mama Cass purred loudly in my lap. I noticed that the broken table was missing, but other than that, everything appeared strangely peaceful.

"I'm going to have to get a new end table," I said.

"I think Pablo's fixing it," Agnes said. "He said he could fix it with new brackets and refinish the wood."

"Mom!" Janey ran into the room. Glen and Clea followed.

I was home. I hugged the kids; the dogs settled in their usual living room places, Yul and Deb on their hallway blanket and Honeydog at my feet. Mama Cass resumed her perch on the window sill. Agnes left for the kitchen. She had prepared dinner for us, and Lara went to help her. The air hung lightly with fried chicken and what I swore was chili or baked beans. I loved the combination of onions, celery, garlic, and green peppers, the base for either dish. I was hungry after two days of cafeteria-style, horrifically bland, overcooked vegetables accompanied by gelatin salads.

The kids told me that Agnes put them in charge of walking Yul and Deb. Clea leashed them and left with her little sister. Honeydog put her paw on my foot and settled in to nap. When you are a twelve-year-old dog, you can choose your walking time. I patted her head and thought I'd take her out after dinner.

Glen had not spoken to me, but sat across from me. Never shy about saying what was on his mind, his silence disturbed me. He might think I wasn't the best representative for welcoming guests. Who was I kidding? He might be figuring out how to fire me. The Friday night incident was enough to scare off guests. It made no business sense to keep me on. He pushed his hat onto his head. "Tansy, before I go, I've got something to say."

Here it comes, I thought. "Sure, Boss." And then I shook my head. "Glen, I haven't asked how you're doing. Is Dina working out alright?"

I reached over to pat Honeydog, feeling her closeness helped me—I knew she'd never fire me, even on her worst day. Years before, a car hit her when she tried to retrieve a ball in the street. As a result, she wore a cone around her neck for a week or two to keep her from licking some open abrasions on her legs. The accident happened a few days before the Fourth of July fireworks that terrified Honeydog.

She was on pain medication because of the accident, so she moved slowly that day. The other dogs slept in the guest bedroom—Yul and Deb were never afraid of loud noises. Clea spent the night with a school friend, and I was home with Janey, who was six months old. I had a great view of the fireworks from the attic loft as they shot out over Portage Bay, so I checked on the baby and Honeydog and left them to view the show from my attic dormer. I was there for about ten minutes when I heard the dog patiently climbing the stairs. She nuzzled my hand as I sat on my window pillow, circled a few times, and laid down on the outside perimeter as fireworks burst one after another. With each burst, she shuddered a little, but no way was Honeydog going to have me endure the fireworks alone.

Today with Glen, and with whatever he had to say, Honeydog was not leaving me for a minute. Simply touching her head made me feel stronger.

Glen stared straight into my eyes. "We can't have this happen again."

My heart sped. Shit, I'm fired. I couldn't blame him. I felt physically sick at the thought of leaving CollinCamp. "You don't have to explain, Glen. Friday night definitely was not good for business. I might need some time to figure out where we'll go, and God, I appreciate—"

"I'm not letting you go. Will you hear me out for once before you come to some half-cocked conclusion?"

I happily shut up.

"I want to know if you are going to press charges." He pointed his index finger at me. " That ex-husband of yours could have killed you. Next time, the outcome could be different. I got a protective order against him because of the hell-raising he did here. You need to sign the papers and get yourself an order, too."

"Yeah, I did. Gloria, the woman from the sheriff's office, told me he won't be allowed within three hundred feet of me."

"Good. That's the main thing I wanted to ask about."

"Thank you for not firing me," I said.

"After all that trouble with Peter, this ain't nothin' but a storm passin' over on a summer night."

"How are you doing, Boss? You never said."

"Dina's keepin' the house so damn clean I don't know where nothin' is." Glen chuckled. "She's a fine lady. That Miz Daniels turned out alright, too. I don't think she has had a decent night's sleep since you got hurt. I can respect a woman like that. You be nice to her. Make her get some rest."

"Since you didn't fire me, can I take Monday off?" I laughed.

"You wait a few more days. Now, Jimmy Andrews, that kid from the Arizona Tourist Bureau, he's comin' by Thursday. You think you can come back to work, then? Share some of your ideas for the brochure?"

"Yes, I'd love that." I swallowed hard, "You don't mind how I look?"

"Come up with a good story."

"Lara told me to say that a bear attacked me, and I beat him up with my face."

"No wonder Alex likes her so much. That's a good one!"

Agnes poked her head from the kitchen. "Glen, you want to eat with us? I'll set a place."

"Dina's fixing me a fancy salad of some sort, and I best be getting' home, but thank you, Miz Daniels."

"Call me Agnes," she said, whisking back into the kitchen.

"You're eating salad, and Agnes and you? Friendly?"

"Best thing you ever did was hire that cook—as for Agnes Daniels, she come around really quick."

"It feels like the plates inside the earth shifted."

Glen nodded. "That's a fact."

The kids returned with Yul and Deb and passed Glen as he headed home. Lara left with him. I think she and Alex had something planned.

I listened to the kids' chatter as we ate fried chicken, potato salad, and chili. Home never felt so good.

Agnes insisted on cleaning up while I got Janey ready for bed. I read *James and the Giant Peach* and *Cloudy With A Chance of Meatballs* and laid down by my little daughter.

"Mommy?"

"Yes, sweetie?"

"Grandma told me Daddy's in time out. Is that right?"

"Yes, that's right."

"If he knocks on the door, how will we know?"

"Rancher Glen's making sure Daddy stays far away until he gets his anger fixed. We're all OK. Do you want Yul and Deb to sleep in here tonight? I know they would love that."

Janey thought that would be a great idea. I called the dogs in, put on her lullaby music, and stayed with her. I drifted off and woke with a start when Clea opened the door.

"It's almost ten, Mom," Clea said.

"Sh." I tiptoed out of Janey's room. I put my arm around Clea's shoulder. "You have any questions?"

"I talked to Dad," Clea said.

A chilly wave circulated inside me. "When was that?"

"Yesterday." Clea's tone was matter-of-fact.

"How was that for you?" God, I thought, how was I going to handle this? I didn't know where Allen was. Still in Tucson at the resort? In jail? I tried my best for an overview outside of my aching head, a forever reminder that part of me was hurting and scared. And where was Patricia? I needed to talk to Agnes. We needed a plan if she were truly an ally; from what I could tell, she had all the particulars.

"Grandma was with Dad in Tucson at the Lasater place, and Alex and Lara were here with us. They planned the call that way, which made it really weird, Mom." A tear fell on Clea's cheek. "We started talking, you know, and it got easier. For a little while, I forgot he hurt you and that everyone in the whole world hates him. I told him I loved him, no matter what because that's what you tell me when things screw up."

"You know," I wiped the tear from Clea's cheek, "your dad has to work on some of his behaviors before things feel less awkward. He's not the only one. It takes hard work on all our parts. Letting your dad know you love him can only help him. Don't you feel better when you feel loved? I know I do."

"So it wasn't wrong for me to tell him I loved him. I mean, I know he—"

"I think it was the right thing to say." I peered over my shoulder and noticed the kitchen door open a smidge.

"He hurt you, Mom. I saw it. And I hate that."

I held up my hand to stop the discussion. "We're good. We're going to make every day the best we can. It's late. You have school tomorrow. Go brush your teeth and get to bed.

I love you 24/7. Never forget that." I laughed. "No matter what."

"I love you, Mom," and off she went.

I went to the kitchen. Agnes sipped tea at the table with the crossword page opened on the newspaper in front of her. She looked up at me. "I think you might have some questions?"

"You heard us?"

"Yes. I wanted to explain the phone call yesterday. You handled Clea so well. She clammed up on me after talking to Allen. I couldn't get a word out of her last night."

"She's twelve, and her feelings have to be super jumbled. All of ours are." I didn't reheat the hot water but poured it over a tea bag and sat across from Agnes, dipping the bag in my oversized mug as I spoke. "I can't thank you enough for all you've done—including the dishes, for God's sake."

She blushed and tapped her pencil on the puzzle. "A quick update. Allen turned himself in at the sheriff's office about when you returned home. He pleaded guilty to assault. He's out on bond. His Seattle lawyer, Max? Is that his name?"

"Max is his guy." I sipped the lukewarm tea.

"He has a friend from law school who practices here. And tomorrow, they'll ask the court for permission so that Allen can return to Seattle while he awaits sentencing."

"So that's how it works." I drank the mint tea and asked, "Where's Patricia?"

"Back in Seattle with that woman."

"Poor little kiddo."

"When I get home, she's coming to San Francisco. Brette agreed to a week's stay. I'm holding my nose, so maybe Brette will let me have Patricia for next summer."

I shook my head. "You are kind of an amazing woman, do you know that?"

"Before you hand out awards, I must tell you I share Clea's dilemma."

"Let's see," I dragged the teabag from the cup and put it on the saucer, "can I guess what the dilemma is?" The kitchen light hurt my eyes.

"You know damn well." She fiddled with her powdery blue silk scarf, tying back her henna-dyed hair. "I made a deal with Allen. I'd provide a lawyer if he pleaded guilty and quit drinking." Agnes's witch-like cackle startled me. "I wanted to insist he breaks up with that woman, but I stopped short of that. I hope he'll break up on his own when he sobers up and reflects on what he did. Meanwhile, we have to consider Patricia." She patted my hand. "I'm on your team, Tansy, but Allen needs help, and I gave birth to him. He's still my dear boy, but to say that makes me want to cry. That's my dilemma. My blood pressure rises every time I think about you in the bathroom, blood everywhere. I am so sorry."

"You love Allen no matter what. I think you made a good deal. Keep me posted—I don't want to lose you."

"That 'no matter what' business applies to you, too. I am paying Lara for all your legal expenses. Don't give me that look! I've already spoken to her and we've struck a deal. We'll get through this together."

"Thank you," I said, "I can't tell you how much!"

"I'm exhausted." She stood and stretched. "Going to toddle over to my cabana. Get to bed now. Don't forget your pain meds."

I watched her leave, flashlight in hand, the quarter moon butter-yellow, and the silent world at peace.

42

The Lovebirds

We walked to the bus stop the following day, and Janey and I waved to Clea as she set out for school. "You know what?" I strapped Janey into her car seat and started my car.

"What?"

"Chicken's butt." It was a family joke. "You know what else?"

"Two chickens' butts," Janey chimed from the backseat.

"It seems like forever since I've seen Rena." I pulled out onto the feeder road that led to the highway and the ten-minute trip to Rena Flores' preschool program. "Are you excited about a brand new schoolhouse?" Before leaving home, I read a note from Rena from last Friday. Today was the first day in her new schoolhouse, custom-built by Rena's son, Miguel.

"Is that today?" Janey asked.

"The note from school said so, and you know what else?"

"What?"

"We're going to be on time."

I pulled up alongside other cars, delivering children to school. Rena stood on the porch of the brick-red little school with a canary-yellow door. Janey wiggled with excitement as I unstrapped her from the car seat. With my sunglasses in place and my hat pulled low, I got her out of the car and walked her to the porch.

"What a lovely hat," Rena opened her arms for a hug from Janey as the child rushed inside. She didn't ask me why I hid my face. I felt deep relief that I didn't have to focus on anything other than her new little school.

From around the corner, I heard footsteps. I turned to see Pablo carrying a sign reading Rena's Little School. "Hi," I pulled my hat an inch lower and turned to Rena, who greeted other children. "Have a great first day!" Uncertain, I left the porch and took some steps to my car. I wanted to talk to Pablo, but this felt awkward.

"Rena?" Pablo held up the sign. "I'll hang it up later. Sorry, I misjudged the time."

"That will work." Rena turned to the last arrivals.

"Don't you dare run off." Pablo turned to me. "Let's go to my place." He placed the sign alongside the door. "You want coffee or anything."

"No, I'm fueled," I said, but thanks." I peered at the sign. "That's perfect for Rena's school. I couldn't tell who was more excited, Rena or the kids."

"Miguel's wife and grandmother are excited to have their living room back, too." He turned his attention squarely to me. "You're not working today, are you?"

"Glen kicked me out until Thursday."

"Are you free, then?"

"I have birdcages to clean, but that's the only thing on my agenda."

"I cleaned them on Sunday morning," Pablo said. How footloose and fancy-free are you right now? Would you like to go on a field trip? I'll have you home in time for the kids. I promise."

"I've been so restless this morning." I felt grateful. How did this kindred soul come into my life? "Thanks for taking care of my birds and breaking Allen's nose."

Pablo shook his head. "I've never had such a thank you before. Give me a hug. Carefully." He gently closed his arms around me, reminding me of our first dance at Ringo's. "Let's go for a ride in Gladys!"

"What do you have in mind," I asked.

"I want it to be a surprise. Trust me?"

"I'm ready."

I called the office from Pablo's living room. I wanted to let Lara know where I was, and I figured Alex would answer the office phone. Lara and Agnes had already left for Allen's court proceeding, and Alex did not hold back on his feelings about Allen. "That asswipe needs to go to jail. It's a good thing Pablo came across him first. I would have—"

"I love you, too, Alex." I broke into what might have started a tirade.

"I'll send Diego to walk the dogs after school."

"Maria's son is such a sweetheart. Tell him thank you. Pablo says we'll be back before three, but I'd appreciate Diego's help."

"Where you two off to?"

"Vegas. We're getting married." I deadpanned.

"What—you better be—"

"You sound more like the boss every day," I looked over at the shocked expression on Pablo's face and laughed. "I'm teasing. I don't know where we're going, but it isn't Las Vegas."

"Be safe. See you when you get back."

I hung up the phone. "Did I scare you?"

"Not the worst idea you've ever had."

"I think we should go on a truck ride. Let's take Diamond!"

The morning seventy-degree breezy clear-skied weather suited me. I thought I should say something about the past few days, so I told Pablo about Gloria. I pulled the bookmark she gave me from my bag. "It's called 'The Eightfold Path,' with eight directives." I read them aloud. *Right View, Right Thought, Right Behavior, Right Effort, Right Mindfulness, Right Livelihood,* and, *Right Concentration.*" Diamond climbed on my lap for a better road view.

"Surprisingly, that helps me explain to you where we are going. Thanks for the reminder."

I scratched Diamond's head. "You said reminder. You know about 'The Eightfold Path?'"

"I do. Nancy, my ex-girlfriend from Toronto, belonged to a temple. I joined it. And, it was a guy there, a man who belonged to a commune in India for years—he was the one who convinced me it was time to go home. He told me I was turning gray—my face, that is. If I was to get my brownness back, he claimed over a bottle of wine that I needed to go home. Then he told me Nancy was sleeping with an ex-monk and had been for weeks." Pablo shrugged and laughed. "Relationships are weird."

"I think you have a point."

We talked about his show, and I was glad to hear that Glen was feeling like himself and that Dina kept him on his diet. The miles peeled away. I didn't ask where we were going; it felt good watching the desert shift as shadows played while the air conditioning kept us cool. Suddenly, Pablo pulled off the road and stopped. "You see that?"

"What?"

"Wait here. I'll show you." Pablo jumped out of the truck.

Diamond and I observed Pablo as he ran, jumped into a small roadside ravine, and held up what appeared to be a gas can, a very old gas can. He held it up as if it were an award, with an engaging smile sprung across his face. He put it in the truck bed, and we resumed our trip.

"That fuel can is from the forties, maybe before. I always find cool stuff on this route."

"You're going to make something out of it, right?"

"An aardvark, maybe." Pablo patted my hand. "What? You don't like aardvarks."

"Quite honestly, I've never seen an aardvark made from the body of a 1940s gas can, but I can dig it."

"Now for the serious stuff," Pablo said, "we're getting close to our destination. I want to talk to you about your lovebirds."

"I'm sorry the cages weren't cleaner. It was a crazy week."

"They're birds. Does it bother you to hear them sing?"

"I'm used to them. I always know it's morning. Home, you know?"

"Don't you ever think they'd like to use their wings?" Pablo drank some water.

"I'll tell you the story of Starlight and Cecilia. You ready?" I opened bottled water and took a drink. "When I was pregnant with Janey before Allen left, we went for a

Sunday drive and stopped at a unique little store that sold fresh fruit and a whole lot more. From the back of the store, I head a chorus, like the Mormon Tabernacle Choir, except everything was discordant but happy. Birds. I went back to show Clea. The store owner said she had just returned to the States with these two little lovebirds. I wanted one without thinking about the consequences. We got a cage and all and set the little bird up. I called him Starlight. I was having some problems with the pregnancy, and they put me on bed rest. Before Allen left for Japan, he set a bed up in the living room across from Starlight. I kept thinking that the little guy looked unhappy and needed his friend. I asked my dad to return to the bird lady to buy the other lovebird. I called her Cecilia. As it turned out, they were mates. I was guilty. After Janey was born, I put a nesting box in their cage, and they made babies. To answer your questions about their wings—I never clip their wings—it sounds cruel. I don't handle them because it feels wrong. When I do, it always startles me how light they are: a tiny cage of bones with beautiful green feathers, and peach-colored faces. I love the royal blue in their tail feathers. They're beautiful."

"Why do you think they sing?" Pablo peered over at me.

"It's their nature, right? And they hear the local birds, and I suppose they sing back and forth."

"Maybe they'd like the outdoor birds to come free them," Pablo said.

"I don't know," I shrugged. "Maybe?"

"You're feeling pretty light-hearted under the sunglasses and floppy hat, aren't you."

"Gloria and the bookmark. I am finally free. I'm not so scared anymore. I'm sure there'll be times, but—"

"You had to free yourself. You can make that decision for yourself. But your little birds have wings, and they need your help."

"Where the heck are we going?" I asked.

"It's a bird sanctuary for exotic birds. I was thinking about your birds when I was cleaning their cages. Glen told me about this place."

"I try my best—"

"I know you and the girls love your birds. I think you'd make friends with any critter you came across. But what about how they see the world? You know what it's like for them. You've been a caged bird."

"Oh, my God, like the Maya Angelou poem?"

"Let's go take a tour of the place and see what you think." Pablo hugged me close. "Tans, you cared for the birds to keep them safe. You kept yourself pretty locked up, too, hoping nothing bad would happen. How did that work out?" He kissed me on the cheek. "It's your decision. I'm here to buy you a chocolate milkshake with a side of fries when we get done with the tour."

We visited all the different aviaries, and I talked to the director. The little peach-faced lovebirds I saw flew from beam to perch to feeders high and low. I talked to a few of the caretakers, and Pablo backed me up. My birds were healthy and as happy as they could be in the close confines of their current situation.

I rubbed the smooth edge of my bookmark and thought about my birds and the past few days. If you have the right view, everything seems to flow naturally. My birds had wings. Like me, they needed to use their wings.

Sitting in the cool adobe-walled office of S. Frye, her badge read, I pondered my situation. Frye handled relinquishments. I hated the word. I could give up the babies, but Starlight and Cecilia? Their chicks needed this place. I chastised myself for putting a nesting box in Starlight and Cecilia's cage. In my heartbroken life and nursing a new baby, my hormones danced with those engaging lovebirds. And when the chicks hatched and finally appeared outside the box on the narrow perch, how darling they were. Downy black and white and nearly full-sized with the innocence of all babies, no matter the kind. Cecilia and Starlight were frazzled like all new parents. Daily, they ate, regurgitated, and fed the chicks. Neither one looked as if they slept. One went into the nesting box while the other rested a bit, after which they switched. Clea and I watched as Cecilia nudged a chick off the perch. The chick fell into the food dish, and Cecilia monitored the little one as it climbed up the side of the cage to the perch. I told Frye the story.

"Hmmm," she said, straight-faced. The slim, petite woman with green and violet shades of hair reminded me of Cecilia. "I appreciate your story and your attachment to your lovebirds. Are you ready to make this decision?"

In reaction to her unemotional response to my story, I said, "Look, I tell every dog, cat, and bird I adopt into my household that I will take care of you your whole life." I peered over at Pablo, seated next to me. "Greater wisdom tells me I'm not being fair to my birds. I wasn't planning on coming here today. It was a spontaneous gesture—"

Frye locked eyes with me. Her desk was in order, her

hands folded. "How would you like to handle this?" she asked.

"We talked to one of the caretakers in the small bird aviary. He told us that you guys have a sponsorship program. Could I sponsor Starlight and Cecilia? And I could volunteer? I would love to bring my kids here to see what you do. I don't live far away. I could come maybe on one of my days off. I could help in the office, maybe, or whatever you needed." I closed my eyes. Tears threatened, but I sniffed them back and did my best to return Frye's gaze. She was sizing me up. The idea of giving my birds up broke my heart.

"Our sanctuary is new. Usually, people enter the door to my office as quickly as they leave. Sign the papers and get rid of the birds. But even so, they are not selling them. I give credit for that. You are taking responsibility for your birds and giving them a shot at a great, new life. Every day is summer camp for them. I love the deal you propose. We could definitely use help in the office, and sponsorship is greatly appreciated. Welcome to our family, Tansy."

When I signed the papers for my birds, I took off my sunglasses, forgetting about my black eye. Frye asked, What happened to you?"

I said, "Well, a bear attacked me, and I slapped him silly with my head. Not to worry, the bear lived. But it was close."

Acknowledgments

I called the crew of peach-faced lovebirds my office managers, and they were in my upstairs room in the old Park Street house when I began writing the first drafts of this story in 1993. Cecilia and her mate, Starlight, witnessed the keystrokes, the frustration, and the joy of story writing. They listened to "To Make You Feel My Love" on a loop as the song poured into my sensibilities. Thank you, dear lovebird friends. I want to thank the Oasis Bird Sanctuary in Benson, Arizona where I sponsor two lovebirds in memory of Starlight and Cecilia.

I want to spotlight my dear friend, Susan Chase-Foster for her blurb and able eyes as she listened to iterations of this novel.

Thank you, too, to my dear friend Janet Bergstrom, for her blurb and support of my writing. And thank you to my Monday crew of IWS writers. You all motivated me to do better and to keep up with your powerful prose.

Thank you to Jill Estes and Lisa Ahmari for agreeing to be beta readers. I sincerely appreciate their effort on my behalf.

Thank you, Brian Estes, for the back cover photo.

Thank you to my dear daughters, Andrea and Samantha. Their input and support make my world turn on course.

And thank you to my little dog, Betty Bananas.

CONFLUENCE

Reviewed by Kathy Stickles for Reader Views

– A Beautiful and Spiritual Story 5 **STARS**

Confluence by Mary Elizabeth Gillilan is the story of Maya Margarita Moore, a woman whose life is about to be changed completely thanks to a letter found in her attic from her mother who has passed away. This is a story and a protagonist who will grab your heart at the very beginning and take you on an amazing ride of fear, hope, and a lot of changes, and it is a book well worth your time. I was happy, sad, and so humbled after having finished it and you will be as well. . . .

Confluence is an amazing and truly beautiful story that will have the reader completely riveted from beginning to end. The descriptions this author gives in her writing of faraway places are so vivid and stunning that one feels as if they are actually there witnessing this beauty, as well as living through the difficulties that Maya has in making the trip. I absolutely loved the way this author tells the story to her readers. It is superb in all ways. . . .

CONFLUENCE

Reviewed by Sarah Hinrichs for Chanticleer Reviews

A journey of unleashing one's own inner strength, and a love letter to a beautiful location and way of life, *Confluence* is a gem of a novel. **5 STARS**